Catamount Unleashed

CATAMOUNT
Unleashed

by
Rick Davidson

Beech River Books
Center Ossipee, New Hampshire

BℝB

Beech River Books
P.O. Box 62, Center Ossipee, N.H. 03814
1-603-539-3537
www.beechriverbooks.com

LIBRARY OF CONGRESS CONTROL NUMBER: 2019956027

Summary: "Near a remote lodge in northern New Hampshire, an old Abenaki curse is reactivated and the terror of a man-killing catamount is released into the otherwise idyllic environs. A ruthless attempt to suppress all information about the mountain lion threatens the guides at the lodge and their guests, but help comes from an unlikely source"--Provided by publisher.

ISBN 978-0-930149-42-7

Cover art by Ethan Marion.

Printed in the United States of America

This book is dedicated to
the wooded "North Country"
of New Hampshire, Maine, and Vermont
and to the people who live there.

Other thrillers by Rick Davidson:

Catamount, A North Country Thriller

Murder at Stillwater Lodge

Acknowledgments

Little did I know that when *Catamount, A North Country Thriller* was finished that subsequent books would feature many of the same characters. *Murder at Stillwater Lodge* and now *Catamount Unleashed* have put these and many new characters into further perilous situations. I hope my readers will continue to enjoy the adventures my characters confront in the north country of New Hampshire. Catamount is back.

As always, I want to thank my wife of fifty years, Jane. What a great companion she has been on this long strange trip called life. She is invaluable as an editor and continuity advisor before my manuscript goes to the professional editor and publisher, Brad Marion at Beech River Books.

How lucky I am to have the love of my three daughters and my seven grandchildren.

Catamount Unleashed is a work of fiction. It is designed to entertain and keep readers on the edge of their seats. By request, some names in the novel are real but their actions within the context of the story are complete fiction and the product of my imagination. The events depicted herein are also fantasy and I hope they remain that way.

"When economic power became concentrated in a few hands, then political power flowed to those possessors and away from the citizens, ultimately resulting in an oligarchy or tyranny."

—John Adams

Chapter 1

The pontoon boat motored out of the confluence of the two rivers into the shallow waters of Lake Mackapague. Two young men in their early twenties were aboard.

"That's it," said Randall Cramer, "that granite ledge. That's the Rock. The island is that way. That is where she is buried."

"You know, I'm not really sure I... I don't think your great grandfather really meant for anyone to use this map," said Bruce Brownell. "Not for this. It's kind of gross digging up a grave and it's probably a sacrilege or something."

"You don't believe that kind of bullshit. This is like... archeology. You know, it's like the pyramids. It's destiny that I found this," said Randall.

"Destiny for what? Do you think you're going to find anything that is really valuable? Both your father and your grandfather kept the secret."

"Exactly. That's why there might be something there."

"Like what? Maybe they just honored the old Indian's wishes. Your grandfather was his friend."

"I don't know what'll be there but I have to find out. Are you going to come with me or not? She had to have been buried with some interesting artifacts."

"That may be," said Bruce. "The old Indian trusted your great grandfather when he came out here to help dig the grave. You're breaking that trust. Other than the Indian, he was the only other living soul to know the exact location."

"Why did he make the map then?"

"Maybe so your grandfather would know where to go. I have no idea. I don't think I want to do this. It seemed like a good idea at the party but now I'm—"

"What do you think? The 'ghost' is going to get us?"

"I just don't think it's right to dig up someone's grave."

"That's not what you said the other night."

"It seemed like it would be an adventure, but now that we're here, I don't like it."

Cramer looked at his friend as he continued to maneuver the boat. The two young men remained lost in their own thoughts as they headed toward the island. Once there, Randall killed the engine and raised the motor.

"You don't have to come. Just help me get this boat ashore."

A few moments later, Randall jumped onto land and secured the boat to an overhanging tree. He took out a shovel and started up the path that led to a nearby remote camping spot.

"Are you sure you don't want to see what we can find?" he asked. "The grave should be just east of this campsite." Randall looked at his compass and then at the map.

"I'll wait here," said Bruce.

Randall bushwhacked around a few blowdowns beyond the remote campsite until he came to a small clearing. He looked at the map. As he moved into the open space, a silence instantaneously invaded the forest. He stopped and looked around. In the surrounding stillness, his footsteps were offensively loud as he disturbed the dead leaves covering the mossy surface of the ancient ground. The echo of his shovel piercing the long undisturbed turf resonated through the wilderness. The young man continued digging. Then he stopped. Deathly quiet.

Randall Cramer never saw the black apparition that sprang from out of the silence. Seconds later, he perished.

In the boat, Bruce heard a soul-piercing, mournful screech that seemed to vocalize all of the bottled up, unexpressed pain in the universe.

Chapter 2

Marion Roberts strolled slightly ahead of her husband Ike. They always walked this way, at least now that they were in their early seventies. In their younger years, they had walked hand and hand in a manner that Ike liked to refer to as "romantic-like." Over the years the two hadn't quite merged into one. While walking, Marion expressed a sense of purpose in her gait. Ike tended to ramble. Everyone who knew them, though—and that included just about everyone in Northern New Hampshire—always referred to them in the plural. Someone might wonder how Ike and Marion were doing. Another might inquire as to whether anyone had seen the Roberts recently. Neither Ike nor Marion seemed to pay much mind to what the individuals in their small world called them. This was especially true now that they—with their friends Rob Schurman and Jade Morrison—spent most of their time twenty miles down a primitive, unpaved logging road, far away from any semblance of civilization. Rob and the Roberts were the owners and hosts at Stillwater Lodge on Lake Mackapague in northern New Hampshire. The lodge hosted hunting and fishing enthusiasts depending on the season. Thanks to Jade's savvy use of the Internet, the lodge now attracted many snowmobilers in the winter and families seeking a comfortable wilderness experience in the summer.

Ike had become involved with the lodge after Marion had decided that fifty years of marriage was enough for any woman. Marion had moved to Auburn, Maine and Ike, deciding that he could not manage the old family farm alone, had pooled his resources with his old buddy, ex-game warden Rob Schurman. The two had renovated the lodge and were managing to keep their heads above water. The staff had consisted of Jade and Sadie. Sadie was an excellent chef and Jade turned out to have management and people skills that made up for what both Rob and Ike may have lacked in those areas. Ike and Rob were both sought-after guides. This mix had all the makings of success—until guests started dying in some decidedly unnatural ways. Had things moved along smoothly, perhaps Ike and Marion would still be experimenting with living apart.

Once Marion got wind of what turned out to be murders (and that Ike had fallen for the murderess), she decided that the two bachelors really could not be relied upon to be on their own. So Marion was now the chef and her home grown culinary skills were legendary. She was even known to admit on occasion that perhaps she had indeed missed her husband during their short time away from each other.

Ike and Marion were taking advantage of the beautiful late June day to take a walk up by Mackapaque before the first families of the summer arrived the following weekend. The black flies were out, but not so bad that the couple would have wanted to stay cooped up inside the lodge. Besides, you could not live up here if you let those airborne blood suckers get to you. Ike and Marion searched out a couple of flat rocks near the edge of the lake. Without speaking, they each sat down. The warm sun broadcasted light off the horizon and shimmered like small diamonds on the surface of the water. As early evening approached, the crickets began the opening stanzas of what would be a nightlong, mostly harmonious concert of northern New Hampshire animal, insects, and birds a capella. Marion took Ike's hand. Then, the sounds stopped. The light continued to glimmer on the water. Silence.

"Why is it suddenly so quiet?" asked Marion.

Ike stood up. "Shit," said Ike. "This reminds me of the kind of quiet that used to happen whenever that Christly mountain lion showed up."

"That was a while ago," said Marion.

"I suppose," said Ike. "But my mood's been spoilt. Let's go home."

As the elderly pair reached the road, the forest sounds return.

Ike shivered. "Marion, it couldn't be happenin' again, could it?"

"I wouldn't think so," said Marion. "That's all in the past."

In the township of Clifford, the private phone in lawyer Peter Schmidt's study rang. The man dressed in expensive, stylish country clothing picked up the phone.

"Peter Schmidt."

"Peter," the voice on the other end said. "We thought you should know."

"What?"

"You remember the tracking device we had on that catamount, that mountain lion that disappeared a few years ago?"

Peter paused. "Of course!"

"We're receiving the signal again. Off and on."

Chapter 3

Eight men and two women, all dressed in dark, expensive business suits, sat around a large, solid mahogany table inside a windowless conference room. After receiving the phone call, Peter Schmidt had left his remote home in Clifford, New Hampshire and driven to Portsmouth International Airport where he boarded a private jet for Washington, D.C.

"Off and on?" asked Peter Schmidt

"It's not regular but we have gotten a signal from that old collar about five times during the past two weeks. Different times of the day and night," answered the younger of the two women.

"Didn't we lose the tracking signal completely last time?" asked Schmidt.

The woman leaned forward. "We did. We assumed the battery had died."

"Would the battery last this long?" asked Schmidt.

"Hard to say," said another man.

Schmidt took the small plastic bottle of Poland Spring water that had been set out at his place at the table. He unscrewed the cap. "Could someone have replaced it?"

"Who?" asked another man.

Peter poured some water into a glass and sipped the liquid. "How should I know? Isn't that your job to keep track of our projects?

"Yes, we have no record of any recent tagging in that area," said the man.

"Are you sure?" snapped Schmidt.

"That's just it. This isn't a new tag," said the young woman.

Schmidt put his glass down. "What do you mean?"

"I wasn't here when…I mean the signal is designated as having been placed on the mountain lion that was supposedly killed. It matches one of the ones we had been tracing in northern New Hampshire sometime before the fire."

"To tell you the truth," said a white-haired man. "We could never be sure if the cat we had placed up there was the same one that caused all the trouble. I thought you knew that."

"But the signal stopped at about the same time, isn't that right?" asked Peter,

"Yes," said the white-haired man. "But—"

"But what?" asked Schmidt.

"The animal we tagged wasn't black. And by all accounts, the rogue lion was black."

"Do black mountain lions even exist?" asked the older woman.

The white-haired man poured some coffee. "As long as we have been following such things, there has been no documented evidence of one. No one, on record, has ever killed or captured one, yet the myth persists—that and a million other mountain lion stories."

"Didn't that old farmer claim that there was a collar on the dead cat?" asked another man.

"Not a very reliable witness," said the elder woman. "He also claimed he saw an old Indian man and woman in the flames. He's just a blow-hard."

Peter Schmidt grimaced. "Yeah, an old blow-hard who has forgotten more about those woods than any of us will ever know."

"Are you saying that you believe him?" asked the younger woman.

"I am just saying that, from what I know of Ike Roberts, it would be a mistake to dismiss him as an old blow-hard."

The man at the head of the table who had spent the meeting listening and taking notes finally spoke. "So, if I understand all of this correctly, the rumors I have heard about a serious mountain lion incident in New Hampshire were true. We managed to create a cover up and we discredited a number of people."

"That is—" interrupted Peter.

"Let me continue," said the man. "Since I wasn't in office at the time, I want to make sure I have this right. The mountain lion—or the catamount as I have heard it called—attacked a number of farm animals and... people."

"Some of the animals were mine," said Schmidt.

"So I understand. The rogue cat was finally killed but then disappeared. And now we are to at least infer that it may be back?"

"We don't know what is going on. That signal shouldn't be there. We don't know what it is."

"Don't you think we should find out what it is?" asked the man at the head of the table.

"Yes sir, Mr. Vice President, we all do. That is why we are here."

"All right then, meeting adjourned. Mr. Schmidt, would you please stay for a few minutes? I'd like to have a word."

The vice president stood up and shoved his chair against the table. He walked across the room and shut the door. He walked back to the table and, using both hands, grabbed one of the chairs.

"Peter, goddamn it. Fix this. Can you imagine, if these people at the meeting knew...? They'd have my—our—hides before we even get started. Our time has come. We are the destined "Lords of the Earth," the "philosophical rulers." We can't let this fiasco with the mountain lion impede our—"

"Sir, I—

The Vice President walked back to the door. He opened it and turned around.

"Mr. Schmidt, fix it."

Peter Schmidt was alone in the conference room. He took out his cell phone.

THE OLD ABENAKI

The old Abenaki appeared semi-transparent in the early morning fog as he pondered the hazy expanse of Lake Mackapaque. This outcrop had been his wife Moll's favorite spot on earth. For him, this place was sacred as was the hallowed ground on a remote island where he had interred the remains of his beloved spouse. The lone Indian cherished the time he spent on Moll's Rock. Somehow, he was now an old man. He was losing his eyesight and he could no longer live up to his local reputation as the most artful hunter and trapper in the North Country.

Although, at first, he had not welcomed the coming of the white men, the old Abenaki had, in the end, accepted or at least tolerated their ways. He had helped the early settlers adapt to the rugged hardscrabble existence that they had chosen in the Granite State. Old age forced him to accept the kindness of those he had helped. They had been very kind.

But here, on this piece of granite, through the filter of time, both he and his dear Molly were very much alive. He could feel her presence. He also sensed but could not clearly see the piercing yellow eyes of the black apparition that had become his guardian angel.

What was it? He also could not explain the vague awareness he had of a future time. In anger, he had cursed the white men who had brought the diseases that had killed his wife and many of the others of his race. He had also wished misfortune on anyone who might disturb his wife's eternal resting place. As he approached the end of his life, he no longer felt the need to invoke heinous hardship on future generations and he felt uneasy that he could not undo the force that had been unleashed.

What was it? Was it the faint image of a black mountain lion that seemed to appear ever more distinctly in his increasingly persistent nightmares? He did not know how, but he could feel the death and he could nearly see the fire that would come long after his own mortality. Would he understand once he had died? He wondered if he had already passed. His existence was a strange combination of past, present and future impressions, not the reality he had once known. Was he to spend eternity haunting this hallowed ground? If that was his fate, he would accept it.

Here he was with his woman. Would Molly's grave on the island always remain undiscovered and untouched? Woe to any living person who would disturb that place of peace! Someone would. But who? He trusted the white man who had helped him prepare this place. That friend had helped the bereaved Indian dig the grave and he had helped him prepare the canoe that would be Moll's hearse.

The Abenaki would be alone with his wife when he paddled that launch to the convergence of the two rivers and then around the bend past Moll's favorite ledge along the shores of the waters known as Mackapaque. His journey would take him to an isolated island. But, could his curses be agents of power? Calamity should not result from unthinking words of anger. How could he recognize occurrences from the future?

His thoughts, as they invariable did, returned to Molly and their time together. A lifetime of isolated moments but where was the thread that held those minutes, hours, days, weeks, months, and years together? What was his relationship to this catamount? He had hunted mountain lions, but he had hunted many things. He was a hunter. That was his life.

The yellow eyes continued to watch the old man.

Chapter 4

Ike's ancient Jeep Wrangler worked its way down the steep driveway that led to Stillwater Lodge. Jade Morrison was raking gravel to improve what passed as a parking lot. It overlooked a boat house. Ike parked the Jeep in a spot next to his rusty tractor. He and Marion climbed out of the vehicle into ankle-deep mud.

He looked at Jade. "Lot a good that gravel's doin."

Jade had put up orange cones to protect the water sodden grassy area that in the summer could be a lawn.

"Them's a waste, too," observed Ike.

For the time being the parking lot was a mosaic of tire ruts and muck. It was mud season in New Hampshire.

"How was the walk?" asked Jade. She leaned on her rake as the elderly couple approached her. She nodded to Marion.

"Seems like he's in a mood."

"Not so good," interrupted Ike.

"Really?"

"Oh he's all twitterpated because he thinks that the catamount is back. That's all he talked about on the way back. You know how he is when he gets an idea stuck in his craw."

Rob Schurman put down the hammer he was using to make repairs on the boathouse and went over to join the conversation. "How was the walk?" he asked.

Marion threw up her hands. "Don't ask."

"You mark my words," said Ike. "That goddamned thing is back."

"What goddamned thing?" asked Rob.

"The Christly mountain lion."

Rob looked at Marion. "What is he talking about?"

"It got kind of quiet while we were sitting by the lake."

"Kinda quiet? I'll say it was kinda quiet. Quiet like when that goddamned cat was around," said Ike.

"It can't be back," said Rob. "We both saw it killed."

"I'm just sayin'," said Ike "I ain't never goin' to forget how it feels when that goddamned thing is around. You can feel it in your bones. It ain't like anything else you ever felt. You know it as well as I do. You was there. That memory ain't never goin' away. I swear that thing's back. You just wait and see."

Ike walked toward the lodge.

Rob, Jade and Marion watched him go in.

"I hope he doesn't bring this up this weekend," said Jade. "We have two families with kids coming as guests."

"I'll talk to him," said Marion. "I hate to do it, but I have to give him his due. It was a little spooky, even if I do say so myself. It sounded like the Australian Outback—you know, peepers and all—then there was no noise at all. You could hear yourself breathe."

New Hampshire Fish and Game biologist Phil Ramsey watched as two troopers carried the body bag to their boat. Another man dressed in a dark suit followed behind.

"There's no question, Roger?"

State Trooper Sergeant Roger Wright shook his head. "Nope!"

"It was a mountain lion?"

"It was," said Roger. "Believe me, I ought to know. I have seen four bodies that looked just like that one. And it wasn't all that far from here, not as the crow flies at least."

"What do you mean?" asked Ramsey.

"Do you remember the rumors about a catamount during the forest fire?"

"I do. I was supposed to come up to help verify the sightings, but then I was told not to go. We got word that the whole things was a hoax. We'd be wasting our time."

"It wasn't a hoax," said Wright. "I was there. I was one of the ones who shot it. It started attacking people. I like to think I saved a woman's life."

"You shot it? Why didn't you say something?"

"I did. They ordered me to keep my mouth shut. That didn't seem like such a bad idea at the time. The animal was dead. Why make people afraid to go into the woods? Why create a panic?"

"What happened to the carcass?"

"I don't know but I heard that it disappeared."

"How could it disappear?"

"I don't know. The goddamned thing had one of those GPS tags on it."

"That's weird," said Ramsey. "I am not aware of any attempts to reintroduce mountain lions into the state."

"Me neither! But, I know what I saw. After the cat was clearly dead, I saw the woman who had been attacked pick up a rifle and shoot it again. Right in the head. It couldn't have survived that. It was dead."

"So it can't be the same one?"

"Not if we are dealing with anything from the natural world," said Wright. "That guy you brought with you is from Washington?"

"Yeah, so he says." said Ramsey. "He's part of some government wildlife agency."

"He seemed awful anxious to make sure that this wouldn't be attributed to a mountain lion," said Wright.

"Yup," said Ramsey. "He did."

Wright crossed his arms. "Refuted everything I said. Do you think a coyote did this?"

Ramsey looked at Wright. "Who dresses like that?"

"Not me. I don't even own a suit, not one that still fits anyway."

"I am no cat expert but this wasn't done by a coyote, no matter what our city friend says."

"So you believe me?" asked Wright.

"I don't believe that guy," said Ramsey. "Does it surprise you that he wouldn't listen to you?"

"No." said Roger. "He's seems pretty much set on attributing this to a coyote. If that doesn't work, he'll probably come up with something else. Probably blame it on the other kid or something."

"That's total bullshit. You and I both know it."

The man from Washington walked over to Roger and Phil. "Nothing's off the table," said the man.

"Come on," said Roger. "You know this wasn't done by any coyote."

"Maybe it was the kid," said the man.

"Yeah right. No human did that."

"The investigation has just begun," said the man. "You shouldn't jump to any conclusions yet. I'll see you gentlemen later."

Phil watched the man walk away.

"So what are you going to do now?"

"I'm going to go see Rob Schurman, the Fish and Game officer that was involved last time. We might want to be careful about who we talk to about this. I think we can trust Rob. He and his partner Ike Roberts run Stillwater Lodge. Rob actually survived an attack by the mountain lion. Ike lost livestock. At least they won't think we are off our rockers."

"Maybe we can get a free meal. You haven't lived until you have tasted one of Marion Robert's casseroles. She's won more blue ribbons at the fair than you can shake a stick at. Both she and Ike are like institutions around here. So's Rob for that matter. Retired game wardens have kind of revered status around these parts, at least among the law-abiding folks."

"I don't think the attempts to discredit Ike, Marion, or Rob held much water with the locals. I can't imagine anyone questioning Marion's veracity. Ike's kinda crusty but he's a lot sharper than he let's on. Rob's girlfriend isn't hard to look at for her age either. That'd be our age group. You want to come along?"

"Yes, I think I do," said Ramsey.

Chapter 5

Piercing yellow eyes watched.

Jake, the Schmidt's hired hand, gazed out over the carnage. The remains of five of Peter Schmidt's prized Scottish Highland cows lay wrong-side up with their bellies torn open. This felt like more than deja vu. The disemboweled bloody masses in the pasture were exactly as before. Black flies and large houseflies swarmed around the remains of the cattle. Congealed blood stuck to the green grass and resembled melting, gummy taffy. Even the red carpet of blood that led to a pile of brush at the edge of the field was the same.

Jake relived the moment that one of the two state troopers had stepped into the squishy entrails of a particular dead animal. He felt the same revulsion he had felt then. Just as he had done in the past, Jake worked his way over to the heap of cut branches in the clearing at the end of the pasture.

Last time, neither he nor the troopers had known what form of animal life had dragged—and then concealed—its prey in the pile of sticks. This time, Jake knew exactly what had done this.

He turned back to the farm. Peter Schmidt and his wife had had the house and barn designed to be an exact replica of the old homestead. But even from this distance, there was a sheen of newness that didn't quite match the charming antiquity of the original New England farm house that had burned.

Jake was not in the past. The grass was green, not the brown tinder that last time had so easily burst into flames and caused massive destruction. The two troopers were both dead. They were later killed by the mountain lion. How could they have known that their destiny would be the same as the dead carcasses they had come to investigate?

Peter Schmidt was due back from Washington this afternoon. Jake followed the fencing on the edge of the pasture and worked his way back to the house.

Mary Schmidt was sitting on the screened veranda enjoying her morning coffee. Jake opened the front door.

Mary looked up at the man who had saved her life when the fire had destroyed the homestead that had once stood in the original footprint of this new building. "What's the matter, Jake?"

"It's back."

"What do you mean?"

"The cat," said Jake.

"Catamount? What do you mean? It's dead. Peter said so."

"I know it can't be the same one, even if it is just like last time. The dead cows, the pile of brush—it's all the same."

"What are you talking about, Jake? They killed the mountain lion. I don't understand what—"

"They never did find the body."

"Peter said it was dead."

"Do you believe everything your goddamned husband says? I sure as hell don't. Half of what he says comes out of both sides of his mouth."

Mary poured a cup of coffee and handed it to Jake. "I can't believe—"

"Mary, you're not listening. They're out there just like before."

"But how? Why?"

"I don't know. Ask Peter. He isn't going to be happy."

"Maybe he already knows," said Mary

"About the cows?" asked Jake. "How?"

"He just called. He's staying in Washington."

"It's not the first time he's done that," said Jake.

"Something happened. He had called me earlier to say he was on his way home."

"How could they know about this in Washington?"

"I don't know. A tracking device? Peter talked about that last time. I don't know, it's just a guess. For better or worse, I do know my husband. Something's up."

"Could be anything. Maybe our new president attacked China. Why would there be a tracking device?"

"Who knows? Everything kind of exists in an alternative universe when Peter is involved. If a catamount is back, I wonder how he and his buddies are going to cover it up this time?"

"Aren't you jumping to conclusions? Whatever is going on, I don't want to get mixed up in any of it," said Jake.

"That's one of the many reason I like you so much Jake. You are so easy and you don't need to change the world."

"They all say that Peter is a great man," said Jake.

"I suppose he is, but I sometimes think that the overly educated geniuses that think they have the answers to the world's problems are actually causing most of them."

"Well, I wouldn't be able to judge that," said Jake.

"No, probably not, but I'll take you over any of them."

"Why don't you leave him?"

"You know why Jake. It's this life… and actually, I do love him in a way."

"You could walk away with plenty of money."

"It's also the life style. I enjoy that. Besides, he's never around and you always are." Mary smiled. "I get to have my cake and eat it too. He provides some of what I need in a relationship. You fill in the gaps."

Jake grinned as well. "Yeah, happy to be of service."

"We all get what we want. Peter gets his fame and God knows what else along with his harem of young political groupies. And I get to have you. Believe me, mister, that is not a put down. This all actually makes for a damned happy marriage."

Jake kissed Mrs. Schmidt on the mouth. "Like I said, it works for me." Jake headed toward the kitchen. "I'll call Doc Varney. I don't know what good a vet can do now, but after what happened with that other mountain lion, I'll bet he'll want to be involved. Can I get some bourbon for this coffee?"

Mary nodded. "Sure. I'll take some too."

Chapter 6

George Mason drove through the tollbooth as E-ZPass recorded his passage. The last time he had had to hand over a dollar bill in order to continue on his trip north. Modern technology did not ease his sense of reliving the past as he made his way up Route 16. His old friend and veterinary colleague, Doc Varney, had called again. A mountain lion, or maybe the mountain lion was back. Could it be the same animal? That damned beast had almost killed him.

Mason had managed to escape, but a number of people had not lived through their encounter with this ghost-like creature. The unearthly creature had somehow disappeared even after it was shot multiple times. It had to have been dead. From the boat, George had seen the lifeless body of the large cat lying face down in the bloody shallow water on the edge of the shore. George had not had the time to check for vital signs but he did not need to be a trained veterinarian to know that no animal could have survived the violence that inflicted on it.

Those people who had been on the shore would not be alive today had they not managed to kill the vicious mountain lion. So what had happened to it? Dr. Mason's reputation as an expert on predatory animals had been sabotaged by the cover-up of the "Catamount Affair." George decided to follow Doc Varney's example and pursue a quiet life as a country veterinarian.

When George had told his wife that there were indications that a mountain lion might be back in New Hampshire, she had tried to convince him not to get involved. What could be gained by getting mixed up in this controversy again? But George had to come. He turned onto Route 3 in Twin Mountain and headed toward Clifford.

"I may be getting old," said Rob, "but I'm still dangerous."

Jade rolled into her lover's arms. "I'll say! You know, I think this actually gets better as you get older. It's nice to just have fun, without all the crap that seemed to go along with it when we younger."

Rob smiled. "Are we in love with each other?"

"Are we?" asked Jade. "Whatever this is, I'll take it. I wonder how Linda Harris and her friends are doing."

"What made you think of them?"

"I don't know. I think their open attitude helped me realize that sex doesn't need to be as complicated as most of us make it. It's natural and its fun and it apparently doesn't need to be exclusive."

"I think about them a lot, too—the ones who died. But most of all, how those people supported each other." Rob propped himself on his elbows. "I hope we never have to go through anything like that again. Between my run-in with that mountain lion and the murders here at the lodge, I've had enough excitement for one lifetime. Any more trouble and nobody will want to come out here."

"I was just thinking that Linda and Roger Harris seemed about as in love as any two people could be. Being open to having relationships with other people seemed to make their marriage even stronger."

"It seemed to. Are you looking to fool around with someone else?" asked Rob.

Jade grinned. "I don't have anyone in particular in mind."

"Not much to choose from out here," said Rob, "unless you got your eye on Ike."

"You never know," said Jade.

"Nope you never do," said Rob. "It certainly was a shame about Roger, though. I have a feeling Linda is bouncing back in spite of everything and, yes, I think I learned something about what matters in life from those two. I hope she and her friends all come back again. I offered them a free stay."

"I don't know if they could face coming back here, but I would love to get together with all of them somewhere, somehow."

"Maybe we can arrange that," said Rob. "But speaking of guests, we got some arriving today. I suppose we ought to get dressed."

Jade kissed Rob on the forehead. "I suppose so."

"Oh, Ed skyped me this morning," said Rob. He is coming out and he is bringing his kids, Cindy and Josey."

"The kids haven't been here in a while. How old are they now?"

"Josey's a teenager! God, I am getting old"

"You wear it well," said Jade.

"Hiring you is the smartest thing I ever did," said Rob.

Jade gave Rob a peck on the lips. "Could very well be! Come on, we got work to do."

Chapter 7

"They're here," yelled Ike.

Rob and Jade came out of the kitchen to welcome their first guests. The Dodge Grand Caravan minivan crept down the long hill and parked next to Ike's Jeep. The side door of the van slid open and three teenagers climbed out. A man and a woman in their mid-forties got out of the front of the car.

Rob noticed the woman at once. Her long legs were gorgeous. Her dirty blond hair defined a face that was not only pretty but also seemed to reveal a deeper character. She immediately reminded him of Linda Harris, the remarkable widow of a guest murdered at Stillwater Lodge.

The man fit well with his wife. He was big but he did not give impression of being overweight. Like his wife, his engaging face seemed to express something deeper within. His eyes looked exceptionally kind, but there was also something mischievous about them. Rob wondered if the man might be a minister. He looked like someone you could tell about your troubles. Rob also guessed that he had a sense of humor.

The three teenagers all looked skeptical of their new surroundings. The young girl was playing with what appeared to be a smart phone, apparently already perturbed by the lack of signal. The middle boy was lost to the music on his device and the oldest looking boy was reading something on a tablet.

Reluctantly, Rob and Ike had listened to Jade and had agreed to let her set up a satellite-based wireless router so the guests could access the Internet. Ike had pointed out that he was "agin' it. People came out here to get away from that foolishness." At least in the case of these three teenagers, Jade's intuition had apparently proved to be correct. Some people—especially younger ones—couldn't imagine life without technology.

We're the dinosaurs, Rob thought to himself.

"We're the Meurets," said the man as he held out his hand. "I'm Pat. This is my wife Holly and these three aliens are Abbi, Cameron and Paul." Pat smiled and inhaled deeply the pollution-free air.

"We've been looking forward to this." He looked at his offspring.

"At least some of us," said Holly.

Jade smiled and glanced at Rob. "We do have satellite Wi-Fi in the lodge. It works most of the time. We lose it sometimes. The phones should work at the lodge but they won't in the woods. Other than that, welcome to the backwoods. There is no cell service. We only have one other family coming as guests and some old friends of ours will also be staying here. They all have kids in the same age group as yours."

Jade looked at the license plate on the Meuret's car. "Did you guys drive all the way from Nebraska?"

"We did. This is our first time in this part of the country," said Pat. "It is beautiful here, so peaceful. We have seen some wonderful places over the years, but nothing quite like this."

"I hope you enjoy yourselves," said Jade.

Pat smiled. "I already feel less stress. It seems so safe here, far away from the problems of the world."

"We are isolated, but we like it. Come on in," said Jade. "We're giving you cabin 4 up there overlooking the lake."

Sixteen-year-old Paul asked if he could drive the car to the cabin.

"Sure," said Pat.

"The number is on the cabin," said Jade.

Fourteen-year-old Cameron and thirteen-year-old Abbi climbed back into the minivan for the short ride up a small hill.

"That must be the other guests," said Rob. A Nissan Xterra with New Hampshire plates worked its way down the hill and parked next to the Dodge minivan.

Rob waved and waited for the Nash family to exit their vehicle.

Karly and Tristan, also an attractive couple in their mid-forties, came over to meet Rob. The three adults shook hands while the Nash teenagers waited by the car. Like their counterparts in the Meuret family, they occupied themselves with their electronic gadgets.

Tristan's six-foot frame looked strong but Rob guessed that his strength came from vigorous activity, not from workouts in a gym. The kayaks and mountain bikes mounted on the Nissan supported this hypothesis. The man sported a full beard that was just beginning to show some gray interwoven into brown.

As he always did when he laid eyes on a good-looking woman, Rob quickly (and he hoped surreptitiously) checked out Karly's five-foot-eight-inch athletic body. He resisted the urge to touch the woman's almost shoulder-length hair. He was especially attracted to the way the red strands curled in on her tanned neck.

Jade's cheerful voice interrupted his reverie.

"Hi, I'm Jade. Welcome to Stillwater Lodge. These are the Meurets."

Everyone exchanged greetings.

"You will be able drive your car up to the cabin," said Jade. Then she turned to the Karley and Tristan. "First, let's get you all signed in. You are going to be in Cabin 2."

Twelve-year-old Kayla, fifteen-year-old McKenzie, and fourteen-year-old Connor waited by the SUV while the four parents accompanied Jade into the office.

Rob and Ike headed toward the boathouse and then turned around. A State Trooper cruiser appeared at the top of the hill.

"What's a trooper doing out here?" asked Ike. "We never see them, just the game wardens. I ain't done nothin'. What about you, Rob? You done somethin'?"

The Dodge Charger pulled into the parking lot. Officers Wright and Ramsey got out of the cruiser.

"I know who that is," said Rob. "That's Roger Wright. I haven't seen him since—"

Chapter 8

Froggy poured himself another glass of Old Mr. Boston Whiskey. He settled into the weather-beaten sun-grayed Adirondack chair that he had built himself in another—more sober—lifetime. He had spent the morning tacking new pieces of tarpaper over the bare patches of wood on the sides of his run-down shack. They had appeared after winter storms had torn off fragments of the outer protection of the walls.

The stove connected to the large ancient stone chimney with a built-in smoking chamber provided enough heat to keep Froggy warm during the cold months in northern New Hampshire. The old man thought about the Abenaki who had preserved his wife's body in just such a smoking chamber. That was long ago. There was no way to bury the dead in winter in those days. The Indian had smoked his wife in this very chimney. Then in the spring, the old Abenaki had taken her down the river to her final resting place.

The locals did not take Froggy's claims seriously. There was no evidence that his hovel sat on the very piece of land that the legendary old Abenaki had once inhabited. Sometimes someone from away seemed entertained by his tipsy ramblings.

It was a good story after all. Froggy had been to where the Indian had buried his wife. He had been at that place many times. He could not remember how he knew the spot; he just did. His old canoe just seemed to know the way. Was the old Abenaki his guardian angel? Whenever he visited the grave, he never felt like he was alone with the dead woman.

The locals around Clifford did not believe much of anything Froggy said anymore. He was the town drunk. That was a good thing for a small town to have. Some of the respected members of the community drank almost as much, but it was a comfort for them to know they had a ways to go before they sunk to Froggy's level of dissipation. Most people did not take his mountain lion sightings seriously either.

If anyone took the time to think about it, the old sot should have died long ago, but he hadn't. He was a community fixture, part of the landscape.

It doesn't matter what they say or what they think, he thought to himself, I'm still here—and so is the old Abenaki. I'm as sure of that as I am of anything. I worked hard this mornin'. It's time for another drink.

Roger Wright and Phil Ramsey got out of the cruiser. Wright introduced Ramsey. The two men shook hands with Rob and Ike.

"So, what's going on?" asked Rob. "It's not often we see you guys our here."

"I betcha, it's that cat," Ike butted in.

"How'd you know that?" asked Wright.

"I can feel it."

Wright looked at Ike. "Well, neither one of us has your supernatural powers of perception, Ike, but it appears you're right. Ralph Cramer's son was killed out on the lake. He was attacked. Having seen what we saw before, it was unmistakable as far as I'm concerned. It was a mountain lion. I'm sure of it."

Ike looked at Rob. "I told ya so."

"The dead kid—Randall Cramer—had a friend who stayed in the boat. He says he heard a terrible scream. It really shook him up. He could hardly talk."

"We all know what that sounds like," said Ike. "You know what? I remember the Cramer kid. He went off to college. Old Ralph was mighty proud of him. Good thing he's not around to see this. Died last year. Heart attack."

"God," said Rob. "So the Cramer kid was on land?"

"On an island," said Roger.

"What was he doing?" asked Rob.

"The other one said they had been looking for Indian artifacts."

"Kind a makes you wonder 'bout them Indians I saw—" said Ike.

"What Indians?" asked Phil.

Rob looked at Ike. "Ike claims he saw an old Indian man and woman in the flames after the mountain lion was killed."

"How could...?" asked Ramsey. "Did anyone else—"

"They couldn't have survived that, and no, no one else saw them. Just Ike," said Rob.

"They was there," Ike insisted. "I saw 'em."

"A mountain lion was on the island?" asked Rob.

"I'd say it gets to go wherever it's inclined to go and I think them Indians have somethin' to do with it," said Ike.

"Well, we do know mountain lions can swim," said Rob, "after what happened out on Mackapaque last time."

"Roger has been telling me about what happened back then. I have to tell you I find this all hard to believe. But you all... How could they pull off this big a cover-up?" asked Ramsey.

"They?" asked Ike. "They is the goddamned government. They does it all the time. Ask me, that's what government's for. Ain't none of them politicians knows how to tell the truth. That's why I voted—"

"Ike, no one cares who you voted for," said Rob. "What we need to do is convince Mr. Ramsey that we have a serious situation on our hands."

"I was just sayin," Ike complained.

"The kid who was with him said the victim claimed he knew where an Abenaki's wife was buried. He was looking for artifacts. Apparently, Randall had a map from his great-grandfather, or something like that."

"Why would he have had a map to that place?" asked Rob.

"The grandfather was a friend of some Abenaki and he was involved in burying the Indian's wife," Ramsey explained.

"We all know the story, at least those of us who live around here. The old Abenaki supposedly buried his wife in a secret place. There are a number of places on the lake named after him and his wife. It's local legend," said Rob.

"Did the kid find anything?"

Ramsey looked out over the lake. "He never got the chance."

"I wonder what he thought he was going to do with the artifacts," said Rob.

"Probably sell them," said Ramsey.

"Do we know what happened to the Cramer kid's friend?" asked Rob.

"Is there a lot of money in old Indian artifacts?"

"Some, I suppose," said Wright. "The so-called authorities still have the Cramer kid's friend. They were in college together. At least, that was what I was told."

"What about his family?" asked Ramsey.

"I was told it's being handled."

"See, that's what happens when you send a kid off to college," said Ike. "They come back with highfalutin ideas."

"What are you talking about now, Ike?" asked Rob. "What happened to the map?"

"No one could find it," said Roger.

"See, it's got to be with them Indians," said Ike. "You just wait and see."

"What Indians?" asked Roger.

"The one's I saw."

"Where?"

"I already told you—in the fire."

"That doesn't—"

The radio inside the cruiser crackled. Static.

"Ain't none of this makes sense," mumbled Ike.

"Hold on," said Roger. He opened the door to his cruiser and picked up the radio. The other men waited in silence. Roger got out of the car.

"Well, that makes it pretty much certain. Peter Schmidt's cows have been attacked."

"Again?" asked Rob.

"What do you mean?" asked Ramsey.

"The mountain lion attacked his cows the last time, too."

"I know what that's like," said Ike. "The cat killed off my best cows. Somehow he knowed which ones was the best ones. Did it out of spite, too. Didn't even eat 'em or nothin'"

— 27 —

"Schmidt changed his story the last time and said that the cows had died of some disease," said Wright. "Doc Varney and the guy from Montana all said different, but they were discredited by government veterinarians."

"I wonder what that was all about. Why would the government go to so much trouble to alter and cover up a mountain lion attack?" asked Ramsey.

"That's the sixty-four thousand dollar question, ain't it?" muttered Ike. "Somethin's goin' on. Schmidt works for the government. I betcha he's involved. If he ain't, I'll eat my hat."

"John Hudson and Ralph Barnes took that call right before they were killed," said Roger.

"They were killed in the fire, right?" asked Ramsey.

"Not hardly," said Ike. "They was killed by that catamount."

Ramsey looked confused. "Really, I read... None of this makes... If I hadn't just seen what happened to that boy, I probably would have thought that you've all gone off the deep end. You know what? I would like to have a look at those cows. Can we do that, Roger?"

"We can."

Jade and Marion came out of the kitchen.

"What's going on?" asked Marion.

"Seems I was right 'bout that mountain lion bein' back," said Ike.

Chapter 9

Doc Varney had parked his Jeep Grand Cherokee and now stood next to a small, barely legible sign that said CELL PHONES WORK HERE. He nodded his head as he spoke into the phone. The cruiser pulled over.

"Who's that up ahead?" asked Ramsey. "What's he doing?"

Wright squinted through the windshield of the cruiser.

"It's Doc Varney."

"Is there cell service up here? He can't be talking on a cell phone, can he?" asked Ramsey.

When he saw the cruiser, Varney spoke into his Android and then waved.

"Actually there are a few places where the signal can get through. The signal is weak but somehow it makes it between the hills all the way up here."

Wright and Ramsey got out of the Charger. Wright introduced Ramsey.

"Have you been to the Schmidts?" asked Roger.

"I couldn't get in," said Varney. "They've got the road blocked."

"What do you mean?" asked Roger. "Who? If it were us, I'd know about it."

"It's not the police—at least, not state or local."

"Who then?" asked Ramsey.

"I don't know. There were a lot of vehicles. They weren't cruisers—SUV's and a bunch of cars, looked liked rentals. Some had out-of-state plates. They were clean and new looking. I could hear helicopters farther up by the farm. They told me that there is some kind of cattle epidemic. The place is quarantined."

"We were told it looked like a mountain lion had attacked again," said Roger.

"That's why I was heading out there. When I told them I was the local vet, they said they didn't need me."

Roger went over to his cruiser.

Varney looked at Ramsey. "I don't know what's going on. I hear that the Cramer boy—Randall—was killed. What happened?"

"I was called in by the university down in Durham," said Ramsey. "He was attacked by something. I don't think it was a human. I have never seen anything like what happened to that kid before. Some guy in a suit tried to convince me that a coyote did it."

"Sounds way too familiar," said Varney, "the cows and the attack. Who was the guy in the suit?"

"I don't know. He mentioned some agency I wasn't familiar with it. That's not necessarily strange. They're a lot of agencies out there."

"You don't think it was a coyote?" asked Doc.

"No coyote I ever saw or heard of."

Roger approached the two men. "We have been called off the case. I asked how come and also why it had taken so long to get back to us. I was told they were verifying the epidemic story."

"Did you ask about the dead boy?" asked Ramsey

"They told me that it was being handled."

Ramsey looked at Wright. "Did you ask about the body?"

"Same story. I was told it's being handled."

"Really," said Varney.

"I wonder about those out-of-state cars. Government guys often use rental cars," said Wright.

"Could have been," said Doc. "Don't those guys usually keep the locals in the loop?"

"Usually," said Wright.

"If there is an epidemic in our area, you'd think they'd want me involved," said Doc.

"You'd think," said Ramsey. "Can I really use my phone over there?"

Doc held up his phone. "I just called my friend George Mason. He knows about mountain lions. He's on his way and he was here the last time."

Ramsey started toward the sign. "I guess I'll call my wife and tell her I might be staying up here longer than I had planned. I'm not sure what to believe, but I sure as hell can't leave now."

Marion served coffee. Roger Wright, Phil Ramsey, Doc Varney, Rob Schurman, Jade Morrison and Ike Roberts sat around two tables that had been pulled together in the dining room of Stillwater Lodge.

"Thank you, Marion," said Doc. "I'm glad to see you haven't lost your touch. You make the best coffee I have ever tasted. Those casseroles you used to make for the fair deserved every blue ribbon they got. Are you going to enter again this year?"

"I appreciate the compliment," said Marion. "You're too kind."

"No he isn't," said Roger. "This coffee is excellent."

Ike took out his old corncob pipe and a red packet of Prince Albert tobacco.

"You're not smoking that thing in here, Ike Roberts," said Jade.

"Wasn't plannin' on it," said Ike. "Havin' my pipe helps me think, and besides, I taught Marion how to make coffee. I don't get credit for nothin' around here."

Marion smiled. "I'm willing to admit that Ike and I make a good team. But I don't know if I can take another fifty years."

"Well, we all have a lot of years in common," said Rob.

"Most of us," said Jade.

"Hell for someone from away, you fit in quite well," said Ike. "The t'other thing we have in common is this godddamned cata-mount."

"Again, except for me," said Jade.

"And me," said Ramsey.

"It's not a pretty story. Rob's lucky to be alive. I can't imagine what Ed and Marty's kid went through. Quite a few people died. Ed's and Marty's marriage fell apart."

"That weren't cuz of the mountain lion," said Ike.

"We know about the affair," said Jade. She looked at the group at the table. She had come to Clifford to fulfill her lifelong dream of liv-ing in the woods. Her boy friend at the time of her retirement from teaching could not understand why she would want to move north. It was not easy to make a break with the life she had built, but she knew it was then or never.

Now in her fifties, she had reached that age where, if you really wanted to do something, you had better get to it. Now, she would never go back. She still stayed in touch with old friends, but Stillwater Lodge fit her like a glove. She had immediately taken to being a hostess, a promoter and the business manager for the Lodge. She would never say so, but she was quite sure that lodge would not be successful if business matters had been left solely up to Ike and Rob. She was the outsider but she had earned her place at the table. She was happy with the life she was now sharing with the man who, she supposed, was still her employer. Rob was like the trees, the lake and the river. He belonged here.

In his younger years, Rob had been away. He had been to college. He had enjoyed many a late evening in the nightspots of Europe, Boston and Montreal. However, he was not made for city life. After a number of different assignments as a conservation officer, he finally landed the position he coveted. He became one of the Fish and Game officers for the North Country of New Hampshire. He never really found the right woman and Jade knew that Rob regretted the repercussions of his brief affair with his best friend's wife. Marty Rollins and Rob had not even had the time to be dishonest with Ed. He had caught them in the act right after the first time. She knew Rob regretted the strain on his friendship with Ed. In the end, the two men seemed to have worked it out.

She also knew that Rob wished that his retirement had not become entangled with the discredited story of the catamount. Rob was a classic North Country persona. Many an angler and hunter envied him his job. To them, he was the ultimate woodsman. Of course, Rob knew the real story. He always said that you learn from your mistakes. Screw-ups in the North Country can kill or maim you. He still bore the scar on his lower ankle from the time his chain saw had kicked back and come close to taking off his foot. He had not told anyone about the time he lost the blades on his outboard while speeding onto the rocks on a shallow area in the lake. He was thrown out of the boat. He knew better, but had not been paying attention. He was a good shot, but he had missed his prey more than once. In spite of his skill with a fly rod, how much time had he spent by the side of a river untangling a line while the fish he had spooked went down deeper or just disappeared?

Fortunately, most of the time no one had been around to witness these chinks in his armor. Someone had been around to catch him in his one and only adventure with adultery. No matter how well you present yourself to the outside world, there are always plenty of ways to mess up. When you do, especially when there is an audience, it is hard to take the sting out of the shame. Rob knew all about that. Sometimes, in spite of all your so-called experience, in the moment, you make the wrong choice. You do the wrong thing. Were his two days with Marty wrong? It had not felt wrong. She belonged to someone else. Does anyone really belong to someone else? Whether we do or not, Rob should not have been playing around with Ed's wife.

There was the time the choke stuck on his outboard. The engine would not stop racing and the kill button did not work. He knew he should have just pulled the gas line, but instead, for some reason, he engaged the engine. He was thrown overboard that time too. The boat sped onto the shore. He had had an audience for that one. Toxic shame. He still had it whenever he thought about that incident—so much for the skillful woodsman. On other occasions, he had reacted just in time to avoid hitting a moose or deer on North Country back roads. There was no audience on those occasions. It is not as if anyone believes you when you describe the big salmon you caught while fishing alone. You make mistakes and hope you continue to learn—at least, until you make the one fatal human error that ends it all. He had shown his mettle during the wild fire that almost destroyed Clifford. He had also survived the encounter with the mountain lion and had the courage to play an important role in stopping the murders at Stillwater Lodge.

Rob had not had much success in his relationships, but Jade had fallen for him hook, line and sinker (she smiled—what a perfect analogy for Stillwater Lodge) and he was obviously attracted to her as well. He had shared all these insecurities with her; that had to mean something. All of these people are classics, Jade thought as she looked around the table.

Ike and Marion shared almost fifty years of farming. The outside of their old farm may have looked weather beaten and dilapidated, but Jade knew the inside had to have been well-kept and comfortable. The house was much like Ike and Marion themselves: somewhat the worse for the wear on the outside but full of decency and warmth on the inside. Ike relished his persona as an old curmudgeon but it did not take long for people to see through the facade. Both Ike and Marion would give you the shirt off their backs.

Doc Varney knew every domestic animal in the North Country. Unlike many modern veterinarians, Doc spent much of his time on the road making house calls. He had gone into a partnership with a younger woman who seemed content to keep office hours. Many of the citizens of Clifford were known to remark that they'd just as soon go to Varney for their own ailments rather than visit the doctors down in Berlin. It was an affront that the Doc was refused entry to the Schmidt farm. Of course, he did not show it. He had witnessed the results of the mountain lion attacks, so he was not on the good side of the authorities.

Roger Wright was imposing in his dark green state trooper uniform. In his law enforcement persona, Wright did not appear to be someone you would want to cross, but his friends all knew him as a "really nice guy." Like Doc and Rob, Roger felt resentment and frustration with the cover up of the cougar attacks. All three also suffered from guilt. They had decided to get on with their lives and gave up their attempts to tell the truth.

Jade did not know Phil Ramsey but he appeared to be knowledgeable and honest. Now, along with the others at the table, he knew what it felt like to have experienced something only to have the official version contradict everything he had seen. Jade watched as everyone calmly sipped his or her coffee. She was sure acquiescence was not on their minds. From everything she had heard about this mountain lion, they had to stop it before it harmed someone else.

Chapter 10

The Meurets and the Nashes had finished settling in. Pat and Holly Meuret and Karley and Tristan Nash were sitting on the wooden Adirondack chairs on the long dock in front of the lodge. The younger generation were diving off the raft a few hundred feet further out in the lake. Despite Ike's repeated protests that a hunting and fishing lodge should not have a raft, Jade had convinced Rob that the float would help attract summer guests.

"The kids seem to be getting to know each other," said Pat. "How long are you folks here for?"

"We're here for the week," said Tristan. "What about you?"

"We booked for the week as well," said Holly. "We are looking forward to some real peace and quiet."

"This looks like the place for that. I just want to read a couple of books and maybe explore some," said Karley.

Pat stretched back in his chair. "Is this your first time here?"

"I've been here a couple of time in the spring with a fishing buddy," said Tristan. "Usually all we do is fish. We live about three hours south of here, so we come up to this area often. Can't afford to stay at a place like this all the time, though."

"This is special for us," said Pat. "We wanted to experience something other than the usual touristy stuff. Everything is flat where we live. You look out from the back door and you can sees as far as the eye can see. This so different, so many hills and trees."

Karley turned toward her husband. "You know what? I would like to go to some those places you fish. They would be fun to explore."

"Can we invite ourselves along?" asked Holly. "I bet you can show us things we wouldn't find on our own."

"Sounds like a plan to me," said Tristan. "Let's go get those sandwiches we ordered and go have a picnic. I do know some neat places."

The adults called to the swimmers out on the raft. Paul pushed his brother into the water before diving in himself. Abbi jumped in. Not to be outdone by Paul, Connor pushed his older sister off the float. Kayla dove in last.

"Do you guys want to do some exploring?" asked Holly. Toweling off, the kids looked at each other and then back at their parents.

"Do we have to?" asked McKenzie.

"No, of course not. You are all old enough to be on your own. It's up to you. We just wanted to ask."

"We want to take the canoes out this afternoon," said Paul.

"Well, we are going to take a ride and visit some of the places where Dad has fished," said Karley. "You said you wanted to do that, Connor."

Connor looked at his siblings and his new friends. "Maybe later. I think I'll stay here."

"Okay. We're going to go get our sandwiches and take them with us. You might want to look into getting your lunches," said Tristan. "I think they're already made. Sandwiches. The big meals are breakfast and dinner. We'll be back for dinner. Make sure you take life vests with you when you go out on the lake."

"Dad, we don't—" began Connor.

"I mean it. Besides, it's the law."

"I'll make sure we do," said Kayla.

Pat, Holly, Karley and Tristan walked into the dining room.

The group at the table looked up with a start.

"Oh!" said Holly. "Hi! Are we…interrupting?"

"No, of course not," said Jade.

"We thought we might pick up our lunches," said Pat.

Marion got up from the table. "I'll have them for you in a jiffy. Why don't you meet me at the kitchen door around the corner?"

The two couples went back outside.

"I wonder what the state trooper is doing here," asked Tristan.

"I wondered about that too when I saw the cruiser come in," said Pat.

"Well, it doesn't have anything to do with us," said Holly. "We're on vacation. Forget the rest of the world."

"Well, it looks like we got caught with our Christly hands in the cookie jar on that one," said Ike.

"Shouldn't we tell them?" asked Jade.

"Are we overreacting?" asked Ramsey. "I know what I saw out on the lake, but do we really know what happened at the Schmidt farm? Maybe there's another explanation for what happened to that boy."

"Like what?" asked Wright.

Ramsey opened his hands. "I don't know. I just—"

"Just what?" asked Ike.

"If you really want an honest answer, all of this is so hard to—"

"Accept?" asked Rob.

"Yes, I guess so," said Ramsey.

Rob looked at the biologist. "We're not crazy. We're not a religious cult."

"No, I don't—"

"Look, we do have a choice. We can pretend a coyote attacked Randall Cramer and accept that some disease killed Schmidt's cows. Is anyone comfortable with that?"

"Not me," said Doc. "George Mason should also be here today or tomorrow. Both of us want to know what is happening at the Schmidt place. If there is another catamount that is anything like the last one, we all know how dangerous that is."

"Don't mountain lions usually stay away from humans?" asked Ramsey. "I thought they were shy animals. I guess your friend from out west must take this pretty seriously, if he is coming all the way here."

"There was nothing usual about the last attacks and I don't think there is anything normal about what is happening now," said Doc. "If I'm right—and I think others would agree—people could die."

Marion opened the kitchen door and came back into the dining room. "I haven't heard everything you said but I don't think we can afford to not be careful."

Rob looked at the state trooper and the biologist. "Do you agree?"

Both men nodded.

"I wasn't around when the mountain lion was here before," said Ramsey, "but I think I would be ready to testify to the veracity of everyone at this table."

Ike pulled out his pipe. "Yup right! A group of discredited dubbers, if I ever saw one. Ain't nobody goin' to listen to us. Government already says we're a bunch of Christly liars. You really want to 'sociate yourself with us? This is your last chance to get out."

"I guess I'm inclined to take my chances," said Ramsey

"So what do we do?" asked Jade.

"I think we should go after it," said Wright.

Rob looked around the table. Everyone seemed to acquiesce.

"How?" asked Marion.

"I think Phil and I should go back to where the kid was killed," said Wright. "At least we know it was there and it looks like they are not going to let us go to the farm."

Ramsey looked at Varney. "I'd like to have your friend from out west with us. He's a mountain lion expert, right?"

"Discredited one," mumbled Ike.

Doc turned to Jade. "If I can use your computer, I can find out when George is supposed to get here."

"He's 'nuther member of the highfalutin discredited club," snorted Ike.

"We're lucky to have him," said Marion. "And put that smelly old pipe away!"

"Ed and the kids should be here soon," said Rob. "He's bringing Virgil."

"Who's Virgil?" asked Ramsey.

Rob smiled. "He's Ed's dog. He's getting old but he sure came in handy last time. Saved Cindy and Josey's lives."

"Who's Cindy and Josey?" asked Ramsey.

"Ed and Marty's kids."

"Is Marty—"

"No," said Rob. "Ed and Marty are divorced."

"So you think this dog—Virgil—might be of some help," said Ramsey.

"Probably not," said Rob. "He has gotten pretty old."

"Kinda like the rest of us?" snorted Ike.

"Speak for yourself," said Jade.

"Does Ed know about what is going on?" asked Ramsey.

"I don't know," said Rob.

Wright looked at Ramsey. "I'm off tomorrow. We can go back out to the island tomorrow."

"Okay," said Ramsey. "Hopefully. Doc's friend will be here."

"What about our guests?" asked Jade.

"I don't think they should be out on their own until we figure out what is going on," said Wright.

"The adults are already gone," said Marion. "I gave them their lunches but I didn't realize they planned to leave. I should have—"

"It's not your fault," said Rob. "I wouldn't have thought that they would take off somewhere this soon after getting here. Maybe the kids know where they planned to go."

"Their kids are out in the canoes. They're just paddling around out by the raft."

Rob got up and opened the door. "I'll go ask them. Don't you think we should try to find them?"

"Yup," said Wright. "Can you and Ike do that? I'd better call in. What do you want to do, Phil?"

"I think I can get away with staying here. I'd like to meet Doc's friend."

Doc came back from using the computer.

"What about you Doc?" asked Wright.

"I've got some calls to make and George's e-mail says he should be in Clifford early this afternoon. He has also told a friend of his who is an Alaskan guide about all this and that fellow is actually going to come with his dogs. He specializes in this kind of hunt."

"Christ, another guy from far away," grumbled Ike. "He don't know nuthin' 'bout these woods."

"It sounds to me like we can use any help we can get," said Jade.

"I'll second that," said Roger. "Plus this guy might have a better chance of tracking the cat. I wouldn't know where to start. Would you?"

Ike fiddled with his pipe. "No, but I'm just sayin' that ain't nobody never listens to me. Every time I think we got things under control, the Christly shit hits the goddamned fan. I'm getting' fed up with it, if you want to know the truth. I just want some peace and quiet."

Rob came back from outside. "I can't disagree with you on that one," he said as he approached the table.

"That fan has spread more than its fair share of excrement in our direction. The Meurets and the Nashes went to check out the places where Tristan fishes when he's in the area. It's probably the usual holes. They shouldn't be too hard to find. Ike and I can go."

"On t'other hand, we ain't had nothin' happen to us," said Ike. "Not yet! We could just see what happens. Let them government guys or whoever they are take care of this."

"Are you saying it's not our problem?" asked Roger.

Ike stuck his pipe in his mouth. "The thing might just go away."

"Is that your considered opinion?" asked Rob.

"Just suggestin'" said Ike.

"As far as I'm concerned," said Doc, "it's my business when I'm not allowed to go visit sick animals in my hometown."

"I guess there is no reason why Ike and I can't go out and see if we can find our guests," said Rob.

"Even kinda knowin' where they might be, that's easier said than done," said Ike. "Lotta roads out there."

"You have a better idea, Ike?" asked Rob.

"Nope! Just pointin' out that things ain't always as easy as they appear. You make it sound like it's a piece of cake," said Ike. "Least it'll feel like we're doin' somethin' even if maybe we aint."

"How about we all get together back here this evening? Can we invite ourselves?" asked Doc.

"Can we feed these guys, Marion?" asked Rob.

Marion smiled. "We certainly can. Beef stew."

Roger Wright went out to his cruiser.

"Dinner's on the house," said Rob.

"Christ, they'll eat us out of house and home," said Ike.

"That's the idea," said Doc. "That's the real reason I'm here."

Ike grunted. "What about them kids?" he asked.

Jade went over to one of the windows. "They brought the canoes in. It looks like they are just playing around down by the lake. I can see them. Last time I looked, they were playing kick the can. Marion and I can look after them while you and Rob go after the parents."

"Playin' outside'll do them kids good," observed Ike. "Reminds me of my childhood. Didn't think kids nowadays played hide and seek kind a games. And here I'd lost faith in kids these days."

"Can you remember back that far?" asked Marion.

"Look who's talkin'," said Ike. "You ain't no spring chicken."

Wright came back into the dining room. "There's been an accident on the road below Clifford. I have to go. I'll see you tonight."

The Xterra crossed the bridge, started up the hill and then pulled off to the side of the road.

"That's the path," said Tristan. "There's actually a picnic table by the first pool. Why don't we have lunch there?"

"Who would bring a picnic table all the way up here?" asked Holly.

Tristan opened the drivers side door. "Who knows? At least a couple of presidents fished up here. Maybe they brought it in for them. I heard they stocked the river so that the presidents would be guaranteed to catch fish."

"Did they catch fish?" asked Pat.

"Couldn't say for sure," said Tristan "but I bet they did. It wouldn't look good for the president to get skunked."

Karley opened the back of the Xterra and took out a small cooler.

"It's only a short walk," said Tristan.

"It is incredibly beautiful out here," said Pat. "I didn't know it got this hot in New Hampshire."

"We get a couple of weeks of this every year," said Karley. She looked at Tristan.

"Is there a place we can swim in the river?"

"I wouldn't call it swimming, but there are places where we could sit in the river to cool off. Did we bring bathing suits?"

Karley shook her head. "They're back at the lodge. What about you guys?"

Pat looked at Holly. "Ours are back there, too.

Chapter 11

George Mason finished filling his metal water bottle then he cupped his hand under the small pipe that served as a conduit for the delicious spring water that flowed from a source deep down in the earth. Water doesn't get any better than this, George thought as he got back into his rented Chevy Malibu. He had pulled over by the side of the road. For a few moments, he watched a couple of people casting lures into the deep water under a bridge that connected with a dirt road on the other side. George wondered where the road led. There was also a father and mother with two young kids cooling off just a few hundred feet down the river. George remembered when he had done the same thing with his own children. They were all grown up now. He wished he'd spent more time with them when they were the same age as that boy and that girl who were splashing water on each other. Even now, just as when he was younger, he seemed to be a victim of time—always supposed to be somewhere.

He checked his watch. Speaking of time, he needed to make some if he was to get Clifford to meet Doc Varney on time. Everything's about time, he thought. Past time, present time, future time, lost time, too much time, daylight savings times... but mostly, not enough time. At his age, time was no longer on his side.

The Malibu navigated the twisty road north. The car seemed made for this kind of driving. George was lost in thought. He was still thinking about his family and about how fast life had flown by. As one of his friends had pointed out, the two of them were now already too old to die young. I guess that is comforting, George was thinking to himself—when something large and black materialized in front of the car. George reacted. It was too late to brake. The Malibu swerved to the left. He missed the object, whatever it had been. Then he heard the air horn and the screech of brakes. He saw the logging truck coming around the next curve. George cut the steering wheel to the right. It was too late. The semi clipped the Malibu sending it spinning on its roof into the rapidly flowing river.

"PB and J! I haven't had a peanut butter and jelly sandwich since I went to camp," said Pat. "I used to love them back then."

"So, is it as good as you remember?" asked Karley.

Pat took another bite. "Not bad. We used to eat this stuff by the tub loads. I remember the summer that the new peanut butter came out. You know the kind that doesn't separate. We thought that was the cat's pajamas."

"Turns out that it's not so good for you," said Holly. "Now we all seem to try to avoid hydrogenated fats. How's that white bread you're eating, Tristan?" asked Holly.

Tristan continued to eat. "I guess white is what you get when you forget to ask for wheat or rye. Actually, just about anything tastes good out here."

Holly lifted her can of ginger ale. "I'll drink to that."

Everyone held up his or her can of soda.

"Here's to vacation," said Karley. "School is still over a month away, plenty of time before the end of August."

"You're teachers right? When do you go back?" asked Pat.

Tristan finished his sandwich and rolled up the cellophane wrapping and put it back into his brown paper lunch bag. He pulled out an apple.

"Officially, the last week in August but I think we both find we need to start preparing for the fall as soon as August comes around. What about you guys? When do you go back to Nebraska?"

Holly took out a good-sized chocolate chip cookie. "We'll start driving back next week. Fortunately, we have enough help to keep the farm running. We can't stay away too long though. Pat's parents ran the place for many years, so it is in good hands. We actually planned this trip for quite some time. We figured we should do it before the kids get too old."

"What do we want to do now?" asked Tristan.

Karley wiped her brow with a napkin. "I'd still like to cool off in that water."

"If we walk up that path, there's a pool that is probably just over our heads."

Pat looked at Holly. "Sounds good to me," she said. "Are we going to skinny dip?"

Karley turned to her husband. He hesitated but then opened both palms in a "why not" gesture. "Haven't done that in years. Pat and Holly, are you okay with that?"

"Actually," said Holly, "works for us. We sometimes go to nudist resorts."

"Wow! Nudist colonies." said Karley. "Doesn't it feel kind of strange in front of all those other people? I'd be nervous. In fact, I am somewhat nervous right now. Where do you carry your wallet?"

Pat laughed. "I don't think anyone calls them colonies anymore. We're not outcasts or aliens from another planet who have colonized earth. You usually don't need a wallet. I only remember going to one place in Europe where you could actually shop in the nude. We carried our money around our necks. I don't really know why, but is very liberating to walk around without clothes. The hard part is getting dressed when you leave the resort. There's nothing to be nervous about. Nobody has clothes on. I'd probably feel more out of place, if I kept my clothes on."

"Clothes or no clothes," said Tristan. "I'm ready to cool off. Follow me. It's not far."

A few minutes later, the two couples arrived at a large deep pool in the river. Pat and Holly disrobed.

Both Karley and Tristan paused. "Wow!" said Karley. "Just like that."

"Just like that," said Pat. "The world hasn't stopped turning."

Tristan and Karley took off their clothes. Pat and Holly started toward the water.

"Ouch," said Holly. "It's pretty rough on the feet."

"Yeah, I'd keep my sneakers on. The bottom is very rocky."

They all put on their sneakers back on. Karley finished lacing hers first.

"I guess we are not completely nude." She worked to keep her balance as she stumble on the rocks out to the deeper water.

"It's like walking on bowling balls," she yelled back to the others as they also staggered on the loose stones. After a few moments, they were all immersed in the cold, clear water.

Pat dunked his head and then reappeared. "This does feel good."

Holly remained under water longer than her husband had. "I could stay in here all day," she said.

"I think I like skinny dipping," said Karley. "I really do feel more free."

"Looks like we may have found a new hobby," said Tristan. "You'll have to tell us about those resorts you go to. Where are they?"

"All over the country. Actually, all over the world," said Pat. "We'll give you some names when we get back to the lodge."

"So what do we want to do next?" asked Pat.

"I'd kind of like to go to Border Pond. I was there the last time I was here. The upper part of the river is up there and we can use the kayaks and the lodge's canoe to paddle to the pond. The owner gave me the lock combinations."

Pat looked at Holly. "Sounds good to us," he said.

The two couple worked their way out of the water.

"I think I remember how to get there," said Tristan.

Karley threw up her hands. "We are in deep trouble if we have to rely on Tristan's sense of direction."

"At least I know the difference between left and right," responded Tristan.

Karley smiled. "I know the difference. You just have to remember that Karley's right means left and vice versa. Easy!"

"I have the same problem," said Holly. "And, at least I know enough to ask for directions if I get lost."

"Your husband, too?" asked Karley.

Holly nodded.

"Well, there aren't any gas stations out here where we can ask for directions," said Pat.

"Don't need one. I'm pretty sure I remember how to get there," said Tristan.

"Famous last words," said Karley.

Chapter 12

"Are you sure?" asked the Emergency Medical Technician. "We really should have you checked out by a doctor."

George Mason sat on a rock next to the parked emergency vehicle. "I am a doctor. Of sorts."

One cruiser drove away as Roger Wright approached the accident scene. He got out of the cruiser.

He approached two officers who were surveying the scene.

"What happened?" asked Roger.

"The guy swerved to miss something and ended up in the river," said one trooper.

Roger looked over to where George was sitting.

"Is he all right?"

"Says he is," said the other trooper. "Says he's a doctor."

Roger looked at George again. "I know who that is. He's a vet."

"He served in the military? What's that got to do with anything?" asked the first trooper.

"No, he's a veterinarian."

The trooper laughed. "And to think, I'm up for detective."

"I won't say anything."

Roger walked over to the rescue vehicle. "You're George Mason, aren't you?"

George looked up. "Yes, you're the trooper who—"

"Roger Wright. Are you okay?"

"I'm trying to convince these guys that I am really okay."

"We should be taking him over to Cold Brook to be checked out," said one of the EMTs.

Roger looked at George. George nodded.

"I'll take care of him," said Roger. "I know him."

One of the troopers approached.

"I'll take Mr. Mason with me," said Roger. "Can we get his things out of the car?"

"The wrecker is ready to tow the car to Clifford. We need to do a couple of more things and then we can open up the other lane."

George and Roger went over to the now-battered-but-upright remains of George's rental car.

An ancient Izuzu Trooper drove by the cop who was directing the traffic by the accident scene in the one free lane that led from south to north. The SUV parked in front of Roger Wright's Dodge Charger.

Ed Rollins opened the driver-side door and got out. Cindy and Josey Rollins stayed in the car. Gray-muzzled Virgil stuck his head out of the back window of the weather-beaten SUV. His tongue drooped out of the side of his mouth and he breathed heavily. Time had taken its toll on both the dog and the vehicle.

Peter Schmidt put down his bottle of Sierra Nevada Ale. A man dressed in a dark suit, white shirt and red tie approached the porch. Three helicopters took off from the field next to the Schmidt's barn.

"The dead cows are gone. The diseased cow is on its way."

Schmidt motioned for the man to come up on the porch. "Are we sure this cow has Mad Cow disease?"

"We can't be absolutely sure until the animal is dead. The symptoms are there. We've created a bill of sale showing that you purchased the cows a couple of years ago. It would take at least that long for the disease to manifest itself. It can take up to eight years. Maybe longer, no one really knows. The blame for the contaminated feed will lead to a place in the United Kingdom. It is out of business because it used animal parts in its feed. The owners are already serving time."

"When should we call Varney?"

"As soon as the cow is here."

"You are sure that the animal can't infect my other cows."

"BSE is not contagious, not unless you decide to feed its brain to your other cattle."

Peter picked up his beer. "Well, I guess just the mention of Mad Cow disease should be enough to divert attention away from what really happened. I like the idea of having Varney verify the diagnosis. You are a genius. You want something to drink?"

"You wouldn't happen to have some coffee, would you?"

Peter called to his wife. "Could you make some coffee for Mr. Smith? And could you bring me the phone?"

"Do you want bourbon in the coffee?" yelled Mary.

Mr. Smith shook his head. "I don't drink."

Back at the lodge, Roger Wright's cruiser and Ed's Trooper were parked between the Meuret's Dodge Caravan and Ikes' Jeep.

"I'll be damned if I know where they went," said Ike. "Disappeared right off the map."

"Your timing was probably off," said Roger.

"Yup, every time we went somewhere, they was somewheres else. We came back 'cuz we figured they shoulda been back here by now," said Ike. "Christ, me and Rob looked everywhere."

Marion and Jade came through the kitchen door into the dining room.

"What'll it be gentlemen? Coffee or scotch or both?" asked Marion.

"It ain't goin' to be scotch. We gotta go look for them guests again," said Ike. "They shoulda been back."

"It is easy to get turned around out there," said Ed. "I've done it myself. The first time I wanted to find Border Pond, I took the Border Pond road. Who knew you couldn't get there using that road?"

"Well, you sorta can," said Ike. "but them roads is all gated."

"On the other hand, a lot of our guests stay out later than this," said Ike. "Huntin' 'n fishin' and stuff."

"Yeah," said Jade. "But these people aren't hunting and fishing and I don't think they would leave their kids this long, especially on their first day here."

"She's right. There are enough of us to recheck most of the roads," said Rob.

"You have hunted and fished out here, Doc. Why don't you and George go check the falls?"

Rob looked at Roger. "How about you? Have you been on these roads?"

"Only once, when we were looking for the cat and Ed's kids. Someone should probably go with me."

"I'll go with Roger," said Ed. "We can check the old dam. Let's take my car. I have both a MURS and a CB radio and I have four wheel drive."

"Okay, Phil and I'll go the other direction toward Border Pond," said Rob. "I have radios in my pickup. Doc, you have them in yours too, right?"

"Yes, I do. Assuming we find your guests, what about tomorrow?" asked Doc. "It appears that I have an invitation to visit the Schmidt place. They supposedly have a case of Mad Cow disease."

"You believe that?" asked Wright.

Doc smiled. "They probably have a bridge to sell me, too. George and I'll go and see what they have cooked up. I think I told you that George contacted a registered guide from Alaska. He is on his way. He has also lived in Montana. Word is, it was too crowded for him there. That's why he moved to Alaska. His name is Hank Harbor."

Jade smiled. "Sounds like my type of guy."

"I hear he is quite a ladies' man," said George.

"I'll keep that in mind," said Jade.

Jade and Marion went into the kitchen

"Sounds to me like he will be a good guy to have on board," said Roger. "I'm guessing his dogs might come in handy. No offense Ed, but old Virgil there is kind of getting along."

Hearing his name, Virgil looked up from where he was sleeping next to Ed's feet.

Ed rubbed the dog's ears. "You're doing just fine, aren't you, boy?"

Virgil lifted his head to accept his master's attention. When Ed pulled his hands away, Virgil looked up at his master and then dropped back down and resumed his snooze.

"Phil and I'll go out and take another look tomorrow at the place where the Cramer kid was killed," said Roger. "It'll also be interesting to see what the official cause of death turns out to be."

"The cops will probably say the Cramer kid was attacked by a wiezen biff," said Ike.

"What's a wiezen biff?" asked Ramsey.

"You know, one of them animals you haveta catch in a gunny sack. It's kinda a cross between a squirrel and a fisher cat. Mean son a bitches, they are."

"Oh, one of those. We call them snipes where I come from."

Ike shrugged. "Well they're called wiezen biffs around here."

"Rob and I'll keep an eye out for wiezen biffs," said Phil. "Maybe there is another logical answer for what happened to the kid and Schmidt's cows."

"You believe that?" asked Ike.

"No, I guess not," said Phil. "I just wouldn't believe any of this, if I hadn't seen what happened out on that island."

"Firsthand experience kind of does make you a believer.

Ike sneered. "What don't kill ya, will make ya stronger."

"Yeah! Screw that," said Rob. "I don't need any more getting stronger. When does this guy Harbor get here?"

"He's a pilot," said Doc. "I wouldn't be surprised to see him fly in to Clifford International tomorrow, probably late in the day."

"Christ, next thing you know, we're goin' to need more runways at the airport. I heard a couple of planes flew in there yesterday," said Ike. "Christ, next there'll be tourist flyin' in from all over the damned world."

"It does seem like we have been getting a lot of visitors in the last few weeks," said Doc. "Clifford's getting to be a popular place. Are we ready to go?"

Marion and Jade came out of the kitchen carrying six thermos bottles of coffee along with twelve sandwich boxes.

"This ought to tide you over. There's enough there for the guests. Beef stew will be on the stove when you get back,"

"Don't nobody want to go out with me?" asked Ike. "I know them roads like the back of my hand."

"Why don't you stay at the base station? That way if we get out of range with each other, you should be able stay in contact with all of us," said Rob.

"I 'spose I can do that," said Ike. "I just hate to miss out on no action."

Ike looked at Marion. "Don't I get no coffee and sandwiches?"

Marion smiled. "I've been kind of busy. Beside if you drink coffee, you'll keep me up all night."

Jade went back into the kitchen and then came back. "Here you go. I'll take care of you." She handed Ike a sandwich and a cup of coffee.

Rob got up. "There isn't going to by any action. We'll probably run into our guests driving back to the lodge. Are we ready to go?"

"Jade and I'll keep an eye on the kids," said Marion. "We can at least give them supper on time."

"I'll tell Cindy and Josey where we are going," said Ed.

"Have you told them about the mountain lion?" asked Rob.

Ed shook his head. "It took them a long time to get over what happened to them, especially Cindy. She still sometimes gets panic attacks in the woods."

"I guess you can't blame them," said Marion. They were pretty young and I have to tell you, I still get a shiver every time I think about what they went through."

"Maybe, I should take them back home," said Ed. "I don't think I can tell them—"

"Tell us what?" asked Josey.

Everyone turn their head as Josey entered the room.

"I was thinking of taking you and Cindy back home," said Ed.

"Mom's in California," said Josey.

Ed stood up. "We could stay in a hotel."

"Why would we do that?"

"Because I think it might be a good idea if we didn't stay here."

"Why not? Something's going on? What? We've just made some new friends and I like being here. Cindy seems to be having fun, too, even if we are in the woods."

"That's just it. I'm afraid Cindy—"

"What? I'm sixteen," said Josey. "We're both old enough—"

"I think you need to tell him," said Jade.

Rob nodded. The others looked at the youth who stood in front of them. Maybe for the first time, Ed realized that Josey was no longer

— 51 —

a kid. He felt a flash of guilt as he also recognized that he was momentarily jealous of his son's strength and vigor.

"Oh, for Christ's sake!" Ike blurted out. "The goddamned cat is back!"

"What do you mean?"

"The Christly mountain lion. The catamount. The thing that tried to kill you."

"It' can't be the same one," said Josey. "I saw it die. So did you. We were there."

"What I know and what is, ain't always the same thing."

Chapter 13

"Maybe if we get out and push," Pat suggested.

When Tristan tried to engage the Xterra in either a forward or reverse direction, the four wheels spun harmoniously, spewing water-logged dirt over the body of the vehicle. The four passengers peered alternatively out through the semi-circular openings created by the windshield wipers in both the front and the rear. It was like being in a tunnel.

"There is no resistance at all," said Tristan. "We are literally swimming in mud. There's nothing for any of the wheels to grab onto."

Tristan put the gearshift into the park position.

Karley glared at her husband.

"I told you this didn't look like much of a road."

"I'm positive—"

Karley rolled down the passengers side window. The dirty glass grated against the rubber molding that protected the interior of the door.

"Tristan, we are in the middle of nowhere! How the hell do you think we are going to get out of here?"

Tristan stared through the windshield. He wanted to pound his fists on the steering wheel, but in deference to Pat and Holly sitting in the back seat, he restrained himself. "Shit!"

Pat looked at his cell phone. "No signal."

"No there wouldn't be," said Tristan. "I'm sorry, guys. I thought this thing would go through anything."

"Should we try and push?" asked Pat.

Tristan turned to Karley. "Do you want to take the wheel?"

"Sure."

"Let's see if we can go backwards. Even if we go forwards, we'll have to come back through this."

Tristan opened the door. He climbed into near knee-deep water. Pat and Holly climbed out of the back seats. They sloshed to the front of the SUV.

Tristan yelled to Karley. She put the Xterra into reverse. Tristan, Pat and Holly pushed. The four wheels slung water, mud and dirt into three frustrated faces. There was no discernible progress.

Tristan spit. "Try again."

The second try yielded the same result. Tristan motioned toward the vehicle. "Well, it was worth a try, I guess. Let's get back in."

Once inside, Karley offered paper towels to the mud-covered trio.

"You guys are always prepared," said Holly. She wiped her face.

"Well, at least it's summer. We're not going to die or anything," said Pat. "What's going to bother us out here?"

"Nothing. We might hear some coyotes but they don't want anything to do with us."

Karley turned around to the back seat. "What do you guys want to do?"

"We could wait here," said Holly. "I assume someone would come looking for us when we don't get back."

"Do you think they would look for us on this road?" asked Karley.

"If this is the Border Pond Road," said Tristan. "I think there's a good chance. On the other hand, they might be more likely to find us, if we were on one of the main logging roads. Actually, I think some of the loggers stay out here in their trucks. They have radios. That last log yard wasn't that far from here. We still have a little daylight left. Maybe someone's still there."

"We could try to find a logger," agreed Pat, "but it's not going to be light too much longer."

"It might be worth a—" said Holly.

"Do want to be out there in the dark?" asked Pat. "It'd be easy to get lost."

Tristan took a drink of water. He opened the passengers side door and spit a mouth full of water outside. He re-closed the door.

"I'm not real worried about getting lost but the wind has gone down. We'll get eaten alive if we're out there now. It'll be unbearable in the dark."

"Eaten alive?" gasped Holly. "What do you—"

"Black flies. They've already started coming out."

"They can't be that bad," said Holly.

Karley turned around to face the Meurets. "Yes, they can be. Drive you crazy. They're relentless."

"I guess we stay inside," said Pat.

Karley pointed behind Pat and Holly. "We have some trail mix in the pack in the back and there is still some water in our water bottles. I guess we won't die of thirst or hunger. And we do have a flashlight. There's even a deck of cards."

"You guys really are like boy scouts. Always prepared!" said Pat.

"We have kids," said Karley

"I understand," said Pat. "We'll be in the lap of luxury."

"Don't know about that, but I'll get the stuff out of the back," said Tristan.

He opened the door and climbed into mucky water. He thought he saw something ahead. He sloshed around the front of the vehicle. With each step he had to fight to keep his Keen Sandals from being sucked into the soft earth below. Six feet in front of him the road was once again dry, rocky and passable. Nothing. His eyes followed the long stretch of green grass that separated the tire ruts that had been created by generations of vehicles—traveling, obviously, to some-where. It didn't look like anyone had used the road recently though. There were no fresh tire tracks. Pat joined Tristan. He swatted a swarm of black flies.

"I see what you mean."

"I thought I saw something up there. Do you see anything?"

"No."

Tristan pointed to the left of the Xterra. "That beaver dam is what flooded the road. That and it looks like it rained not too long ago. I am still sure this is the right road."

"I guess it doesn't much matter," said Pat, "if we can't get the car out."

"If I am right, the river and the pond are not far from here. There's a canoe there. There are a couple of houses on the pond. Maybe someone is there. They probably have radios."

"This doesn't look like the kind of road that would lead to someone's house."

"No, they get in from the other side. You can only reach the houses by water from this side. We could use the lodge's canoe. We have our kayaks. What do you think?"

"What about these damned black flies?"

"I have survived worse, but you're right. Best to stay right here."

Karley and Holly both opened their doors. Karley hesitated. Holly jumped into the puddle. That's all it was really, but it was just long and deep enough to hold the powerful four-wheel-drive vehicle hostage.

Holly moved forward. "Pat, what are you doing? I thought—"

Pat and Tristan waited for her to wade out of the water. They watched her stop. Time seemed to slow as the two men watched Holly's face contort first into surprise and then alarm.

"Pat! Tristan! Behind you. Karley get back in the car! What's—"

Holly froze, her mouth open and pointed.

Tristan and Pat turned around. Time had still not returned to its normal cadence. Crouched low, a large, sleek, black form with intense fire-like yellow eyes seemed almost to be floating towards them.

"In the car!" yelled Tristan.

Time was now moving much faster. Holly jumped back in the car. Karley slid over to the drivers side front door. Both women watched as the animal gracefully sprang. Again, time slowed. Karley saw the black phantom floating in the air. It had to be a figment of her imagination. Had to be, but…. She had no time to think but she knew she was watching a monstrous black cat that was about to slaughter her husband and Pat Meuret.

Both women threw open the drivers side doors. Both men sprang into the car. The angled edge of the front door hit the cat just below the throat altering its trajectory. Tristan and Pat slammed their doors shut. Momentarily, the cat almost looked like an oversize house cat as it stood on the side of the road looking up at Tristan. That illusion was shattered by the penetrating yellow eyes that looked as if they might bore through the glass and metal that was the only thing that was protecting the four terrified humans inside the impotent SUV.

The cat paced around the vehicle and then let out a mournful wail that pierced through the early evening air like an Abenaki arrow.

Rob pulled the pickup to the side of a well-traveled logging road.

"If we go straight, we'll come to a gate. The Canadian border is only about a half mile beyond that. If they went that way, they'd just have to turn around. If we go right, the same thing. The lumber company is fixing the road up there. It's not passable, even with four wheel drive."

Phil Ramsey looked to his left. "There was a hell of a sunset somewhere but it's gotten dark here fast. If it weren't for the trees... What's that over there?"

"That's the road to Border Pond and the upper part of the river."

"It doesn't look like it gets used much."

"Actually, more than you would think. One of the local game wardens keeps a canoe up there. It's good fishing. Not everyone knows about it. It doesn't get as much pressure as the fishing holes down below. I can't remember the last time that anyone maintained the road. It does look like there are some fresh tire tracks. Worth a shot."

"Okay.

The pickup's headlights swept around to the west and illuminated the tunnel-like entrance to the Border Pond Road. Low hanging branches on both sides of the pathway brushed along the sides and top of the slow-moving vehicle.

"There they are," said Ramsey.

Rob stopped the pickup. The headlights illuminated the Xterra,

"It looks like they're stuck," he said.

Both men started to get out of the truck.

"Oh shit! We have to warn them," shouted Pat.

"Is it still out there?" asked Holly. "It's too dark to see."

Tristan turned on his lights. "It's still there. What—"

Pat rolled down his window. "Get back!" he yelled.

"What did he—" asked Phil

"Get back into your car!" screamed Pat.

"What?" yelled Rob.

"Get back! There's—"

"Oh shit!" cried Tristan. He blasted his horn. He turned on his emergency lights.

Pat continued to holler out his window. Tristan and Holly watched the black form slither alongside the drivers side of the car. It was impervious to the yelling and the ear-piercing blasts of the horn.

"What are they doing?" cried Ramsey.

Rob approached the Nissan.

"Oh no! Not again. They're trying to—"

Rob dove under the car. "Get under—"

Ramsey stopped. Immobile, he watched as the long sleek silhouette seemed to float through the air toward him. His mind had never processed anything like this before. He couldn't move. Suddenly, he comprehended.

"I'm dead!" Then his body responded. He started to move. Both his arms flew up and crossed in front of his face. It was too late. The mountain lion assaulted Phil Ramsey. Instinctively, Rob felt impelled to help. He had no weapon. He crawled out from underneath the vehicle. He started jumping up and down, shrieking and waving his hands. The animal's eyes seemed to bore into Rob as the cat turned away from Ramsey's wounded body lying motionless on the ground. Holly opened her door.

"Get in," she yelled.

Rob continued to try to frighten the cat away from its prey. He threw a fist-size rock. It fell short. He picked up another smaller rock. This time he hit the mountain lion in the midsection of its body. The catamount snarled.

Tristan rolled down his window. "Get in the car!"

Then the cougar inched toward Rob. Once more, it bared it's bloody teeth.

"For God's sake! Now!" yelled Tristan.

Rob turned and jumped into the back seat of the Xterra and slammed the door shut.

The cat circled and re-circled the car. Then he returned to the body on the ground. Tristan, Karley, Pat, Holly and Rob watched as the cat dragged the biologist into the woods.

Chapter 14

Ed and Roger climbed up the hill from the old dam.

"They aren't here," said Roger. "What now?"

Ed climbed into the Izuzu. He picked up the mic for his two-way radio. He tried Rob. There was no response.

"That's odd," he said. "Rob shouldn't be out of range."

Then he called back to the lodge. He asked Ike if he had heard from Rob.

"Nope," said Ike. "I ain't heard nothin'"

"Okay," said Ed. "The guests aren't here, so we are going to head up toward Border Pond."

"Suits me," responded Ike. "Doc and George didn't find nothin' up the falls neither. They did find one of them nametags Marion put on the lunches though. It had the Meuret's name on it. It musta fell off. Anyways, it seems like them guests was there."

"What are Doc and George going to do?"

"Kinda drive around a bit more. They're headin' back to go check out Long Pond."

"Okay, we'll keep in touch."

Ed started the Trooper, turned on his headlights, and put the SUV in gear.

"Have they found our parents yet?" asked Paul Meuret.

"Nope, not yet," said Ike.

"Have you heard from my Dad?" asked Cindy Rollins.

Ike nodded. "Yup, he just called in. He's headed up to Border Pond."

Cindy was sitting at the table with Cameron and Abbi

Meuret. Kayla and Connor Nash pulled up chairs next to the group. Paul Meuret, McKenzie Nash, and Josey Rollins were standing by Ike.

"We could help, too," said Paul. "Josey and I both have our driver's licenses. We could—"

Jade came out of the kitchen with cold soda. "I'm sure they will find your parents," she said. "It's best if you stay here. You don't know the area and we don't want to have to go out looking for you."

"I suppose," said Paul.

"I do know the roads out there," said Josey. "I have been out there with my Dad."

Jade looked at the three older teenagers. "No one else is going out. Everyone is going to be fine. I am sure your parents just got lost. There are only so many places they can go."

"What about the mountain lion Josey told us about?" asked Paul.

Ike butted in. "There are a few thousand acres out there and one Christly mountain lion. They ain't likely to run into it."

Marion brought out some cookies from the kitchen. "Ike, will you please watch your language."

"I was just makin' a point."

Marion passed the cookies to the kids. "He is right. I am sure your parents will be back before you know it."

"It found us the last time," said Cindy. "It was…"" Cindy wanted to cry but she held back. "Please, Josey, don't go out. I don't want to be here without you or Dad. I wish we could go home."

"He'll come back," said Josey. "I'm not going anywhere. Everything will be okay."

Abbi got up and went over to Cindy. She hugged her new friend. Cindy glanced around the room. She knew everyone here cared but none of them could offer the comfort she needed. She couldn't go home, not yet anyway. Her Mom was in California and her Dad was out in the woods. The mountain lion was out there too. She knew what it could do.

The room was quiet except for the nervous creak of a wooden chair or the soft crunch of a piece of Marion's homemade cookies. Paul pulled the tab on a can of soda. Everyone looked over at him.

Then Rob's voice came over the two-way radio. "We found them!"

Ike picked up the mic. "Where?"

"Up by.....Holy Sh....! We'll get—"

"What's goin' on?" cried Ike.

There was no answer.

Ike tried calling again and again. There was no response. "Shit!"

Cameron, Abbi, Kayla, and Connor all rushed over to where the adults were standing.

"What's happening?" cried Cindy.

Jade turned toward the frightened girl. "I'm sure everything is all right. We often lose radio contact," she lied. "Where are Paul, Josey and McKenzie?"

A motor started in the parking lot. Jade ran to the window. The Meuret's Grand Caravan was making its way up the hill.

It wasn't easy to impress Hank Harbor, but there was something about flying his rented Husky over Mount Washington, New Hampshire's highest peak, that triggered the same sense of awe that he felt every time he flew the Alaskan Bush in his PA-18 Super Cub.

He loved flying. Whenever it was possible, he preferred to be the pilot. He liked to be in control. He did not like being a passenger. Passengers were at the mercy of someone else and Harbor didn't care for that. He hunted everything, from grizzlies to elk. Where he lived, there was no supermarket. He had a free-range diet.

He was happy living in the Alaskan Bush where he had built his own home. Most of all he enjoyed hunting for prey that just might fight back. Harbor knew that someday his time would come, yet his mortality did not concern him. You have what you have while you have it. He welcomed the fact that his chosen lifestyle would most likely not lead to an old age spent slowly dying in a nursing home. He had watched both of his parents die passive, lingering deaths. He had seen the future and it was not pretty. Once you are gone, does it really matter how long you were here? Someday, the time would come. Something he stalked would turn on him. He hoped for that, at least. It would be poetic justice. He would die in the wilderness, Hank Harbor would make sure of that.

Hunting for a rogue mountain lion in northern New England was his kind of challenge. This was especially true since it was next to impossible to find a track during the summer months. Mountain lion hunts that Hank had guided had all been in the winter. Hank enjoyed finding the track and working with his dogs to tree the cougar.

Mountain lion hunting was not for sissies, thought Harbor. The process, although challenging, was straightforward. Once you found the track, it was time to hunt. The dogs chased the cat. It was up to the hunter to find the treed animal and then shoot it. This was usually in rough country. Most mountain lions didn't want to be found. This one that Hank Harbor had come to capture was different. It showed itself and it attacked. That will be its fatal flaw, thought Harbor. I just need to figure out where it will attack next.

Three of Harbor's black-and-tan hounds had been flown to Manchester airport and would be transported north by a canine unit of the New Hampshire State Police. Someone had suggested that he tranquilize the cat. That was, at best, a tricky solution. The effects of tranquilizing are not always immediate. That makes the animal even more dangerous. This cat was not going to be relocated. It killed human beings. It had to be killed.

Harbor carried a relatively small caliber .243 Winchester to bring down this catamount. Harbor counted on his ability to make an accurate, clean shot. He sometimes hunted with a bow or a muzzleloader. He did carry a high-powered handgun in case he got into a tight situation where he couldn't count on his hunting skills. He was not ready to die yet. He was still in his prime. He was at the top of his form.

THE OLD ABENAKI

The aged man was not at peace. The remains of his beloved wife rested nearby but something was... He envied Molly's repose. He did not have that. He was not at rest. He seemed to be in some kind of future. It was not the present exactly. The future and the present seemed to be the same. The past was separate. He remembered that. He was at her place. He was here often, but he could not say how he got here. He just seemed to be wherever he was.

Without knowing how, he knew someone else had been in this place too. That person had died here. This sacred ground had been violated. He was aware of the presence. The piercing yellow eyes were watching. For a moment, the Abenaki was a hunter again, his eyes and nose were those of a young man. He sniffed. He could smell the animal. He saw it and then the vision vanished.

He returned to his aged embodiment. What he had seen was majestic, but it was wrong. This was not the sacred mountain lion of his tribe. The white men had hunted those magnificent tawny animals to extinction. The Abenaki had always respected his prey. He had always given thanks for the power he had taken from the animals he had killed. They provided sustenance when he was alive. He had never hunted sacred mountain lions.

This phenomenon was different. Was it evil? Good and evil did not make sense in the same way now that he wasn't... Wasn't what? Alive? He did know that somehow the black apparition had to be stopped. Did he have the power? Was he responsible? Had he ever meant for his curse to take on a reality such as this? He knelt down to pray to the white man's God. He had long ago given up calling upon the divinities of his own people.

Chapter 15

The pickup continued to idle. Through a light mist, its headlights illuminated the interior of the Xterra. Inside the air was thick and stale. The five trapped people regarded each other. Each one was looking for an answer in the other's eyes. Eventually, they were able to speak.

"What do we do?" asked Holly.

"Is it gone?" asked Karley.

"It's been a half hour," said Pat.

"It's gone," said Rob. "When it's around, you can feel it. It's the same feeling you get when someone is creeping up behind you. It's what people claim to experience in a haunted house."

"That didn't seem like a ghost to me," said Holly.

"Me neither," Tristan agreed.

"It's real," said Rob, "all too real, but it's a reality that shouldn't be. It's a mountain lion, a catamount."

"There are mountain lions out west but I've never heard—" said Pat.

Tristan looked out the window. "I've been going into these woods since I was a kid. Except for getting lost or being unprepared in the cold, one of the things I always liked about these places was that they were safe. I have never been afraid before now. Never!"

"Shouldn't we have been warned about—" asked Holly.

"Wasn't there supposed to have been something…? I mean back when the forest fire burned near here. Holy shit! All of that was true!" said Tristan.

"What are you talking about?" asked Pat.

"Look," said Rob. "Let's get you out of here. I can hook a

chain to your tow hitch. We can talk about all of this when we get back to the lodge. I am going to turn my vehicle around. I'll be right back."

Rob opened the door. Holly grabbed his shoulder. "What about that man?"

Rob got out of the car. "Once we have you out, we'll look. I survived exactly the same thing."

"You?" gasped Holly.

"We'll look," said Rob and closed the door. The four people in the SUV watched as the pickup slowly backed up out of sight.

"He wouldn't leave us here, would he?" asked Karley.

"No, I don't think he would do that," said Tristan.

"I wish they had told us about…" said Holly. "Don't you think they should warn you that something like this could happen."

"This isn't exactly normal for around here," said Tristan. "I don't think they thought—"

"It's normal enough that this is not the first time for that guy who owns the lodge. He just said that he survived being attacked," said Pat.

"Here he comes," said Karley.

The red taillights of the pickup approached the back of the Xterra. For a moment, Holly flashed back to the fiery yellow eyes of the black cat. The brake lights brightened and the vehicle stopped. Rob went to the back of the truck and took out a short chain. Tristan rolled down his window.

Rob attached the chain to the stuck vehicle. "Let me get into my truck, then put yours into reverse and I should be able to pull you out."

Rob climbed back into the pickup, engaged the four-wheel drive and shifted into the first gear. The truck groaned but inched forward. The stuck SUV seemed to float. The wheels sprayed water and then grabbed solid ground. The Xterra popped out of the water. Rob stopped, opened the door, got out and unhooked the chain.

Tristan leaned out of his window. Rob took a flashlight out of his jacket pocket.

"I'm going to look for Phil. I can't go back without seeing if I can find him."

"Do you need help?" asked Tristan. He started to open the door.

Rob waved him back. "No, you stay here. You're safe in the car. I'll look quickly. If I don't see anything, we'll come back tomorrow."

Rob pointed the light in the direction that the cat had taken the biologist. He hesitated. He looked around. Nothing. He felt his last meal move way too quickly through his intestines. He pushed through the underbrush to a small clearing.

At first, all he saw was a pile of brush. Then he saw the arm. Rob moved the flashlight back and forth from left to right. Nothing. He approached the pile of scrub and started to remove the sticks. The body underneath twitched.

My God, he's alive, thought Rob. Then he heard something move right behind him.

The Grand Caravan crossed over a sturdy wooden bridge and then started up a steep hill.

Paul slowed down. "I thought you knew where to go."

Josey looked out of the back window. He leaned forward. "I sort of do. It looks different and I haven't been here in a while... Pull over right there. There's enough room to park. That's the path down to the falls."

McKenzie looked out the drivers side door. "This can't be the place. Their car's not here."

"I know," said Josey. "I'm just trying to find the places where they would probably go. This is on that old guy's map."

"So where should I go now?" asked Paul.

Josey sat back into his seat. "I don't know. Maybe this was a bad idea. What are we going to do anyway? I am scared. It's like I am going through all of it again. That thing was a killer."

"I didn't think mountain lions want anything to do with us. And what was it, I mean is it, doing around here?" asked Paul.

"It must have been horrible!" said McKenzie.

"It was! If it hadn't been for Virgil, neither Cindy or I would be here."

"That old dog you brought with you?" asked Paul.

"He wasn't old then."

McKenzie pulled something out of her pocket. "Hey guys, you want to share this with me? It helps me when I am nervous or afraid."

"Why not?" said Paul.

McKenzie opened the door. "We better do it outside. I don't want my parents to smell it in the car."

The three teenagers each took their individual turns until the joint disintegrated into ash.

"Wow! That does help," said Josey. "I feel like I could face that mountain lion all by myself. You know what I want to be when I grow up?"

"A mountain lion hunter?" asked Paul.

"No, a Fish and Game officer."

"I want to be Captain America," said Paul.

"I'm serious," said Josey. "I want to work in the woods."

"Don't be so serious," said Paul. "We can be the invincible three. Who are you going to be McKenzie?"

The girl extended her arms, shoulder height in front of her body and pretended to fly. "I'm Super Girl"

Paul clenched his left fist and held up his right hand. "I'm Captain America but I can't find my shield." Paul started to giggle.

Josey pretended to climb up the side of the car. "All right, so I'm Spider Man," he said as he fell backwards onto the ground. Paul and McKenzie doubled over, chortling uncontrollably. Josey joined in writhing on the ground.

Then they heard it. The sound was mystifying, yet familiar. What was it? A cat purring? But it was too loud. Josey knew the sound.

"In the car!" he screamed.

McKenzie jumped in the drivers seat. Paul and Josey dove into the back seat.

"Go!" cried Josey. "Do you know how to drive?"

"I'm learning! I can't find the keys."

"In the ignition," yelled Paul. "I didn't take them out."

"Oh!" said McKenzie. She turned on the ignition. The car started to move. The headlights panned from the woods to the road.

There it was. McKenzie braked. There it was. The large, beautifully sleek, black ghostlike figure stood there for a moment. The reflected light shimmered in the cats burning yellow eyes. They reached deep into the stoned paranoia of all three teenagers.

Josey was the first to react.

"Go!"

"Where?" sobbed McKenzie. "It's in the way."

"Go as fast as you can!" yelled Josey.

The girl hit the accelerator. Dirt spewed up from the back tires. The cat seemed to float into the forest. It was gone. McKenzie sped up the hill. She almost missed the sharp curve at the top. Then the road straightened out into a flat stretch.

McKenzie gave the car more gas.

"Where are we going?"

"Just keep going," said Josey. "Let's just get away from here."

Paul leaned toward the front seat. "Are you all right?" he asked McKenzie.

"I think so."

"What's that?" screamed Paul.

"It's big," said McKenzie.

Josey braced himself. "It's a moose!"

Chapter 16

Rob spun around. A shiver of alarm rushed up his spine. Nothing there, at least not that he could see. His nose registered the sharp smell of cat pee that came from the pile of brush behind him. The catamount had staked its territory. Rob was standing in that territory. The rustling in the brush grew closer. Was it the cat? His reason told him no. If he were the prey, there would be no warning. Mountain lions do not signal their intent. Yet, primeval instinct gripped his intestines. He wanted to turn around, to reach for Phil Ramsey, to save the man, to pull him out from underneath that God forsaken pile of brush, to get out of here before that damned thing returned to claim its evening meal. Rob did not move. Something was coming. Rob wanted to run but he remained immobile.

Ed Rollins and Roger Wright appeared in the clearing.

"Shit!" said Rob. "I thought—"

"Are you okay?" asked Ed.

"Is Phil—" asked Roger.

Rob pointed to the pile of brush. "He's alive! I saw him move. I was—"

"Let's get him out of here!" said Roger.

The three men grabbed the dead branches that covered Phil Ramsey's limp body. They threw the brush aside.

"Are you sure he's..." asked Roger. "He looks dead."

Rob knelt down. "I saw him move. I know I did."

Rob felt for the man's pulse. "He is alive!"

"Should we move him?" asked Ed

"We can't leave him here," said Rob. "It doesn't look like he has any obvious broken bone but we need to get those wounds taken care of. You can see the teeth marks. Roger and I can carry him out. Go tell the people with that SUV to put the back down. It looks like they've got room."

Ed headed back to the vehicles. Rob and Roger turned the unconscious man onto his back. Roger lifted Ramsey's head and neck to a sitting position. Using both arms, he secured the injured man's upper body. Rob crossed Ramsey's legs and picked them up with his left hand. Then Rob and Roger carried the man back to the waiting vehicle.

Jade and Ike were sitting on the stoop in front of the back kitchen door. A stretcher was leaning against the side of the wall. They watched as three sets of headlights materialized at the top of the hill. Ike grabbed the stretcher.

"Let's get him."

Ed and Roger got out of the old Izuzu and went over to the Nissan. They opened the rear hatchback.

"He's in here!" yelled Roger. "Ike, you and Ed get the stretcher ready. Rob and I will lift him out."

George came running out of the front door of the lodge.

"Take him inside. We got a bed ready for him on the porch. Let's not move him any more than necessary."

Jade held the door as Ike and Ed carefully carried the stretcher onto the porch.

"Keep the weight close to your body," instructed Roger.

Once inside Roger and Rob lifted the severely wounded man onto the bed. George inspected the lacerations and checked Ramsey's vital signs.

"He gonna make it?" asked Ike.

George turned around. "I'd say that he is one lucky guy, but we do need to get him to a hospital. Ike, get on that radio and get an airlift out here."

"I already got an ambulance comin'," said Ike. "I don't know why it ain't here yet."

"It's here," said Ed.

"We need a helicopter!" yelled George. "The ambulance'll take too long." Ike looked outside.

"Get the 'copter!"

Ike went back to the radio.

Red flashing lights seem to float down the hill amidst the whoops of a wailing siren. The vehicle stopped. Then there was silence. The staccato of red and black illuminated and then darkened the interior of the porch. The EMTs rushed onto the porch. They examined the man on the bed.

"We're way too far away," said one of the EMTs. "We're going to need an airlift."

"It's on the way," said George.

"Good," said the other EMT.

Chapter 17

Jade came out of the lodge onto the porch. A tall imposing figure stood next to her.

"This is Hank Harbor," she said. "He's the guide from Alaska."

Harbor held out his hand. Rob felt the controlled strength in the man's hand as he shook. The two men appraised each other. Rob looked at Jade. How did he compare to this man? Rob let the thought go. If the man noticed Rob's momentary lapse in self-confidence, he did not let on.

"Good to meet you," said Harbor.

"Likewise," said Rob. "I see you got the only rental truck in town."

"Yup, quite a relic, isn't it?"

"Yeah, it is," said Rob. "But old Bill Holiday keeps her running smoothly. Other than fish, about all he does is work on that beat up Ford. He's never had a dissatisfied customer as far as I know. Lots of people have rented that truck. Bill is quite an angler. His son and his wife now own a fly shop. Runs in the family I guess. He got his mechanical skills in the army—I think he was a colonel or something like that. Young Bill comes up here from time to time."

Harbor smiled. "The engine sounds good and the brakes work."

"Well in any case, you're better off with Bill's pick-up than Ike's Jeep. I'm surprised he hasn't tried to con you into renting that."

Harbor smiled again. "I haven't been here long enough, I guess. I did meet Ike. He didn't mention the Jeep."

Jade interrupted. Rob looked at her. Hank Harbor was a good ten years younger than Jade but Rob could not help noticing the tall man and the attractive white-haired woman beside him would make an intriguing couple.

"We have another problem," said Jade.

"What?" asked Rob.

Harbor watched Rob.

"Josey, McKenzie, and Paul are gone."

"What do you mean gone?"

"They took the Meuret's van and drove off."

"Really?" asked Rob.

"Really," said Jade.

"My parents are going to kill me," said Paul. "This car is almost brand new."

Paul, McKenzie and Josey stood outside the wrecked Dodge Caravan. McKenzie still held a towel she had used to wipe the blood off her face.

"It's my fault," she said. "I didn't see... I'm so sorry."

"No, it's not," said Josey. "It happened so fast. That's how it is. A moose is right there in front of you. Then it's too late. I almost hit one right after I got my license."

McKenzie was still shaking. "It was like driving into a cement wall."

"It's not dead," said Paul. "It's twitching."

"It must be in pain?" said McKenzie. "I didn't mean to—"

The bloody, comatose moose lay over the damaged hood of the van. Most of the front windshield was shattered, yet more or less intact. The fragmented safety glass had bowed in where the moose's developing velvet antlers had broken through. Blood and another yellowish, sticky fluid dripped through the hole in the glass. The van was covered in moose excrement.

"I don't think it is now," said Josey. "But if it comes to, I'm not sure what it'll do. That's a big fucking animal. If we'd been going any faster, that thing would be in the front seat."

"So what do we do?" asked Paul. "We can't move it."

"Do you think the car will start?" asked Josey.

Paul turned around and inspected both sides of the mangled vehicle.

"The wheels seem okay. The hood is bent way in. I don't know if it is hitting the motor." Paul opened the drivers side door. "The steering wheel and everything look all right. You can't see anything through the windshield though. All you see is moose, gross blood...and shit. I don't know what that other stuff is. Are you thinking we should drive back with it on the car? I don't think I can stand the smell."

"What else are we going to do? It's a long walk. Do you have a better idea?" asked Josey.

"If we wait or start back, someone'll come after us."

"But no one knows where we are. What about the mountain lion?"

"Shit!" said Paul.

McKenzie continued to try to wipe various fluids off her face and clothing. "I just want to get out of here. I want a bath."

"I have an idea," said Josey. "What would happen if we got up some speed and we slammed on the brakes? Wouldn't the moose get thrown off the hood. We do have one head light left and you can drive with your head out the window. The road looks pretty straight."

Paul opened the front door. He looked back. "Can I have that cloth?"

McKenzie wiped her hands and then threw the soiled towel to Paul.

"It's not very clean," she said.

"It's better than nothing," said Paul. "The steering wheel and dashboard are really super gross."

"Tell me about it! You weren't sitting in the front seat!" yelled McKenzie.

Paul got into the car. He turned the key. Nothing! A moment later, he tried again. The engine turned over and started. Paul stuck his head out the window.

"Get in," he yelled.

McKenzie and Josey got into the back seat.

"Should I try to get rid of it?" asked Paul.

"Do it," said McKenzie.

Paul put the Dodge into drive and hit the gas pedal. The van lurched forward. Paul stepped on the gas pedal, accelerated to almost thirty-five miles an hour.

"Now?"

McKenzie and Josey braced themselves.

"Now!" yelled McKenzie and Josey.

Paul hit the brakes. The moose's body bounced off the windshield but its head remained stuck in the glass. Blood and the sickly yellow fluid sprayed over Paul's face and torso. The animal resettled even deeper into its previous position. He slammed the steering wheel with both hands.

"This really sucks! I...I think I'm...I'm going to be sick." Paul opened the door and vomited. Then he closed the door again. "Any other ideas?" he asked.

"How about if we try to break the glass," said Josey.

"What do you mean?"

Josey opened his door. "We could use a rock. If we could get the head out of the hole, maybe my idea would work then."

McKenzie got out of the car. "I'm going to wait out here. If I stay in there, I'll blow lunch too."

Josey and Paul both found sizable, but manageable, rocks.

"Is it still alive?" asked Paul.

"I don't know," said Josey. "It still twitches sometimes."

Paul went over the passengers side of the hood. "Do you think it is safe? What if it comes to? Those hooves could kill us if it started kicking."

"Come on. Let's do it quickly." The two boys hammered on the remnants of the windshield. McKenzie watched. The elastic safety glass absorbed the hits and then gave. The moose sank deeper into the concave depression its bulk had created and settled on the dashboard.

"I guess that was kind of dumb," said Josey.

"It wasn't like I tried to stop you," said Paul. "Looks like we drive back with the moose. Do you know how to get back?"

"Not really, but I'm pretty sure we want to go back that way," said Josey.

"What about the mountain lion?" asked McKenzie. "It might still be back that way."

"It could be," said Josey. "It could be anywhere, but do we want to wait for it to find us here? I'd say this moose makes us a mountain lion magnet."

No one spoke as the three teenagers got back into the car.

The large object turned backwards, stopped, and then moved in the opposite direction. As the single headlight panned through the underbrush, it briefly reflected in two yellow eyes. Paul did not notice. He leaned his head out of the window as he used the lone beam of light to guide his driving.

He had driven far enough down the road that he also did not notice the sleek black apparition that emerged out of the woods. An animal was near death. That animal was vulnerable. The catamount was hungry but she held back. The cat made a strange sound as it disappeared into the darkness.

Chapter 18

Outside, the clicking hum of the helicopter blades faded away to silence. Roger, Doc, George, Rob, Ike and Hank Harbor came into the dining room. Pat, Holly, Tristan and Karley sat at a table in the middle of the room. A canister of coffee and porcelain cups were distributed on the table. The Meuret and the Nash children had pulled up chairs next to the table. Pat put his hand on Holly's as he sipped his coffee. Holly stared at her cup. Tristan and Karley mirrored their new friends' aspect. Cameron and Abbi Meuret and Kayla and Connor Nash watched their parents, waiting. The parents had hugged their progenies but there had not been much conversation since the four adults had returned from their encounter with the mountain lion. Ed sat at the next table. His daughter's head rested on his shoulders. Cindy was trembling.

"It's all right," said Ed.

"Dad," said Cindy, "I wish I had never come."

"I just wanted some time with you and Josey. I didn't know—"

Marion and Jade came out of the kitchen carrying sandwiches. Ed and Cindy declined Jade's offer of sustenance. Marion set one platter on the guests' table and Jade set the other on a large empty table.

Pat, Holly, Tristan and Karley acknowledged the arrival of the food.

"Thank you," said Pat.

"Is there anything else we can do?" asked Marion.

"Thank you," said Holly. "We're fine." She picked up one of the sandwiches and took a small bite. Then she set the sandwich back on the table.

"If there is anything, please let us know."

Holly nodded.

After coming in the porch door, Rob, Ike and Roger went over to the guests' table. Hank, George and Doc went over to the larger table, sat down, and each man picked up a sandwich.

Rob pulled up a chair. Ike and the state trooper remained standing.

"I'm so…" said Rob "I don't know—"

"You should have told us," said Karley. "You knew!"

"We just didn't think… and you left before we had—" said Rob.

"What's going on?" asked Tristan. "Even as a kid, I spent time in the woods up here. I never saw or heard of anything like that, not around here."

"This goddamned cat! It's supernatural or sumpin'," said Ike.

"We'll get it," said Roger. He pointed at Hank Harbor. "That man makes his living hunting mountain lions. He'll get it."

"What do you mean by supernatural?" asked Holly.

Ike started to speak.

"He doesn't mean anything," said Rob. "Tristan's right. This kind of thing doesn't happen around here."

"Well, it happened to us," said Karly. "I want my daughter back and then I want to leave."

"We're going to go back out and find your kids right now," said Rob.

"Should we—" asked Pat.

Rob stood up. "You need to stay here with your families."

"I'm too afraid to walk to our cabin," said Karley.

"We can arrange for you to stay in the lodge. We can get your things and bring them here."

"No! We'll wait right here until our kids get back, then we'll see what we want to do."

Rob looked at Ed. "Do you want to come?"

Cindy moved closer to her Dad.

"I know you'll find them. I'll stay here with Cindy."

Jade came over to Rob. She hugged him. "Please be careful."

"I will," he said. "I bet those kids will come down the driveway anytime now."

"I hope so," said Pat, "but they don't know those roads."

"Josey does," said Ed

"It's dark," said Holly.

"We'll find them," said Rob. "George, why don't you come with me? Roger, you and Doc can go the other way. Mr. Harbor, what do you want to do?"

"I'll go alone."

"You don't know them roads," said Ike.

"I will before I come back," said Harbor. He pointed to a piece of paper in his shirt pocket. "And I have the map that Ike drew for your guests."

Rob looked at Ike.

"I know. Sit by the Christly radio," said Ike. "It ain't like my map did them other guests no good. It seems like no one never pays no attention to that Christly map. I was wastin' my time makin' it."

"I'll pay attention," said Harbor. "I'll let you know what I think of it when I get back."

"It's good," said Ike.

Harbor looked at Ike. "I'm counting on it."

THE OLD ABENAKI

The old Abenaki turned away from the chimney. His wife was nestled securely in the smoking chamber. He knew the smoke would preserve her remains until spring. Again, he cursed aloud the coming of the white man and the diseases they had brought from far off places. Almost immediately, he wanted to take his words back.

The words seemed to echo far away before they faded to nothing. He was at his cabin but he wasn't. How many times had he repeated this moment? How many times had he paddled a canoe to where his wife's smoked body, still preserved, lay beneath the ground. She was there and she was here in the chimney. How many... he started to ask himself. But he was beginning to know that whatever his state of existence was, it had nothing to do with time.

What was the black paper-like material that covered the outside of the shack? There was someone else inside. Who was it? The footprint of the Indian's ancient log cabin was still faintly visible. The implausibility of what he perceived did not trouble the old Abenaki. The piercing yellow eyes that seem to be always watching did. It would not hurt him, but he knew this apparition was capable of causing great harm.

Chapter 19

Hank Harbor drove the old, dented, green Ford F100 up a long hill. He crossed a sturdy but simply constructed wooden bridge. He stopped and got out. He took out a powerful flashlight. The dirt road was solid from heavy lumber truck traffic. In spite of this, two ruts revealed that someone had spun their tires when driving away. Hank went over to the soft, sandy shoulder to his right. He knelt down. He had not expected to be so lucky, but there they were: three distinctive mountain lion tracks.

Harbor got back into the truck. He circled Fall's Pool on Ike's map. He noted the time, 11:00 PM. It was getting late. He continued up the hill and around a sharp corner. The road appeared to straighten out. He checked the map. He put the truck into gear and let out on the clutch. Then he saw something in the distance. A single beam of light grew larger and brighter as he drove on. At first, he thought someone might be out here on a motorcycle. Then, he realized he was approaching a vehicle with only one functioning headlight. Hank stopped. His headlights revealed a minivan and a huge object embedded in its hood and windshield. Paul's soiled face protruded out of the drivers side window. The Dodge pulled up next to the old pick-up.

"We need help," said Paul. "We ran into a moose and—"

Hank nodded. "You're the kids from the lodge! Your parents are pretty worried."

"Are you from... I don't remember seeing you. Are our parents okay?"

"Your parents are fine. Yes, I'm staying at the lodge. I got there right after you left. My name's Hank."

"I'm Paul." The two other teenagers opened the back door and climbed out of the van.

"That's McKenzie and Josey."

Hank nodded. "It looks like you were moving along."

"We were trying to get away," said Paul. "From a—"

"What?"

"You won't believe us," said McKenzie.

"Try me," said Hank.

"It was a mountain lion," said Josey. "Just like—"

"Last time," said Hank.

"Yes," said Josey. "How did you know?"

"Look," said Hank, "that's why I'm here."

"You're the guy from Alaska they were talking about," said Josey.

"That would be me," said Hank, "We need to get you three home."

"Are we in big trouble?" asked Paul. "Look at the car."

"Well you know," said Hank, "I bet they'll get over it. Right now, they are more worried than angry."

"Wait until my parents see the car," said Paul.

Hank looked at the minivan. "I have to admit you did a pretty good job of it, but it's only a car."

"It's still drivable," Paul insisted. "I'm pretty sure we can get back."

"I think you can," said Hank. "Look, I have another idea. You take my truck. That moose you hit might make my job easier. Mountain lions normally only eat what they themselves kill but I wonder if this cat can pass up something as fresh as this. Of course, this cat isn't exactly normal. In any case, I'm going to wait and see if it can resist checking this out. I'll bet it's watching us right now."

"Aren't you scared? How do you know so much about mountain lions?" asked McKenzie.

Hank smiled. "Always a little scared," he said. Carrying a rifle, he got out of the old Ford. "I respect the animals I hunt. It's my job to know about them."

"How are you—"

"Don't worry about me."

Paul, Josey, and McKenzie all climbed into the front seat of Hank's truck.

— 83 —

"Shit!" said Paul. "This thing has a clutch. I don't really know how to... My dad has an old tractor but—" Paul looked out the window.

Hank Harbor had disappeared.

"It can't be that hard," said McKenzie.

"Okay, I'll try," said Paul. He started to turn the key.

"Wait," said Josey. The truck jerked in place.

"I think you have to push down on the pedal first," said Josey. "My Dad's truck is a standard. I've driven it a few times. Do you want me to try?"

"Give me one more time," said Paul. "I drove my Dad's tractor a couple of times."

He put his left foot on the clutch and pressed it to the floor.

"Okay, turn the key now," said Josey.

The engine rumbled.

"Sweet," said Paul. "Now what?"

"For now keep your foot on the clutch," said Josey. "Make sure you are in first gear."

"How? Where's the gear shift?"

Josey leaned in front of McKenzie. "I think it's that bar thing behind the steering wheel."

"How do I put it into first gear? This is different from the tractor."

"I don't know. Maybe that guy left it in first."

"We should have asked him," said McKenzie.

Paul pulled on the lever. "It seems to pull down toward me, then up and then down. My foot is starting to shake."

"Where was it before you moved it?"

"Down towards me."

"Try that," said Josey. "Let your foot up slowly and also give it gas."

"At the same time, right?" asked Paul.

Josey nodded. "Yeah."

Paul started to pull his foot up. The truck lurched forward. Then he pushed his foot back down on the clutch. The engine raced.

"Take your foot off the gas," yelled Josey. The vehicle careened forward.

"Don't take your foot off the clutch," yelled Josey.

The truck jerked to a stop. The three teenagers held out their hands to avoid smashing into the dashboard and the windshield.

"Now I see why seat belts are a good idea," said McKenzie. "Maybe you should try, Josey."

"Let me try one more time," said Paul. "I think I can do it. Okay. Clutch in. Wait. Shift down. Give gas slowly. Let up on the pedal." The truck jerked forward. Paul pressed down part way on the clutch. The motor raced but continued to move forward. He let the clutch all the way out. The transmission whined but the old Ford continued on.

"Put in the clutch and put it into second," said Josey.

Paul reengaged the clutch and moved the gearshift upwards. Then he pressed on the accelerator lightly and let the clutch out. The truck remained in motion and gained speed.

"It's easier once you get going," said Paul. "This is fun."

"We're going the wrong way," said McKenzie. "Now we need to turn this thing around."

Paul stopped the truck.

"Shit!" said Paul. "How do you put it in reverse?"

"Try pulling in and then up," said Josey. "I think."

Chapter 20

Roger Wright started the cruiser and headed up the hill. Rob and George checked the dam.

"They're not there. And they're not here at the falls."

"Well, I guess this is still the most likely road, isn't it?" said Doc.

"I'd say so," said Roger. "I haven't spent as much time out here as I would have liked. I'm relying on Ike's map."

"That can't be good," said Doc.

"Actually, it's pretty—"

Doc smiled. "I know. I've used it every time I have come out here. I trust Ike more than just about anyone I know."

"For God's sake, don't tell him that," said Roger. "We'll never hear the end of it. Someone's coming." Roger pulled over. "Isn't that Bill Holiday's old truck? It must be that guide. He's going kind of fast."

The old Ford sped by the cruiser and then stopped short before it stalled.

"Guy's not much of a driver," said Doc.

Roger opened the door of the cruiser. Doc got out of the passenger side just as the three teenagers jumped out of the truck.

"Are you guys all right? How'd you get the truck?" asked Roger.

"We switched with the mountain lion killer guy," said Paul.

"He's not exactly—" said Doc.

"No, we are not all right," said McKenzie. "I'm tired, hungry, thirsty and I can't stand my own smell."

Doc moved toward the truck. "You all do smell a little ripe," said Doc. "What'd you try to do, gut a deer?"

"We hit a moose," said Josey.

"Been there, done that," said Roger. "It happens more than you would think. Looks like you had a bumpy ride back."

"That car has a clutch. It's the first time—"

Roger nodded. "Nobody learns how to drive a standard anymore. Crazy! How'd you hit the moose?"

"I can't believe I'm saying this! We were trying to get away from the mountain lion," said McKenzie. "I was driving. I was going pretty fast. The car and the moose are kind of a mess.

"Kind of? Smells like it. Are you sure you saw the mountain lion?" asked Doc.

"We saw it and it saw us," said Josey. "So we were trying to get away as fast as we could. McKenzie was nearest to the drivers seat."

McKenzie looked at the state trooper. "It was like hitting a cement wall. The moose was huge. It flipped right up onto our windshield. It was gross."

Doc approached the three teenagers. "Are you all right? I can smell you, for sure, but you look like you're all in one piece."

"You sort of get used to the smell after a while," said Josey.

"Not me!" said McKenzie. "I'm never getting out of the shower when we get back." Paul looked at Doc.

"We are all fine but we would really like to get back."

"Where's your car?" asked Roger. "Where did you run into the guide?"

"Back there, up the hill. He stayed with our car," said Paul.

"Is it drivable?" asked Roger.

Paul nodded. "Sort of, the moose is in the windshield but we were driving it when we ran into Mr.Harbor. We tried to get the moose off but we couldn't."

"It was super gross," said McKenzie. "Mr. Harbor told us to take his car. He said not to worry about him."

Roger looked at Paul. "What's your name son?"

"Paul."

"Can you drive the truck back to the lodge?"

Paul glanced at his friends. "I think so. Josey knows the way."

Josey nodded. "I'm pretty sure."

"I tell you what," said Doc. ""You go back with Mr. Wright. I'll drive the old truck."

"What about the guide guy?" asked McKenzie,

"You said the car is drivable, right Paul?" asked Roger.

"Yes, sir," said Paul.

"Okay! I think Mr. Harbor can take care of himself. In fact, I think he prefers it that way. Let's go."

Roger, Josey and McKenzie got in the cruiser.

Roger yelled to Doc. "I'll let everyone know we found the kids."

Chapter 21

Hank Harbor knew he was vulnerable. The cat was certainly aware of his presence. He waited. Would it suddenly appear out of the darkness and attack him instead of the moose? He carried a Ruger 44 rem mag on his hip for just such a scenario. He would not be able to wield a rifle successfully, if attacked. This high-powered hand gun would save his life. He waited. He knew his Winchester .243 could kill the cat from a distance and he preferred the idea of bagging the animal with his lower caliber rifle.

Still he waited. He was a patient man. His instincts told him that the mountain lion was nearby. He could sense it. He did not exactly smell the lion's almost skunk-like odor, but he occasionally caught it in the air. He wished he had the cougar's acute sense of smell. Was it getting closer? He cocked his pistol. He waited. Still nothing. If the cat approached the van, he would pick up his rifle. For the moment, he held the handgun, ready to fire. Then he saw it, the flick of a long tail. The smell was intense.

It was not coming for the moose.

It was coming for him!

A large body seemed to fly out of the tall grass on the edge of the forest.

Hank Harbor fired.

Chapter 22

Two vehicles came down the long driveway and parked in the small parking area next to the lodge. Jade came out of the kitchen door and walked outside.

"They're here," she yelled.

Pat, Holly, Abbi and Cameron Meuret and Karley, Tristan, Kayla and Connor Nash all rushed out of the porch door. Ed and Cindy Rollins followed behind. Paul, McKenzie, and Josey hesitated before moving toward their parents and siblings.

The younger brothers and sisters stood back while Pat and Holly hugged Paul. Karley and Tristan embraced McKenzie and Ed hugged Josey.

"Are we in—" asked Paul.

"Where's our car?" asked Pat. "You shouldn't have gone out there. We asked you not to."

"We hit a moose," said Paul. "The car is—"

"What?" asked Pat.

"A moose," said Paul. "We were trying get away from the mountain lion. And we were going—"

"You saw the mountain lion?" asked Holly.

"It was right in front to us," said Josey.

"The guide, Mr. Harbor stayed back with our car. He said he would drive it back," said McKenzie. "He was going to look for the mountain lion."

Tristan looked at McKenzie, Paul and Josey. "I don't know what you three were thinking."

"I don't know. We just wanted to help find you," said Paul. "We didn't really think about it."

Roger came over from the cruiser. "I thought you should know. They handled themselves well."

"But still," said Tristan.

Karley took Tristan's hand. "They're safe. That's all that matters right now. We can talk about the car some other time."

"I'm sorry Mom... Dad," said Paul.

"We all are," said McKenzie.

"Come on," said Pat. "Let's go inside. You guys need to take showers and we'll get you something to eat. Wait!"

The Grand Caravan with the one lone headlight came down the hill and parked. Hank Harbor got out. "It's in there." he said.

He opened the back of the minivan. A dead mountain lion lay in the back.

"Well, at least I'll be able to sleep tonight," said Holly.

"You coming?" asked Doc Varney. "One of us can ride in the back with the cat." Hank and George pushed the dead cougar toward the back of the old pick-up truck. George slammed the tailgate shut. It sprang back.

"It doesn't stay shut," said Hank. Roger stood next to his cruiser.

"Did you tell Concord?" asked Doc.

"No! They told me to stay out of it. The Feds are supposedly handling it. I think I ought to be there though."

"Christ, I'd like to be there when you dump that cat in their Christly laps. Like to see the look on their faces. Mad Cow Disease, my foot! How stupid do they think we are?"

"Well," said Doc. "George and I are the only ones that have been invited. We don't need to bring the whole neighborhood."

Ike glanced back at the Lodge. Marion stood in the doorway to the kitchen. She shook her head.

"I ain't got permission to go anyhow. Looks like them guests might be changin' their minds now that you got the catamount. They might be stayin'"

Rob and Jade leaned against the side of the bed of the pickup. "That thing really does stink," said Rob. "I guess I was too out of it to notice the last time."

Jade nodded toward the dead animal. "It doesn't look so dangerous anymore. It almost looks kind of pathetic really."

"Once you take the life out of any animal, us included, what's left
isn't much," said Harbor. "Look at it. The magnificence is gone."

"Do you regret taking that away?" asked Jade.

Hank looked at Jade. "Some, but not too much. It's what I do. I
don't take it lightly, though."

Jade looked at Harbor. She seemed to want to say something more
but didn't. Rob was not sure why but he felt a momentary flash of
jealousy. Had something more than information just been communi-
cated between Jade and Harbor?

Let it go, thought Rob, but why do I feel so inadequate around
this man?

Ike grunted. "Well, if I don't get to go, I guess someone 'sides
Marion should be tendin' to them guests."

Jade looked away from Harbor. "It looks like they all got a good
night's sleep. They're talking about staying."

Hank Harbor smiled. "A good night's sleep can certainly change
how the world looks in the morning."

He climbed into the pickup. Doc pulled himself into the back of
the truck. Roger and George got into the cruiser.

Ike stepped back. "I'd still like to be a fly on the wall when those
shitheads from Washington see that cat. Mad Christly Cow Disease!"

Hank leaned out of the truck window. "Rob, do you want to come
with me?"

"I'm not invited."

Rob looked at Jade. She nodded.

"Neither am I," said Hank.

"I'll go help Marion," said Jade."

Chapter 23

"Anyone like more coffee?" asked Marion.

Pat, Holly, Karley and Tristan all held their hands over their cups, indicating that they were satisfied.

"I think we're good," said Pat. "That was an excellent breakfast."

"We aim to please," said Marion. "Fish and Game are coming for the moose. They should be here shortly. Do you have any other plans for the day?"

"We need to do something about our car," said Holly. She looked at her husband.

Pat leaned back in his chair. "I guess it is drivable. I could—"

Holly grimaced. "I'm not getting into that car. I makes me sick just thinking about that smell."

"Do you have AAA or something like that?" asked Marion. "I can radio Bill Holiday. He can come get it with his wrecker."

Holly looked at Pat. "We did re-up that, didn't we?"

"Yes, we did. I have the card right here."

"I tell you what," said Tristan. "Why don't I drive Pat into town so he can deal with the car? We can talk to Bill Holiday. Let's see what he has to say before we ask him to bring out a wrecker. The girls can stay here and enjoy the water."

"Sounds good to me," said Karley.

"Is that okay with you, Pat?" asked Holly.

"Yup. We might as well make the best of it. I suspect Bill Holiday will have to come out here, but I'll take a couple of pictures with the phone. He can get idea of what the damage looks like."

"What a beautiful day," said Holly. "Looking out there right now, it looks like paradise."

Marion nodded. She put some empty cups on a tray. "I'll let Bill know you are coming." She turned to the next table.

"What are you guys going to do, Ed?" Marion set the tray on the table and sat down next to Cindy. She took the girl's right hand. "How are you holding up, dear?"

"I'm okay, I guess. I e-mailed my Mom. She's coming to get us. She's coming from California. She's angry at Dad for bringing us here. I want to go home and meet her there but Mom told us to stay here because there is nobody at home."

"You're safe here, sweetheart," said Marion.

"I know, Mrs. Roberts, but—"

"What are you all waiting for?" called Ike standing in the doorway to the front porch. "I thought you kids wanted to learn how to fish. We can't wait around all day."

"I'm ready," said Paul.

"I want to learn," said Abbi.

"Me, too," said Kayla.

"We're all coming," said Cameron.

Ike started out the back door. "Let's go then. Everythin's ready. Marion even packed us a scrumptious lunch."

Josey stood up. "Can McKenzie and I go to the old dam? I'd like to teach her myself. Can I use our car, Dad?"

Karley looked at Tristan. "What do you think?"

"I guess there's no... Is it safe?"

"Should be," said Ed. "With the mountain lion gone—"

"That's what you said last time," said Cindy. "You said we were safe in the woods but we weren't."

"But the catamount is dead," said Josey. "I know how—"

Ike butted in. "I got an idea."

"Uh oh!" said Marion.

"For Christ sakes, it's a good one."

"Stop swearing in front of the kids," said Marion.

"It's a god... ah, compromise," said Ike. "I was goin' to take Rob's pickup, but it'd be pretty crowded in the back with all them kids and all that equipment."

"You're planning on carry the kids in the bed of the truck?" asked

Jade. "Isn't that against the law?"

"You see any cops around here? Roger is over at the Schmidts. I hope he don't get mixed up in that triangle over there."

Jade looked at Marion. "What's he talking about now?"

"Jake and that Schmidt woman got something goin' on," said Ike. "Only one don't know it is Schmidt. He must be number than a hake."

Marion shook her head. "What's that got to do with anything? Ike, no one here cares about what is going on between those people. Probably the most dangerous part of this excursion is letting the kids go with Ike."

"I was just commentin' on the state of morals in this country."

"Good Lord," said Marion.

"When I was a kid at camp," said Tristan, "we all rode in the back of a truck. It was fun. What's your idea, Ike?"

"Let Josey and that girl go in Ed's car. They can do their fishin' or whatever nearby where the rest of us are fishin'. That'll free up space in the truck."

Pat noticed Karley hesitate. "How about if Paul goes with Josey and McKenzie?"

"That would make even more room in the truck," said Ike.

"Okay with you, Josey?" asked Ed.

Josey nodded. "Sure, we were going to ask Paul anyway."

"Okay, you can take the car," said Ed. "I'd appreciate it if you didn't hit a moose though. I'm kind of partial to that old piece of junk. They don't make SUVs like that anymore."

"Don't worry! We don't need to go through that again," said Josey. "I still haven't gotten rid of the smell and I have showered three times since we got back here."

Ike looked at Ed. "What are you going to do? I could use some help trainin' these young whippersnappers."

"I should probably—"

"Cindy is fine with me," said Marion. "I'm looking forward to spending time with her. We got some pies to bake."

"Is that okay with you?" asked Ed.

"I'm fine here, Dad."

"Are you sure?"

"Yes, I like being with Mrs. Roberts."

"Couldn't be safer than with her," said Ike. "You kids ready?"

"Well, Karley," said Holly, "while the men go to town, I think we should get into our bathing suits and sit down by the water. I got a book I want to read. Is that okay with you, Pat?"

"Sure. We'll join you when we get back. Staying here for the rest of the week is looking better and better and we haven't got a car in any case. It's a beautiful day. Someone should get a chance to enjoy it. Looking out there today, who'd...? I mean that's why we came here. Have fun, ladies."

"We will," said Holly.

She and Karley went out the front door.

"What do you think?" asked Karley. "If we went over there to that clearing beyond those trees, I bet we could take off our bathing suits, maybe do some skinny-dipping."

"So, we are succeeding in corrupting you guys."

"Whatcha got there?" asked Froggy. Rob finished putting gas into the old pickup. Froggy steadied himself by leaning against the bed of the F-100 and leaned forward. He pulled back the tarp that covered the dead mountain lion.

"When did ya get it?"

"Yesterday," said Rob.

"You get it?"

"No!"

Froggy turned toward Harbor. He leaned against the side of the truck in order to preserve an illusion of maintaining a sense of balance. He pointed at Harbor. "It was him!"

"Yes."

"Wellp, I wouldn't send him back to wherever he comes from quite yet."

"How's that?"

"I saw one of them this morning, just as live as could be."

"What are you talking about, Fr—"

"It's okay, Mr. Schurman. You can call me Froggy. Everybody else does. Yes sir, I saw one looked just like that dead one this morning."

"Have you been—"

Froggy smiled. "Mr. Schurman, you know I don't drink… much."

Rob opened the passengers side door. Froggy moved away from the truck. "Don't say I didn't tell you so."

"Okay Fr—" said Rob. Froggy ambled down the street.

"It's okay to call me Froggy. Like I said, everybody does."

"Who's that?" asked Hank.

"I guess you could call him the town drunk. It's funny, I can't remember his real name after all these years."

"Should we believe him?"

"Well, I didn't believe him once before. It turned out to be a mistake."

Hank put the truck into first gear. He followed Roger Wright's cruiser out of town.

"I guess we should take care of this business before we do anything else."

Chapter 24

"So, we all set?" asked Peter Schmidt.

Mr. Smith took a sip of coffee. "You had a case of Mad Cow Disease. We're here to help and we have it under control.

"What about the other kid that was in the boat?"

"It's all taken care of."

"And the biologist?"

"Peter, don't worry. You do your job. We'll do ours. They're here."

Peter and Mr. Smith went out to the driveway.

Roger and George parked their respective vehicles.

Doc got out of the cruiser.

Mr Smith held out his hand. "You must be Doc Varney. I've heard a lot about you."

Doc took the man's hand.

Peter held out his hand as well. "How's it going, doc? I apologize for not getting you out sooner, but I think you should see what we have to show you." Peter turned to Rob and shook hands. "Who's that with you in Bill's truck?"

Rob introduced Hank Harbor. "I think you know Roger Wright and that's George Mason. He's a veterinarian from Montana."

"Of course. Why are all of you...? Ah, good to see you, Roger. This is Mr. Smith from Washington. He's here to help. I believe you have been apprised of the situation. Mr. Smith is an expert on BSE."

"I can't say that I have any experience with Mad Cow," said Doc. "But George spent some time in England to familiarize himself with it. He also went to Alberta when the disease appeared there."

"Have you had the brain tissue tested for the PrPsc protein?" asked George.

"We have," said Mr. Smith. "That is the reason we waited so long. We want to be sure. The animal couldn't stand before it died but I wanted verification before we acted. The cow was bought in England a number of years ago. It appears that the company is now out of business. The cow is over here."

The four men looked silently at the dead animal.

"It looks like the one I saw in Canada," said George, "but the proof is in the lab's findings."

"I have that right here," said Mr. Smith.

George looked at the slip of paper and nodded. "That's only one cow," said Doc. "Jake said something about five. He said it looked like a mountain lion had attacked again. Where's Jake?"

"He's in town. We destroyed those animals. Just to be safe."

"To be safe from what?" asked Roger.

"From Mad Cow."

"Have you been feeding animal parts to your cows, Peter?" asked Doc.

"Of course not!"

"Did you destroy all of your cows?" asked George.

"Yes," said Peter.

"Why, if they were not eating contaminated feed?" asked Doc. "Aren't all your animals grass fed?"

"Once they got here," said Peter. "But the cows all came from the same place in England."

"We felt it was best," said Mr. Smith. "We don't know what they were fed before Mr. Schmidt purchased them."

"That's a lot of money," said George.

"I can handle it," said Peter. "I'm just happy that we didn't slaughter and eat any of the meat from these cows."

"So?" Doc asked. "You're really sure about the Mad Cow Disease? I'm surprised you didn't check out the breeding history of the cows."

"I did," said Peter. "The company falsified the paperwork. Believe me, I have learned a lesson."

"We're positive about the diagnosis," said Mr. Smith.

"I see," said Doc. "Well, we have something to show you. It's in the truck."

The men walked back to the house and went over to the pick-up where Rob and Hank were waiting. Hank lifted the tarp. Peter looked at Mr. Smith.

"What's this? Why are you showing it to us?"

Doc nodded his head toward Hank. "Thought you might be interested. Mr. Harbor shot it yesterday."

Chapter 25

A forest-green pick-up drove into the Schmidt's driveway.

"That'll be the guys from Concord," said Doc. "They're here to take the cat. George and I will be going with them."

"I'd like to go, too," said Rob.

"There's room in the cruiser," said Roger.

Doc looked at Mr. Smith. "We didn't want to trouble you federal guys with such a trivial local issue. We'll have our guys do the autopsy."

Peter glanced at Mr. Smith. "Probably just someone's pet," said Mr. Smith. "I think that's what Fish and Game usually claims when something like this happens."

"I've heard that," said Doc.

Mr. Smith looked at Rob. "Is that what you say, Mr. Schurman? You used to be a conservation officer, if I'm not mistaken."

Rob smiled. "I'm of a different opinion. But I suspect you already know that."

The two officers got out of their pickup. They acknowledged Rob.

"Bruce, Al. How are you doing?"

"Can't complain. How's retirement treating you?" asked Al.

"Working harder than ever," said Rob.

"Yeah, me and the wife have been thinking about coming up to your place to do some fishing."

Rob nodded. "Anytime, just let us know. We'll set you up with the best guide in the area."

"Would that be Ike Roberts?"

"Yup," said Rob.

The man grinned. "It'll be an interesting day"

"You'll catch fish."

"I suspect so."

The man approached the old truck. "So that's the critter. Are we putting it in our truck? That truck doesn't look like it would make it to Concord."

"It would," said Rob, "but yes, you guys can take over. Mr. Harbor is going back to the lodge. Doc, George and I will head down to Concord in the cruiser. We'll see you there."

Peter and Mr. Smith watched Rob, Hank and the two conservation officers transfer the dead animal to their truck. They covered it with the bull tarp.

"I could use a cup of coffee," said Mr. Smith. He started back toward the house. He turned back. "Good luck gentlemen," he said.

Peter Schmidt followed the man into the house.

The Fish and Game truck drove away from the farm.

"What was going on there?" asked the driver."That one guy looked like something out of a bad FBI movie."

"That other one, the guy who shot it," said the other man. "He looks like he came out of a movie, too."

"What about the released pet theory?"

"What about it?"

"Do you buy it? Do you know where someone might buy a mountain lion as a pet?"

"Can't say as I do, but I believe there are places where you can. I've seen picture of leashed mountain lions on the Internet. Actually, I don't know that it is illegal to buy something like that. I don't think it is."

"Does that mean you buy the theory that this one was a released pet?

"Nope! I mean who put the GPS tracker on it?"

"The equipment looks old and broken to me. Is there a way to trace where it came from?"

"Don't know. Maybe. That's above my pay grade."

"How long has Rob Schurman been retired?"

"I don't know. A while."

"Wasn't he involved in that other conspiracy about a mountain lion?"

"Yeah, there were a bunch of people mixed up in that. They were all discredited. I always kind of wondered about it. Those two vets were part of it too, I think."

"They didn't strike me as being wackos. And we got ourselves a mountain lion in the back. I think that trooper was involved before too."

"Do you think they put the cat there?"

"To prove they were right last time?"

"I don't know, seems kind of farfetched."

"I got a cousin that claims to have seen one."

"What?

"A mountain lion?"

"Yes."

"I've heard a lot of stories. There's a couple of lists floating around. Some guy named Rollins wrote a book and has a presentation on mountain lion sightings. I heard it was pretty interesting."

"The book's fiction, isn't it?"

"Yeah, I read it. It's not bad. I couldn't put it down."

"From what I've heard, there are a lot of reliable people that supposedly have sighted them."

"We've got reliable people who have seen UFOs and Bigfoot, too."

"I'm still not sure I buy all of this," said the driver. "I'm just not sure what I don't buy."

"What about the Mad Cow thing?"

"Yeah, that too."

"And Mr. Smith?"

"Him, too."

"You want to grab a coffee in town?"

"I could use one. Let's park outback. We don't need to attract any attention."

Chapter 26

Hank Harbor got out of the old pick-up. He started toward the lodge, changed his mind and then went out on the dock. He sat on the old bench that afforded a panoramic view of Lake Makapague. He had to admit that he was looking out over a truly beautiful expanse of water. He knew the wind could more often than not turn the now tranquil, glass-like surface into choppy whitecaps. He could as well be contemplating his home waters in Alaska, and for the moment, he was glad for the serenity of this place. No grizzlies, he thought to himself, but who would have ever thought he would have been called upon to hunt and kill a mountain lion in one of the New England states? There was something uncomfortable about that.

He had always thought of nature in this part of the world as relatively benign. Sure, you could fall through thin ice on your snowmobile. You could die of exposure on Mt. Washington. You could be in the way of a rutting moose or corner a black bear with her cubs. Although Mother Nature can turn on you no matter where you are, he supposed wilderness deaths in these parts were mostly the product of being ill prepared or downright stupidity. Humans were at the top of the food chain and he had just shot a cougar. There was a certain exhilaration in the killing. What was it about catching a gorgeous trout, or bagging a big buck, that was so thrilling?

There was also often a brief sense of regret. Why had he just taken this being's life? He did not feel that regret this time. Someone needed to remove the animal from this environment. He regretted that the catamount had been here and that it had taken a human life. Was that old drunk right? Was there another one? Was his job done or would he be going out again? Somehow taking this cougar had been too easy.

Suddenly the dock rippled to life. Hank turned around. It was Jade. I wouldn't mind knowing this woman better, thought Hank. I wonder... She's probably taken though. It seems like the good ones always are. Why would he say something like that? He knew a number of good one who weren't—

"Hi," said Jade. "I didn't mean to interrupt. I thought you might like something to eat. Maybe a cup of coffee?"

He looked at Jade. She did not look away.

Self-confident, thought Hank. I like that. She was a teacher. I suppose if you spend a good portion of your life staring down a bunch of teenagers every day, you have to be confident. I wouldn't have the courage to do it. Living here and running this place required something as well. He also appreciated the tank top and shorts that she was wearing.

"I was just enjoying your beautiful lake," said Hank. "You know, a cup of coffee would hit the spot. I know it's a bit early, but you wouldn't happen to have a little bourbon to go with that, would you? And would you join me?"

Jade smiled. "It's got to be 5 o'clock somewhere, right? I'll be right back."

"It's gotta be. Do you need help?"

"Nope, you stay right there."

"I take mine black," said Hank.

"I figured," said Jade.

Jade headed toward the lodge. Hank watched her go. When she got to the end of the dock, Jade glanced back. Oh shit, she thought. She whispered, "Oh shit!"

Hank watched as Jade entered the lodge and then came back out carrying a tray with two cups of coffee and a fifth of Wild Turkey.

Hank got up and approached Jade. He took the tray and put it down next to the bench.

"Allow me," he said. "Have a seat."

Yeah right, "allow you," thought Jade. She sat down and crossed her legs. Hank open the bottle and poured a splash into each cup. He sat down next to Jade. His thighs touched bare thighs as he handed her one of the cups. Jade's first thought was to move her leg away, but she knew she didn't want to and the bench was too narrow for her to slide over anyway. Hank lifted his cup.

"Here's to a beautiful lake and a—"

Jade lifted her cup. The man and the woman sipped their drinks. The whiskey first burned, and then mellowed, as it went down.

"And what?" asked Jade.

"I was going to say 'and a beautiful woman,' but I guess that would be a bit forward."

Without really thinking, Hank leaned toward Jade. His hand rested lightly on her knee.

"Not as forward as that hand on my knee," said Jade. She swallowed the rest of her coffee. Hank pulled his hand back.

"Oh shit! I didn't know I had... I didn't mean—"

"Yes, one side of me hopes you did mean it. But I suppose... I shouldn't think that, should I? Rob and I... What about you? You're not exactly unattractive yourself."

"I'm not married. I do have someone in Alaska. We enjoy each other's company when we can be together. 'Can' is kind of the key word. She runs an outpost in the bush and I do what I do. We don't see each other all that often, so there are no strings, at least not at the moment."

"Hank, I don't know if I have strings or not. I have no desire to run off with you, but sitting here with you is... That mid-afternoon drink feels nice. Too nice. I'm a little bit drunk. A roll in the hay with you wouldn't change my feelings for Rob, but I don't exactly have permission."

Hank took Jade's hand. "I understand."

"A roll in the hay is all it would be. Too bad we can't have that."

"It is," said Hank. "It is." He kissed Jade on the cheek. He looked up to the lodge.

"Are you expecting someone?"

"That must be Ed Rollin's ex-wife, but I didn't expect she'd be here quite this soon."

Chapter 27

A state trooper sat outside the hospital room. The corridor was deserted. Then the twin doors at the end of the hall opened. Two men approached the trooper.

"FBI," one of the men said. "We're here to replace you. How's he doing?"

The trooper stood up. "Doctor says he's stable. Can I see your IDs?"

"Of course."

The other man took out a needle and stuck it into the trooper's arm. The trooper slumped back into the chair. The two men looked at the sign outside the door. It read Phillip Ramsey. They entered the room.

Chapter 28

The Class C RV pulled into the remote campsite. A man and woman in their mid-sixties got out of the camper.

"Nice spot," said the woman.

The man looked around. "A good place for our first time out. How do we want to park this thing? I'm still not completely comfortable driving something this big."

"Can you back it in over there? It looks like there is enough space. That way we can face the river and the fire will be in front. It'll be nice to sit by the fire tonight."

"Hopefully, the bugs won't be too bad. There is a breeze; that should help. I'll see if I can turn the camper around. Then, you know what? I'm going to take a nap. Isn't that what retirement is all about? I have an idea about what else we could do before I take a nap."

"We could do that, too," said the woman.

The man climbed into the cab and backed it out onto the road. He pulled forward enough to allow enough room to put the vehicle in reverse, turn the wheel and back into the campsite. The woman signaled left, right, and back. After a couple of tries, both were satisfied with the camper's position.

"Want a beer?" asked the woman.

The man opened the storage compartment in the back of the vehicle. He pulled two outdoor lounging chairs, set them up facing the water and sat down.

The woman came out of the camper carrying two bottles of beer. She handed one of the bottles to her husband and took her seat.

"This is the life," said the man. "That's what my Dad used to say every time we went camping."

The woman held up her bottle. "Here's to retirement. And this is just the beginning."

"It hasn't really hit me yet. Maybe it will when September comes around and school starts again."

"Do you think you'll miss it?"

"Forty years in the same school... I'll miss the kids. I'll miss my colleagues. I won't miss teaching for the test. The Department of Education and corporate reform are milking the creativity right out of teaching. I guess I'm glad that I'm at the end of my career. I don't think I could do it as a young teacher today. I'm still proud to call myself an educator, though."

"You should be. And you don't have to convince me."

"I know. It just seems like teachers are blamed for everything that's wrong in this country."

"Well, I don't know about you, but I'm not going to spend this trip worrying about all of that. We've paid our dues."

"Oh, I think we had a pretty good life, you and I. The time has gone by so fast."

"Forty years and we're still doing all right," said the woman. "Let's celebrate."

The man and the woman walked got up and climbed into their mobile home.

"We need to fix this door. It won't stay shut," said the man.

"We'll look at it afterward," said the woman.

"Oh shit!" said Bruce.

The two Fish and Game officers came out of the restaurant and approached their truck. The bed of the pickup was empty. There was no tarp and no mountain lion.

"Christ!" said Al. "I thought we might attract a crowd. It never dawned on me that someone would steal the damned thing."

"What do we do now?" asked Bruce.

"Call in and have dispatch tell those vets that they might as well come back. Also, put out an alert for someone transporting a mountain lion."

"Yeah, right. You want to be the one to tell them that?"

Marty got out of the car and looked around. The lodge looked abandoned. She saw two people out on the dock. She didn't recognize either the man or the woman. She started to head toward the porch and then hesitated. The two figures walked together down the dock toward her.

"Hi," yelled Jade.

"Hello."

Jade stepped off the dock and held out her hand. If this was Ed's ex wife, she could see how Rob would have fallen for her. She was mature, but still attractive. And she was single, available, the one woman from Rob's past he had never gotten over. Would he...? She had been told that Marty Rollins would come to pick up her son and daughter, but until now, Jade had never really considered that Marty Rollins might come here. She was in the past. She was not supposed to be a threat, yet here she was. She glanced at Hank. It was obvious that he had also made his own appraisal. Jade had to smile. Only moments ago—

"Hi, I'm Jade. You must be Josey's and Cindy's mother?"

Marty was surprised to see the smile but it helped her feel better. She was not sure how welcome she would be.

"Yes, I am. I'm Marty Rollins. I'm here to—"

"To pick up the kids. By the way, this is Hank Harbor." Hank and Marty shook hands. "He's the one who shot the mountain lion. Thanks to him, things are back to normal, more or less."

"I guess we have something in common. I shot the last one. Where are—?"

"Oh, Cindy's inside with Marion."

Hank wasn't sure how to respond. He had heard the stories about the last one but—

"Marion Roberts? My goodness, I haven't seen Marion in so long. How is she?"

"She's great. She's our cook."

"Then you and your guests must be eating well. And Ike? Is she keeping him in line?"

Jade grinned. "She is. Ike hasn't changed."

"I hope not," said Marty. "They were—are—two of my favorite people."

"Well, let's go inside," said Jade.

"Where's Josey?" asked Marty.

"Ike and Ed took some of our guests fishing. Josey is with them."

"Ed went fishing?" Marty looked at Jade and Hank. "Ed went fucking fishing?" she whispered.

Jade glanced at Hank. "I know this must be hard."

"Must be hard?" screamed Marty. "Goddamn right, it's hard! I never wanted to come back here. Ever! I almost died out here. I almost lost my children out here. And Ed brings my kids back here again and the same thing happens. This place is cursed, I swear it. And goddamned Ed goes fishing!"

Marty wanted to cry.

"I'm—" said Marty.

Hank stepped back.

Then the kitchen door opened and Marion and Cindy came out onto the small stoop.

"Mommy," yelled Cindy. She started to run.

Marion saw Marty. She held Cindy back and took her hand. "Let's go together," said Marion.

Marty watched Cindy and Marion come down the driveway. She looked back at Jade and Hank.

"I apologize. I don't usually... Actually, there are things I do miss about these woods. Sometimes I think I'm manic depressive or something."

"It's okay. I understand," said Jade.

Marty ran toward her daughter and her old friend. She threw her arms around both of them and began to cry again.

Hank looked at Jade. "I expect that my dogs will have arrived in town by now. I'm going to go get them. We probably won't need them, but I'll be glad to see them."

"Probably not?" asked Jade.

Hank headed toward the old pick-up and got in.

Chapter 29

Josey Rollins retrieved a good-size brook trout from the pool. Nearby to his right, McKenzie Nash and Paul Meuret were casting less effectively. Paul jerked his rod backwards and forwards numerous times before lifting it upwards allowing the line to twirl into a jumble just in front of him. McKenzie was only about twenty feet away from Josey. Her back cast was somewhat smoother and she was able to plop the fly about six feet out into a small pool. She turned and watched Josey release his latest catch.

"You make it look so easy," she yelled.

"Just slow down and let the line cast back before you—"

Without any warning, McKenzie's rod bent toward the water and the line was yanked through the ferrules deep into the water.

"I got one!" she yelled.

"Lift the rod. Pull the line tight," yelled Josey. McKenzie tugged on the line.

"Not too tight! I'm coming. Give the fish some room to move."

Josey approached the girl. "Not too much. Nice and slow." The fish was still underwater. The line jerked. "Keep the line tight but let enough out to give the fish some room to move. Then try to bring it in a little bit closer. You're doing great."

Suddenly the fish rolled over on the surface of the water, splashed and then disappeared again. McKenzie let the line out again.

"That's a good-sized fish," said Josey. "Keep doing what you are doing. See if you can get it in closer, so I can get it into the net."

The fish splashed again, this time closer. Then it disappeared again. Josey took out a small camera. McKenzie managed to strip even more line. This time the fish emerged out of the water only a few feet in front of McKenzie. Josey grabbed a couple of pictures and then he stepped into the water next to the girl. He pulled his net from behind his back. The net's lanyard did not quite reach.

"Try to keep it right there,"

Before Josey could get close enough, the trout took off back into the pool.

"Oh no," cried McKenzie. "What... It's getting away."

"It's okay. It's still on. Keep the line tight and just bring him in like you did before."

Josey moved closer to the girl. He watched as the fish emerged and submerged a number of times. Finally, it was close enough. Josey waded in front of McKenzie and dipped his net into the water under the fish. He pulled the fish out of the water and then lowered it back in.

Paul came running up.

"Grab the camera out of my vest," said Josey.

Standing next to Josey, Paul got into position.

Josey knelt. "Come here McKenzie. Quick!" Josey wet his hands and then lifted what had to be a three-pound brook trout out of the water.

McKenzie hesitated.

"Come on. Wet you hands."

McKenzie approached the net.

Josey held the net. "Gently! Take it out. Hold it up so Paul can get a shot. This is your fish. Wet your hands. Pick it up under its belly and hold the tail. That's it."

Smiling, McKenzie did as instructed. The fish cooperated long enough for Paul to record the moment. Using forceps, Josey eased the barbless hook out of the trout's mouth.

"Put it back in the water."

McKenzie lowered her catch back into the pool and it was gone.

"I lost it," said McKenzie.

"No you didn't. That counts." said Josey. "It was time for the fish to get back into the water."

"Bravo!" came a voice from the shore. "Nice fish!"

McKenzie turned to the elderly woman standing on the path.

"My first fish ever."

She turned to Josey and gave him a hug. "I couldn't have done it without you." She kissed the boy on the cheek. Josey felt an unexpected thrill tingle through his body.

The old woman watched the three teenagers. Their youthfulness was palpable. She leaned on her cane. Where had her girlhood gone? She remembered her first fish. It was not as grand as this one. She had been just as excited as this young girl when her husband had helped her land her first catch. It was much like what she had witnessed and she, too, had given her man a meaningful peck on the cheek.

"That's quite a fish," said the woman. "I caught my first fish right in the same spot. My husband and I fished here for over fifty years. We made the path you came in on. He's gone now and I can't fish anymore."

"I'm sorry," said McKenzie.

"Oh, don't be," said the woman. "We had our time. It's good to see you young people on the river. It's yours now, at least for a while." The woman looked at McKenzie. "Make the most of it."

"Thank you for making the path," said Josey.

"We're happy to see it used." She started to walk away.

"Make the most of it," she repeated. "Life, I mean."

Then she was gone.

Ed, Ike, Abbi, Cameron, Kayla and Connor waded down from upstream.

"Who was that you was talkin' to?" asked Ike. "I didn't see nobody."

"It was an old woman with a cane," said Paul. "Said she had been fishing here with her husband for over fifty years."

"Huh," grunted Ike, "that sounds like Martha Kipling. I thought she was dead. Guess not. Some other guests have claimed to run into her. She must be over a hundred. You catch anything?"

"We did," said Josey. He held up the camera. "Do you want to see what McKenzie caught?"

"Nah," mumbled Ike, "we didn't catch nothin'."

"I want to see," said Cameron.

"Course I do too," said Ike. "It's not every day someone catches their first fish." Ike looked at the screen on the back of the camera.

"Holy shit!" he said.

Chapter 30

"As far as I'm concerned, that car is totaled," said Bill Holiday.

"The guy I talked to at the insurance company doesn't share your opinion," said Pat. "I appreciate you coming all the way out here."

"Well, I'd invite him to come take a look," said Bill. "Last time we had something similar to this, the agent wouldn't get near the vehicle. He took one look and quickly came around to my way of thinking. As far as coming out here is concerned, I'd drive twice the distance to partake of Marion's cooking. I don't know what she sees in that old codger of a husband of hers, though."

Ike shrugged. "She's got good taste in men is all. Ain't no wonder we pay so much for insurance. They pay someone to drive all the way up here just so's they can verify what Bill's already told them."

"More coffee?" asked Marion.

Bill held up his hand. "No, thank you. As always, that was a great meal and the coffee was excellent."

Rob pulled up a chair. "You can stay the night, Bill, if you'd like. We have a free room. No charge."

"Christ almighty!" said Ike. "How in hell we goin' to make a livin' iffin' we don't charge for rooms? Christ, we're puttin' up those vets too! Least Roger went home. For some reason, he'd rather be with his wife than mooch off of us. I suspect he'll be comin' back up North seein' as how the cat was stolen right from under those game wardens' noses. And what about that Ramsey fellow? Disappeared out the hospital for Christ's sake! Put the guy that was guardin' him under. Wonder what that's all about? We got catamounts, cows and biologists disapearin'. Gotta kinda wonder, don'tcha?"

"Does seem kind of fishy. You know what, Rob, I just might take you up on the offer. Just to spite Ike. Besides, it's a long drive in the dark. I'm not in the mood for dodging moose. I don't want to total my vintage Chevy.

"Vintage Chevy," huffed Ike. "That piece of junk is in worse shape than the dilapidated clunker you conned that guy from Alaska into renting."

"Weren't for my mechanical skills, that poor excuse for a Jeep of yours would have gone to the junkyard years ago."

Ike mumbled something incomprehensible.

Bill leaned onto the table. "You want to play some cribbage, Ike? I doubt it, but maybe you've learned something since the last time we played."

Ike took out his corncob pipe. "Just got a bunch of crappy cards last time, that's all. I'll get the board."

"Ike, put that pipe away!" said Marion.

"Christ, I was just contemplatin'," said Ike. "Looks like I gotta go outside for a while. Man can't even smoke in peace in his own place no more. A man's home used to be his castle."

Marion smiled. "Really!"

"Before my time," grumbled Ike. "I don't know what they were thinking when they gave women the right to vote."

"I'm not going there," said Bill. "But I'll join you. I brought along a good cigar. I'm not allowed to smoke at home either."

Bill and Ike got up and headed for the door.

"Get as far away from the lodge as possible," said Marion.

"The world ain't what it used to be," said Ike. "Christ, houses used to even have smokin' rooms."

Rob leaned back in his chair. Marion continued to offer coffee as she moved around the room.

Josey, Paul and McKenzie were sitting together across the room near the door to the porch. Karley, Pat and Holly sat at the next table. Marty was sitting with Cindy over by the fireplace. Abbi, Cameron, Kayla and Connor were all sitting in the dilapidated couches in front of the wood stove. They were thumbing through ancient books and old hunting and fishing magazines. Ed was sitting with Tristan.

"Where's the guide from Alaska?" asked Tristan.

"He's outside with his dogs. He's getting ready to go back tomorrow. Even though someone stole the cat, I guess his work is done."

Tristan got up. "It looks like things are getting back to normal. I guess I'll go see what my wife is up to."

Back to normal, thought Ed. I could use some normal.

Jade took the last of the dinner plates into the kitchen and then returned to the dining room. "I'm going out for some air," she said. "I wonder where Doc and George are."

Ike looked back as he headed for the door. "Probably outside smokin'. Bein' in here is like bein' held hostage."

"I don't think either one of them smokes," said Jade.

"Well, they oughta." Ike closed the door.

Marty and Cindy walked over to Ed. "Cindy's going to bed. I'm taking the kids home first thing in the morning."

Ed stood up. "Can't we—?"

"Ed, I'm taking Cindy and Josey home.

Cindy squeezed her mother's hand.

"This is supposed to be my time with... Can't we talk about this later?"

Cindy let go of Marty's hand. She moved away to hug Ed. "Why can't we all be together?"

Ed moved closer and hugged his daughter. "Good night, sweetheart," he said. "I wish that too, sometimes."

"I don't want to go home. I'm old enough to make my own decisions," said Josey. He got up and went out the door to the porch. The door slammed behind him. McKenzie and Paul followed.

Marty regarded her ex-husband. "Do you mean that, Ed?" Marty turned to Cindy, "Go ahead and go to bed. I'll be right in to say good night."

"In spite of everything, I still—"

"I don't know what to say," said Marty. She started to follow Cindy, paused and then went over to Rob.

"Can we talk after Cindy goes to bed?"

Rob nodded. "Of course."

Ed looked away

Pat, Holly, Tristan and Karley headed for the door.

"Anyone up for a beer?" asked Pat. "I have some in a cooler in the cabin." Pat turned back to Rob. "Can we get some more ice?"

Rob got up. "Sure," he said.

Back to normal, he thought. Wouldn't that be nice?

Chapter 31

"Those are beautiful dogs," said Jade.

"They are," said Hank, "but beauty isn't their main calling. They earn their keep." One of the two Black and Tan Coonhounds started to get up. "Down!" said Hank.

"Are they friendly?" asked Jade.

"Oh, they like people, but they have to respond to my commands." Hank knelt down and rubbed both dogs behind their ears.

"You love them, don't you? More than most people, I suspect."

"Yeah, maybe. I don't have anything against people. I just like to be by myself. I work better alone. I can work with the dogs, though, better than with people. These two have treed a number of mountain lions. We just tree the cats nowadays. Used to be there were some panther dogs that would actually fight the cougars and then hold them down by their ears until the hunter arrived."

"That's sounds kind of brutal," said Jade.

"Nobody does it anymore."

"Even treeing the cougars seems kind of unfair."

"You're not alone. I sometimes have mixed feelings. I grew up in a different world. Could be I'm a dying breed. Feels like it sometimes."

"Does it bother you to be here?"

"Not here. The older I get, the more I wonder—"

"You're not that old."

"It used to be easier. I also think about what I might be missing. I used to be so sure; now, not so much. I'm not the man I used to be, maybe I never was. I think Johnny Cash said something like that. I'm not sure where I heard it, but I think it's true. You won't blow my cover, will you?"

Jade shook her head and smiled. "Are you leaving tomorrow?"

"Yes. It doesn't look like my skills are needed here anymore."

I'm not so sure about that, Jade thought to herself.

Hank took Jade's right hand in both of his hands. He gave her a kiss on the lips. Then he pulled back. "I suppose our moment has passed," he said.

"Yes," said Jade "I guess it has."

"I wish it hadn't. I wonder—"

"Wonder what?"

"Could we have accepted it for what it was?"

"What was it?"

"Animal attraction? For me, it was damn powerful. Can a woman feel that too? You're a beautiful lady, Jade Morrison, and no, I don't just look at you as an animal. There's a lot more going on."

"You do seem to know something about animals, Mr. Harbor. Thank you for the compliment and yes, as a woman, I do know something about animal attraction." Jade smiled. "But we women are not supposed to admit it."

"Does that bother you?"

"Starting to. I'll see you in the morning. And you know something?"

"What?"

"I think I missed out on something good."

"We both did," said Hank. "We both did."

"Good night," said Jade. "I'm going to look for Rob."

Well, at least someone will benefit from all of this, thought Hank as he continued to scratch his dogs' ears.

"Rob's a lucky man."

Jade kept going.

Marty entered the dining room and walked over to where Rob was sitting. Rob started to get up. Ed went out to the porch. Virgil groaned and with some effort got up and followed his master.

"You don't have to—"

Marty took Rob's right hand with both of hers and sat down. "It's good to see you, Rob. This place suits you, doesn't it?"

"Yes, it does"

Jade came in from the outside. She started toward Rob and Marty. She hesitated and then went back out on the porch.

"And you?" asked Rob. "How are you?"

Marty let go of Rob's hand. "Oh, I'm all right, I guess. I don't have any major illnesses. The business is making money. I'm just kind of... I don't know. I'm in limbo. Bored?"

"Anybody in your life?"

"Not at the moment. Twice divorced. I don't know that I'll try that again."

"Getting married?"

"I've dated a few guys since the divorce, even dated a woman for a while."

"Wow, how was that?"

"Actually, pretty nice but—"

"But?"

"I guess alternative lifestyles aren't the answer to everything."

"It looks like you might have found someone," said Marty"

"Yes, I think so. We're just getting started really. It took both of us a while but I think we're good together. No grand romance. Maybe a little more mature, I hope."

"I'm happy for you, Rob. That's hard to find. I know you didn't have anything like that before."

"No, I guess I didn't."

"I guess we've changed roles." said Marty. "I was actually pretty content with Ed. If he had not been so unhappy."

"He seems pretty content now. Not everyone is meant to do what is expected. I have to give him credit for realizing he was doing the wrong thing. I wouldn't do well trying to do something I hated just for the sake of a sense of security."

"Ed had to work through all of that. Unfortunately, I had to be a part of the process. It wasn't easy. All I thought I wanted was a decent life for all of us, just a sense of stability and safety. I didn't want the Sturm und Drang of Ed trying to find himself. I get it now, I really do. I put the business up for sale and it looks like I have a buyer. Now I'm the one who found that what I was doing wasn't satisfying. After what happened up here, I could never really go back. I tried, but here I am. And life is kind of short, isn't it? Too short to waste it trying to make a profit doing something you find you don't like."

Rob smiled. "Yes it is, way too short. At least you made a profit. For us, I guess the goal is to break even. I got my retirement and both Ike and Marion are on social security. Jade has some retirement from her teaching. It's not always easy, but we have all chosen to be here trying to make this iffy undertaking work. Just read the newspaper. Look at all the people in our age group in the obituaries. Ike and Marion never made any real money with the farm either."

"Isn't this place profitable?"

"Yes, in a way. I mean we have enough to eat. We have a roof over our heads. Most of the money goes right back into it."

"But you like what you do?"

"Yes, we all do."

"Even Jade?"

"I think especially Jade. This was a conscious decision for her."

"I envy all of you," said Marty. "Breaking even doesn't sound so bad."

"So what's next if you sell the business?"

"I'm not sure. I'm alone. I'll have the freedom to do whatever I want. But I don't feel free. Ed and I were a team. We wouldn't have survived the search for the kids, the mountain lion attacks and the fire if we hadn't been together. Somehow, when everything returned to normal, our marriage couldn't survive that. Do you know what I mean?"

"Yes, I do. None of us will ever be what we were before," said Rob. "That's not all bad. Do you think you and I had—"

"No, we weren't cut out to become a couple. I don't think Ed was all that upset with what we did. He knew I would never have wanted to live with you. You're an attractive man but I never wanted to run off to faraway places with you. I never imagined moving up here or having you come back to Massachusetts."

"It wasn't about that, was it?"

"We both know what it was about and it was great even it was short-lived. Anytime you'd like to—"

"I'll definitely keep that in mind," said Rob.

"Not tonight, though," said Marty.

"No, not tonight, but it's a nice thought."

"You know what is really strange, Rob? I think I still love Ed. No one in the world pisses me off like he does, but still—"

"Maybe you should talk more. It's not for me to say, but I don't think Ed ever got over you either."

"He never did find anyone else, did he?"

"Nothing that stuck. Are you leaving tomorrow?"

"Yes."

"Can we convince you to stay another day? I know Josey isn't ready to leave. I think he's in love. Marion would welcome having Cindy around for another day. It would make me happy if you stayed. No charge."

"Josey is in love? So, the next generation starts. Is it all worth it, Rob?"

"You know it is," said Rob.

"Yes, I guess I do. It's good to see you. Do you think your new love would share you for one night?" joked Marty.

"It's a long story, but she just might."

"Interesting. I'll sleep on that."

Chapter 32

The two anglers emerged out of the bushes and waded into the river.

"This is it," said Eli Hodge. "Last time I fished from that campsite across the way. No one was camping. I caught some really nice trout."

"Someone's on the campsite now. I see a camper but I don't see anyone," said Joe Hampton. "They got a fire going though."

"I don't think we'll bother them. If we see anyone, we can ask. We've only got about an hour before it is too dark to fish anyway. I just saw a couple of rises over there. They're yours. I'm going to explore upstream a bit. I won't go far."

Joe took out his wading stick and felt his way along the rocky river bed until he found a spot where he could comfortably place his feet. He saw the rise. He released the fly from his rod and drew some line. After one false cast, Joe aimed and the line shot out toward the circle on the surface of the water. The fly just barely touched down on the edge of the rise. The fish hit. Joe set the hook. He held the line tight, occasionally allowing the large trout the freedom to move away. Finally, he was able to strip enough line to net a nice, colorful brook trout.

He looked around for his friend. Eli must have moved up the river. Joe reached into the net, unhooked his catch and released it. He cast a few more times and caught a couple more good-size brookies.

It was time to go. Eli should be coming back. When Joe got back to the shore, there was no sign of his friend. Joe took out his headlamp. He turned it on and panned the light across the river and over the foliage on the side of the riverbank. Yellow eyes appeared and then disappeared. Before Joe could respond to what he had just seen, the large black apparition leapt out of the woods and tore into his throat.

So ended Joe's last day of fishing and his last day on earth. He would not return to his wife and two sons. Nor would he return to finish the house he had contracted to build. Nor would he return to his seat on the New Hampshire State Legislature. Using his headlamp, Eli poled his way back down stream just in time to catch a glimpse of the cat dragging his friend, Joe Hampton, into the forest.

Momentarily, the cat turn around. Its eyes fixed on the lone fisherman standing in the water. The cat screeched. The faces of the man and woman in the trailer appeared in the small back window. The cat and its prey disappeared into the darkness.

Ed was eating his breakfast alone at a small table for two. He held his coffee cup with two hands and looked out the window at the lake. He loved the north woods. He had winterized his cabin and was living the life he had always wanted. However, he had to admit to himself that he was not basically a hermit and after a while being alone got old. He sometimes missed having someone with whom to share things. It was good to be at the lodge and to be with friends. It was actually nice to see Marty. He was always happy when he could spend time with his kids, but most of the time that meant that he had to go down to Massachusetts.

Maybe I should ask Rob if there were some odd jobs I could do around the lodge, he thought. At least I would be around people some of the time. I am not as much of a loner as I thought I was.

Was he jealous of what Rob and Jade seemed to have with each other? Not jealous, but envious maybe. He was happy for them. He sincerely hoped everything would work out for them.

He had had his chance with Marty. That had not worked out. In spite of the divorce, she was/is a part of him. He had not even felt jealous when he discovered Rob and Marty together, just hurt by the betrayal and dishonesty. He had felt an even stronger sexual attraction to Marty after the affair. That had not been enough to keep them together though. They had both responded differently to the mountain lion attacks.

For Ed, everything had changed. Marty had wanted to go back home and attempt to recreate the past, to go on as if nothing had happened. That experience had convinced Ed that going back was exactly what he did not want. Yet here he was back with some of same people who had been there when what could not have happened did happen.

Jade was new. The tracker from Alaska and the two families were new. The others know the truth. Everyone in this lodge now knows the truth. Didn't Ike say that the mountain lion had been stolen. The biologist had disappeared. Shit, thought Ed, it's happening again! The evidence is disappearing. Will it be enough to discredit us this time?

He looked around the room. Josey was having breakfast with McKenzie and Paul. It was obvious that something was going on between his son and the young girl. The three teenagers were totally into themselves. I can't help but envy those adolescents a little, Ed thought to himself. To be young... On second thought, I don't need to go back to that. I'm happy enough with who I am. Cindy was laughing at a large table with her new friends, the younger Meuret and Nash kids.

The four parents were also clearly hitting it off with each other. Marty was sitting with Rob. Ike was sitting with George, the guide and Varney. He was gesticulating, apparently trying to make some point. Everyone else at the table looked skeptical.

Marion and Jade were clearing the breakfast tables. Rob got up to help. Ed looked over at Jade. Even though he had chosen to sit by himself near the window, he felt so isolated and alone. He looked around the room. These were the people in his life. He gazed out the window at the lake. There was comfort in both. I'll talk to Rob later about odd jobs, he thought. I'd work in exchange for some of Marion's cooking.

"Do you mind if I sit?" asked a woman's voice. Ed turned around. "Hi Ed," said Marty. She pulled back the chair. "Is it okay? You look lost in thought."

"Yes, of course."

Marty sat down. "Ed, I'm sorry we didn't talk again last night. I got talking to Rob."

"I saw that."

"How have you been, Ed?"

"I'm fine, Marty. How about you?"

"Okay, I guess. I have a buyer for the business. I'm ready for something new. I don't know what, but yeah, I'm doing all right."

"Do you have anyone new in your life?" asked Ed

"No, not at the moment. You?"

"No, it's not all that easy, is it?"

"No, it isn't always," said Marty. "It is good to see you though, Ed. We did have something, didn't we?"

"Yes, we did. I guess neither one of us could be all of what we needed to be for the other."

Marty looked out the window. "Maybe we didn't know that we didn't have to be everything to each other. Maybe we tried too hard."

"Maybe," said Ed. "For a while there we did have a good run, but we changed. At least one of us did. We wanted different things."

"We both changed after what happened up here. We realized that life is so short and so precarious, that we had things to do before it was too late. We made our choices and here we are. Did we do the right thing? I had to go back there to be where I am now. Do I regret it? I can't, because I had to do it. Wasn't it the same for you? You had to see if life up here is what you wanted. Is it? I did love you Ed. You are a big part of my life."

"And you, mine. I do like living here, but I'm... Can I admit this to you?"

"What?"

"Sometimes I feel a little lonely."

Marty and Ed looked at each other. The silence was palpable.

"Everyone has asked me to stay at least one more day," said Marty. "I mean, Ike and Marion and Rob and Jade. Is that okay with you?"

"I would like that," said Ed. "It would be nice to see the kids for a little bit longer."

Marty looked at Ed. "I guess I could—"

Marty stood up.

"Maybe we could all have dinner together," said Ed. "You know, as a family."

"I would like that," said Marty. "Speaking of the kids, where are they?" Marty and Ed looked around. They were the only ones left in the room.

"Probably outside with their new friends."

"It's good to see Cindy having a good time. She took everything that happened so hard. Josey is coming into his own, but I've worried about Cindy. I think the divorce was harder on her than on Josey."

"I know," said Ed.

"Christ, Ed," said Marty. "Why does everything have to be so complicated?"

"I don't know. Things just are, I guess. We get what we think we want and still—"

"Do you have what you want, Ed?"

"I thought I did."

"Yeah, me too. Well, time to try again. Do you think we'll find what we're looking for?"

"I hope so, for both of us," said Ed.

"Me too. Dinner tonight? All of us?"

"Yes, if we can break Josey away from his newfound love."

Chapter 33

Jade and Rob finished cleaning up in the deserted dining room.

"It looks like everyone is having fun," said Jade.

Rob wrapped his arms around Jade's waist. "Yup, back to normal. Want to celebrate?"

"You're on for later. I told Hank I'd take a walk with him before he leaves. Is that okay?"

Rob hesitated. "No. That's fine. You got something—"

"No, of course not. He'll be leaving. I'll... we'll probably never see him again. He wanted take a walk on the path that goes along the lake. He just asked me to come along. I think he likes it around here."

"I bet he does."

"You're not jealous, are you?"

"Oh, a little. There is something between you two, isn't there?"

"Are you asking me not to go?"

"No, of course I want you to go."

Rob smiled. "Have fun. I do expect to see you later, though."

"That's the plan." Jade went outside.

Rob went over to the coffeemaker and grabbed a cup of coffee.

"Mind if I join you?" asked Marty from behind.

"Please. Let's go over and sit on the couch." The pair walked over toward the fireplace and sat next to each other on the old piece of furniture.

"I just had a nice conversation with Ed. You know we really did have some good times together."

"It always seemed like that to me."

"Rob, I need to be very direct. I don't want to get into a deep discussion. I need to do one more thing before I move on to whatever I'm going to do next. I'm feeling about as good about myself as I have ever felt, but I need to do this one thing."

"Okay?"

"I don't want to mess up what you have going with Jade but I want to finish what we started. One time. Do you have a free room that no one is using?"

"You know I do."

"It's beautiful here," said Hank. "I can see why you like it here. Not quite as vast as where I come from, but it has its attractions."

They were sitting cross-legged on soft pine needles in a small clearing that overlooked the lake.

"It was always a dream of mine to come up here," said Jade. "It's worked out better than I ever thought it would have. Sometimes I wish I had made the decision sooner, but I guess it might not have worked out the same way if I had. I wonder why it takes so long to make the right decision. Once you have made it, you look back and realize how much time you wasted."

"Funny how that goes," said Hank. "You know, usually when I finish a job, I can't wait to get back to Alaska. I'm having a hard time—"

"What?"

"You know, leaving."

"Will you be leaving?"

"I will be."

"Oh man!" said Jade.

The water lapped against the shore. A warm breeze rustled through the trees. Hank leaned forward.

"Is this our second chance?" asked Jade.

Hank nodded and took Jade's face into both of his hands and pulled her lips to his. Then he pulled back just a little and whispered.

"If I didn't take this chance before I leave, I would regret it for the rest of my life."

"I know," said Jade. "I know."

They kissed again and rolled over together onto the comfort of the wild pine needles.

Chapter 34

"Mr. Smith, what are you doing here? I wouldn't have thought that you'd be interested in petty local crime scenes," said Roger Wright.

"The missing person is a friend of the Schmidts. Thought I might be able to lend a hand. I've been involved in missing person cases before."

"I thought you were some kind of Mad Cow Disease expert."

"I have some experience in that area as well."

"Are you FBI?"

"No, I'm on a special task force."

"Do you have an ID?"

"I do."

"Could I see it?"

Mr. Smith reached into his pocket and pulled out his ID. Roger looked it over and handed it back."

"Looks like the real thing. But then it would, wouldn't it?"

Mr. Smith pocketed the document. His eyes met Rogers. "What do you mean by that?" asked Mr. Smith.

"Oh nothing," said Roger. "Just been a busy couple days. It kind of gets to you, if you know what I mean."

"Yeah, we don't have easy jobs. Do we?"

"No, we don't. So, what have we got this time?"

"Two guys were fishing: Eli Hodge and Joe Hampton. Both of them are involved with state government. Peter Schmidt has worked with both of them."

Roger nodded. "Interesting. So, what happened?"

"The two guys were fishing at dusk. Hodge apparently went upstream and Hampton stayed over there, in front of the camper. When Hodge got back, Hampton was gone."

"Did Hodge see anything?" asked Roger.

"No, he just said that his friend was gone."

"Where's Hodge now?"

"He's at the Schmidt's," said Mr. Smith. "He's pretty shaken."

"I bet. What about the people in the trailer? Did they see anything?"

"They claimed they heard a coyote scream. Another trooper has their statement."

"Well, we do have coyotes around here," said Roger.

"Yes, I believe you do. I'm not a big expert on wild animals."

"Just domestic animals, I guess. Do you mind if I look around?"

Mr. Smith regarded Trooper Wright. "Why not? For now, the state police are handling the case. I haven't asked for your ID, but judging from the uniform it looks like you're a member of the state police," said Mr. Smith. "I don't believe this is your case, though."

"Well, you know how it is. Like you, I just happen to be in the area."

"My task force is always ready to cooperate with local authorities when asked."

"I've never heard of your task force. Have you been asked?"

"We have. I don't think you, personally, have been asked though."

"I guess I'll just have a chat with my colleague over there by the camper. I take it both sides of the river have been checked?"

"Thoroughly. We got here as soon as we were notified."

"Who's we?"

"My associates and I. As you know, we were nearby at the Schmidt's. We were able to get here before the state police or the sheriff. You guys have to cover a lot of territory up here. It was auspicious that we were around."

"Very auspicious. I wouldn't have thought that you would have had jurisdiction until asked."

"I already told you. We were asked. We got the call from Concord."

"That was quick work. Very efficient."

"Yes it was, officer. Officer Wright, correct?"

"Right."

"Well, Officer Wright, can I be of any further assistance?"

"No, I don't think so."

"We're always happy to help whenever we can."

"I'm sure you are.

"Officer Wright?"

"Yes?"

"You don't want to piss me off."

"I don't?"

"I think you need to work on your sarcasm, officer."

"Thank you for your... your advice Mr. Smith."

Roger walked over to the camper. A man in dark suit started to get into an unmarked cruiser, but he didn't drive away.

"Hey Alex, got a minute?"

Alex Hall turned around. "Hey Roger, how's it going? How's the family?"

"We're all fine. How about you?"

"All good."

"What have you got?"

"Not much. The guy just disappeared."

"That doesn't make much sense," said Roger. "Where would he go? I assume they only had one vehicle."

"That's right. His friend said he just wasn't there when he came back from fishing upstream."

"So what did he do?"

"Apparently, he tried his cell phone but there was no signal. Then he drove into Clifford and called 911 from the store there."

"How'd the Feds get here before you guys?"

"I don't know. They were nearby I guess. I can't prove it, but I think some time went by before we were notified. The people in the camper said the Feds were here quite a while before we got here."

"What did the fisherman say?

"I don't know. He was taken to the Schmidt's before I had a chance to question him."

"The campers? Did they see anything?"

"They thought they saw something in the woods and they heard a loud scream. I think that agent—or whatever he is—convinced them it was a coyote."

"Why do you say that?"

"They're pretty shaken up. I don't think they want to believe what they saw. Anyone who uses one of these remote sites isn't going to be worried about coyotes?"

"What do they think they saw?"

"I don't know, but I don't think it was as coyote. We've asked them to stay in the area but they don't want to stay at the campsite. They want to go to a more populated campground."

"Do you think whatever they saw may have had something to do with the missing person?"

"They said the fisherman looked upset. Like he didn't know what to do. He even started toward the camper and then went back to his car. If they really did see something, it would be kind of a coincidence, don't you think? At least it should be investigated."

"One would think. So what's next?"

"Normal missing person stuff. There are some strings being pulled on this one."

"I'd sure like to know what that fisherman had to say," said Roger.

Alex nodded. "Yup, me too."

"Alex, did you hear anything about the mountain lion attack up here. A young kid was killed."

"I heard it was a hoax. Turned out the kid's friend may have killed him.

"What? You believe that? I was on that case but—" said Roger.

"They took you off?"

"Well, I don't think they liked my version of what happened."

"The kid didn't kill his friend?"

"No."

"How do you know?"

"I was one of the first ones there. That victim wasn't killed by a human being."

"Mountain lion?"

"It wasn't a coyote."

"How do you know?"

"This isn't the first time that I've seen the results of a mountain lion attack.

"Where'd you see that?"

"Up here in Clifford. Do you remember the forest fire?"

"I was young, but yes, I do remember that. I thought the mountain lion part was also a hoax."

"Sound familiar?"

"Shit!" said Alex. "They're going to let that kid go to jail then?"

"It looks that way doesn't it?" said Roger.

"But why would—"

"I don't know. I would like to find out. Blaming that kid is too extreme. I can't just shut up and let that kid spend the rest of his life in jail. That's intolerable."

"Roger, you know I trust you. Hell, you helped train me. But, it's hard to believe that a mountain lion attack would be worth all of this effort to cover up. I mean, I know the official position is that they don't exist. If any evidence turns up, then they claim it must be from a released pet or some such thing. It's not like they are saying it's impossible."

"There is a difference between trying to explain a sighting and an actual attack."

"There would be but—"

Roger looked over at Mr. Smith's black vehicle. Mr. Smith was still sitting in his car.

Alex looked at Roger. "I suppose someone might release a pet mountain lion when it wasn't cute anymore. I guess it could happen. Look at what's going on with those snakes down in the Everglades."

"This was no released pet," said Roger. "Neither was the last one."

Alex sneered. "I wonder if it's the Vice President's pet catamount. He seems like the type who would...I really don't like that guy."

"Damn!" said Roger. "Neither do I, but I wonder.—"

"You don't really think the Vice President had a pet mountain lion, do you?

"No, I don't think that, but...Not his personal pet anyway."

"What do you think?"

"I don't know exactly. Somebody in Washington seems awfully interested."

"Yes, they do," Alex agreed. "What are you going to do?"

"I don't know, but I hope we can find out what really happened here. Do you think you could interview that other fisherman? I know they won't let me near him. Have they notified the next of kin? Was the deceased married? What about the other guy?"

"They're both married and have kids. Mr Smith took care of that. It should be my job to interview the victim's friend. They have him at Schmidt's place. I'll see what I can do. I'm not exactly feeling a lot of cooperation."

Mr. Smith started his car's engine. Alex and Roger watched as the man drove away.

"I'm going to take a look around. You said the couple in the trailer said they thought they saw something over on that side?"

"That's what they said. I don't think they really know what they saw. A reflection that looked like yellow eyes. They were surprised when I informed them that I was told it was probably a coyote."

"Alex, do me a favor. Be careful"

"Yeah!"

"Just be careful. Our Mr. Smith knows you have talked to that guy. I'm not sure we are on the same side. And if something should happen to me, I'd do some wondering."

"Do you really think—"

"I don't know," said Roger. "I hope not. There was a biologist that was also there when we investigated the scene where Randall Cramer was killed."

"Is that the guy who disappeared out of the hospital? His name was Ramsey, right?"

"Right."

"Actually I know him," said Alex. "I've worked with him a couple of times. Good guy. Knows his stuff."

"He does. Guess what his conclusion was."

"Mountain lion?"

"Yup."

Alex opened the door of his cruiser. He leaned against the car before getting in. "Roger."

"What?"

"You take care too."

Alex drove away. Roger went down to the river.

THE OLD ABENAKI

The old Abenaki was losing his awareness of the past. His sense of consciousness was changing. How had he not known that he was dead? Had he forgotten that he had died? When did he die? How? He had been old. He had been very old. He had not been killed. He had just stopped living. His Molly, his Moll was gone. Maybe he was going to move on.

It was not his curse that had caused such pain. He did not have the power to conjure the black mountain lion. He had been just a man. The living had fashioned this chaos. He no longer belonged to that group. The time was coming and time was also of the living. The old Abenaki was no longer of time and space but somehow he still had been. His sense of guilt was fading and so was his faculty of perception.

It should have been so simple, but it had not been. He only had to forgive himself for something that was not his fault. He watched the dark, but not quite black, figure as it moved away from the river. One green-and-tan vehicle was on the road near the black one. The other was in front of the metal house on wheels.

The black vehicle did not move. The man was talking into a thin, flat object. The other two men who were dressed in green-and-gray uniforms were talking into a black, square object. One started toward the river. The old Abenaki wanted to shout out, but suddenly his world became an oddly comfortable swirl and the dimension of the living faded to black.

Peter Schmidt and Mr. Smith were sitting on the Schmidt's front porch. Mary served them both drinks. Jake came out of the barn as Alex Hall drove up to the house.

"Thank you, Mary," said Peter. "Why don't you go see if Mr. Hodge would like anything?"

Jake turned around and went back into the barn. Mr. Smith leaned back in his chair and took a sip from his ginger ale.

"You ever worry about Mary and that man you have working for you?"

"No, I know what's going on. Keeps her happy. When she's happy, I'm happy."

"She's a good looking woman," said Mr. Smith.

Peter nodded. "Yes, she is. I have good taste. She and I both do our jobs. It's a good arrangement. Speaking of arrangements, what are we going to do about our nosey state trooper? I don't think we can afford any more disappearances."

"I suppose not," said Mr. Smith. "Any number of things could happen to a man up here in these woods though, don't you agree?"

"Things do happen," said Peter Schmidt. "Speaking of disappearances, what about our biologist?" He took a sip from his drink.

"Everything is falling into place," said Mr. Smith.

Inside, Jake and Mary stood by the kitchen window and watched the trooper walk up to the porch.

"We were just having a drink," said Peter. "Would like to join us?"

Chapter 35

Lying on his back on an antique four-poster bed, Eli Hodge heard a vehicle pull up on the gravel driveway outside. His hands were coupled together behind his neck. His arms spread out like wings on the patchwork down comforter. The dark window shades were pulled down but sunlight slipped in around the edges. He got out of bed, went to one of the windows and pulled up the shade. The bright sunlight momentarily blinded Eli's dilated pupils. He pulled back the white lace curtains and looked down over the roof of the porch. He saw the trooper. Alex glanced up toward the window and then walked toward the porch. Eli could hear unintelligible voices. He thought he heard his name. Maybe this trooper was here to take him home.

The Schmidts had been kind to take him in, but Eli wanted more than anything in the world to see his wife and two sons. Why hadn't Marie called? Peter said he had contacted her and that she would call back. There was no need for Eli to call. Maybe his wife was coming here. Why?

Why couldn't he just go home? He wanted to talk to Joe's wife. It wasn't going to be easy, but that is where he should be, not here. Eli went over to the door. He turned the knob. The door was locked. He rushed back to the window. He saw the trooper walk toward his cruiser. Before he got in, Alex looked up and got into his car. Eli waved but the trooper did not respond.

Josey and McKenzie paddled around the point of land. Stillwater Lodge was inscribed just above three small patched holes on the side of the blue canoe. The brown-stained exterior of the Lodge looked richer in the early evening sun.

"It really is beautiful here," said McKenzie.

"If I had my way, I'd live here all of the time," said Josey. "I'd like to become a Fish and Game officer like Uncle Rob."

"I don't think I would mind living up here either. I don't know if I would get tired of it. I'd miss my friends. My family spends a lot of time in the North Country. I'm usually not ready to go home when it is time to leave. I didn't know Mr. Schurman was your uncle.

"Not my real uncle. Cindy and I just always called him that. You know what is weird? I think my Mom and Uncle Rob had something going on."

"I guess it's kind of gross, isn't it? Is that why your parents got divorced?"

"One of the reasons, I think. Not just that. I never heard them talk about an affair or anything. It's hard to think about your parents having sex. I think they broke up because my mom wanted to stay in Massachusetts and my dad didn't. They wanted to do different things, especially after whatever happened up here. Do your parents still have sex?"

"I think they do," said McKenzie. I guess it's kind of cool that they do. It's just weird to think about. Why do you think Mr. Schurman and your mother had something going on?"

"My mom was supposed to be up here alone one weekend. My Dad decided to come up at the last minute. He surprised Mom and Rob at the cabin. After that, everything changed. Dad stopped talking about Uncle Rob. Mom and Dad acted as if they hardly knew each other. They had trouble looking at each other in the eye. They started arguing about just about everything. I was kind of young so I didn't understand exactly what was going on, but I heard them talking about stuff."

"Like what?"

"Dad would start to say something and Mom would say things like I chose you or it's over. Stuff like that. They didn't think I could hear what they said. I remember Rob stopped by the cabin right before Cindy and I got lost. Rob and Mom were acting really weird together."

"You got lost?"

"We kept going around in circles. If our dog Virgil hadn't been with us, I think the mountain lion I told you about might have killed us."

"That must have been really scary. Is that the old dog that came with your Dad?"

"Yeah, Virgil. He's getting old, but what a great dog! He really did save our lives. So did my parents and Uncle Rob. That trooper Mr. Wright, Ike Roberts, and the two vets were all there. Some people actually got killed. Cindy never got over it."

"What about you? How did you get over it? I can't imagine going through something like that when you were that young. I am still shaking from seeing that animal. There' something about it that's just not right. The idea of meeting a mountain lion is scary enough, but that thing was terrifying. It looked like it actually hated us. It wanted to kill us, I'm sure of it. The moose was gross, but I'll never forget the way that catamount looked at us. Never."

Josey took McKenzie's hand. "You learn to live with it. At least you know its dead."

"Hug me," said the girl.

Josey pulled the girl close. "One side of me wants to cry," he said. "The other feels almost invincible because we survived. We handled it."

"Funny, I know what you mean. I almost feel more alive." McKenzie only slightly pulled back from her hug and kissed Josey on the lips.

"You know what I would like to do," she said. "I would like to sleep outdoors at the campsite that we just saw back there. It's probably only a five minute walk from the lodge."

"I would be up for that. I don't think our parents will let us go alone, do you?"

"I am sure they wouldn't, but I bet my Dad would go," said McKenzie. "He likes to camp. Paul might like to come to."

"Actually, how about if you and I took all the kids. We're almost old enough to be camp counselors. We could sit around a campfire. We could roast marshmallows. We'd be just around the corner. It wouldn't be like going way out into the woods."

"If my Dad goes," said McKenzie. "he'll want to show us how much he knows about camping and stuff. I saw hand-held radios in the office. We could take one of those. Then we could check in. They can come see us before we go to sleep if they want to. I'll ask my Mom and Dad. I think they are happy to spend time with Paul's parents. They all seem to like each other. So maybe they will let us go. They were already drinking when we left."

"I'll ask my parents," said Josey. "They actually seemed to be getting along at the moment. They want to have a family dinner tonight. I will probably have to go to that first. Actually, I kind of want to."

"It must be hard that your parents are divorced."

"It sucks," said Josey, "but you get used to it, in a way. I love my parents but I hate having to spend time with them separately."

"I hope my parents don't get divorced," said McKenzie. "So many kids at school have divorced parents."

"Your Mom and Dad seem happy."

"Yeah, most of the time."

"Most of the time is pretty good, isn't it," said Josey.

"You mean I don't get a prince in shining armor?" said McKenzie."

"Are you sure you want a prince in shining armor?" asked Josey.

McKenzie smiled. "Doesn't every girl want to be Cinderella?"

"I hope not," said Josey. "Anyway, I don't have any shining armor."

"That's good because I don't have a little glass slipper. What's that old song? 'Girls Just Want to Have Fun'. I'll go with that for now," said McKenzie.

Josey guided the canoe to the small beach area in front of the lodge. McKenzie jumped out and pulled the canoe on to the shore.

"Let's go see if the other kids want to come with us," said McKenzie. "We can go after supper. All we really need is our sleeping bags. It doesn't look like rain. There was some wood next to the fireplace. I bet Mrs. Roberts might have some marshmallows."

"You know what I would like to do tomorrow," said Tristan.

"What?" asked Karley.

"I'd like to go back to that place where we went skinny-dipping. You know, kind of start over."

Karley sipped her drink. "You just want to see Holly naked."

"Well, there is that," said Tristan. "But I think I have gotten bitten by the bug. I liked swimming without a bathing suit."

"I told you that you would," said Pat. "The hardest part of leaving a nudist resort is to have to put clothes back on. The best part, when you first get there, is to take them off."

"I would love to go back to that spot," said Holly. "We could bring lunches again and spend the day there. Karley and I took our bathing suits off for a while this afternoon while you guys went to town."

"Shit, I'm sorry I missed that. Holly and I have to go to Coldbrook to get a rental car in the morning but we can all get together in the afternoon. Bill Holiday doesn't do AAA so some guy from Berlin is coming to tow the car to Bill's place. The insurance guy can't make it up for a couple of days."

"Looks like we have to stay," said Holly.

"No choice," said Pat.

"Uh oh, here comes all of our kids together. I wonder what they have in mind."

"We want to go camping," said McKenzie."

"You do? Where do you want to go?" asked Pat.

"There's a campsite about five minutes from here. It belongs to the Lodge. We asked. Mrs. Roberts even has some marshmallows. Mr. Schurman said we could take a two-way radio."

"Does everyone want to go?" asked Tristan.

"I think so," said Cameron. "I'm not sure about Cindy, Josey's sister."

"It sounds like fun," said Holly. "You are all old enough to act responsibly. Don't blow it by doing anything stupid."

"We won't," said Paul.

"Okay, have fun," said Karley.

"We will," said McKenzie.

"Our kids are growing up," Holly observed, "way too fast."

"Yeah and we're getting old way too fast," said Pat.

"Well, we'll have an evening without kids. Want to play some cards?" asked Karley.

"Strip poker?" asked Tristan.

"Not quite what I had in mind," said Karley.

"Rummy?" asked Tristan,

"Boring," said Pat. "We could play in our cabin. We have fixings for gin and tonic."

"Sounds good to me," said Tristan.

"Really?" asked Karley. "You want to play strip poker?"

"It's not like we aren't going skinny-dipping tomorrow," said Tristan. "What's the difference? Besides no kids. Let's live on the wild side."

"I don't know, but there is a difference," said Karley. "You can go if—"

"Never mind," said Tristan. "We can play Rummy."

"I'll go get the gin and tonic stuff," said Holly.

"Oh the hell with it," said Karley. "Let's go to your cabin. You guys are going to corrupt me."

"That's the idea," said Pat.

"Shouldn't we have dinner first?" said Karley.

Chapter 36

Mr. Smith and Peter Schmidt watched as Alex Hall's cruiser backed up and drove away.

"Damn it!" said Peter. "They're not going to leave this alone. I am not so sure we should have taken the biologist out of the hospital. That's kind of messy. We can't keep Eli Hodge here forever. All of this could came back on us."

"Not if we handle it right," said Mr. Smith. "I know what I'm doing."

"I sure hope you do"

"Well, Peter, you're the man with the power and the money. How important is it that all of this gets resolved?"

"Very important."

"My job is to solve problems," said Mr. Smith. "Do you want me to solve this problem?"

"Yes."

"No matter what?"

Peter looked out over the fields next to his house. A warm gentle breeze whisked over his face. "Someone has to get hurt?"

"I think so," said Mr. Smith. "Yes, I believe so."

"It's for the greater good?"

"It is."

"I should go back to Washington?" said Peter.

"You should."

"What about the dead cat?"

"We have it back. Nothing to worry about there."

"The old drunk saw the other one."

"Again, nothing to worry about there," said Mr. Smith. "I have already set things in motion. Do you want to know more?"

"No, I don't," said Peter Schmidt.

"It is nice to have the family all around the same table again," said Marty.

"It is," agreed Ed.

"Are you getting back together?" asked Cindy.

"Let's just enjoy the moment," said Marty.

"What do you think about McKenzie, Paul and I, and the other kids sleeping outside overnight? We'll be just around the corner."

"Couldn't we have dinner before we discuss that?" asked Marty. "It's not like we get to do this often."

We never do, thought Josey, because you got divorced.

"I just wanted to know if it would be okay," said Josey. "I really want to and we should go out before it gets too dark."

"You still have a little over an hour of sunlight," said Ed. "Sleeping outside is part of being in the woods. So, as far as I am concerned, you may go. What do you think Marty?"

"Sure, fine, but let's enjoy our meal now."

"I don't want to sleep outside," said Cindy. "I feel safer inside. Do I have to go?"

"Of course not, you can stay here," said Marty.

"Can I ask Kayla if she will stay with me? I'll be right back."

Before anyone could answer, Cindy got up and walked across the room. Then she came back.

"Kayla and I are going to work on a puzzle together. Is that okay? Kayla is finished eating."

McKenzie approached the table. She held a large bag of marshmallows.

"Our parents said it was okay. Let's get our sleeping bags. Are you sure you don't want to go, Cindy?"

"Kayla and I are going to do a puzzle," said Cindy.

Kayla came over to the table. She held a battered puzzle box.

"You could just come for the marshmallows. Josey and I will walk you back so you don't have to sleep outside."

"Why don't you come?" asked Josey. "You like marshmallows."

"I do but... I also don't like the bugs."

"The bugs aren't so bad. It gets a lot cooler at night and there is a breeze. You like marshmallows, don't you, Kayla?" asked Josey.

"I think we should go have the marshmallows and then come back," agreed Kayla. "Let's do that."

"Okay, as long and Josey and McKenzie walk us back."

Josey started to get up. "We will."

"Don't you want dessert?" asked Marty.

McKenzie held up the bag. Marty smiled.

"All right, see you guys," said Ed. He turned to Marty. "I guess it's just you and me. Our kids are growing up. They have their own plans."

Marty lifted her wine glass. "Here's to you and me."

Chapter 37

Hank Harbor stopped the old truck. A large, dark Ford Explorer blocked the road. Two armed men approached. Harbor recognized the government-issue Heckler and Koch MP5/10 machine guns that they held pointed toward the ground. They also wore Glock 40 S&W pistols as side arms. He wondered why they looked as if they just stepped out of an L.L.Bean advertisement. Harbor turned the window handle on the old Ford. Slowly the window groaned open.

"Please step out of the vehicle, Mr. Harbor," said one of the men. The other man stepped back and raised his weapon.

"What's going on?"

"Please, just open the door and step out. Are you armed?"

"Why would I be armed? I'm heading home."

"Where are your guns?"

"In the back of the truck."

"Okay, I just need you to get out. Then turn around and raise your arms against the cab."

Harbor did as he was told. The man who had been doing the talking patted the Alaskan Guide down.

"What is—"

"Now I want you to get back into your truck, Mr. Harbor. Let's make this easy. My colleague will be joining you. You're not going home just yet. We'll take the dogs. Very slowly, I want you to put them in the back of our vehicle. Please don't try anything. If you do, I will shoot the dogs, and believe me, I have no problem if I have to shoot you."

Hank pulled the driver's seat of the old Ford forward and called his dogs. They jumped out of the pickup and followed their master to the back of the Explorer.

"We'll also be taking your firearms."

"Now get back in the truck."

Hank Harbor did so. He did not say a word.

Alex Hall fumbled with his keys. Then, he realized he hadn't locked his cruiser. He climbed into the driver's seat and started the engine. He felt something hard and metallic against his neck.

"Shit!" he said.

"Hand me your gun." Alex followed the man's instructions. "Now drive to Stillwater Lodge."

"But—"

"We don't need to discuss anything. Just do it."

Alex put the car in gear.

A blue Buick pulled up behind the parked Class C RV.

A man was in the driver's seat of the RV and the woman who sat next to him was looking at a Delorme's Map.

"There's a camping place across the border in Maine. Maybe they will have an available site."

"Hal, those two men are walking toward us. They have guns."

"Are they cops?"

"I don't know. They don't look like it."

One of the men motioned for the woman to roll down the window. The woman pressed the button.

One of the men leaned into the window. He looked at the woman. "Ma'am, would you very carefully open the door to your camper. My partner will be getting in. He will tell you where to go."

"But—" said the woman.

"He'll tell you where to go."

"Who's that in the SUV?" asked Al.

"Looks like they want us to pull over," said Bruce. "They don't look like cops." Al pulled the green Fish and Game truck over to the side of the road. Two men got out of the SUV. They were dressed in plaid shirts and blue jeans. They had guns.

Froggy heard the car approaching. He cracked open the front door of his cabin. He slowly closed the door. He climbed up into the ancient smoking chamber above the old fireplace. He heard the knocking on the door but he did not respond.

Roger Wright emerged from Morrison's Store carrying a large coffee mug. A man who looked like he had just stepped out of an L.L.Bean catalogue was standing next to his cruiser. The clothing did nothing to conceal that the man was not a local. The man walked up to the trooper as if he were meeting an old friend. He wasn't

"Officer Wright, I'm not messing around. I am armed and I really have no problem with the idea of shooting you. I could make this look like I'm just another deranged cop killer. You do understand?"

Roger nodded.

"I want you to take out your gun and your Taser and put them in the back seat. Then get in the front seat. I will be sitting next to you. I'm serious. Don't try anything. I am authorized to kill you."

"Authorized? By whom?"

"Just get in the car. Now."

Roger opened the door to the cruiser. The man in the overly elaborate backwoods clothes got into the passenger's seat. The cruiser drove off.

Doc and George came out of Morrison's.

"I thought Roger was going to wait for us," said George.

"That's what he said."

"I guess he must have gotten called out."

"I guess," said Doc. "I just wanted to get his take on the mountain lion. I don't feel like it is resolved. Do you?"

"Of course not. We got one mountain lion missing and what's his name, the old drunk, says he saw another one. I don't know—"

"Speaking of the devil," said Doc, "he's coming this way."

"You two need to get the hell out of here," said Froggy.

The old man pushed Doc and George back into the store.

Doc put his arm on Froggy's shoulder. "It's okay, Mister," said Doc. "Calm down."

"It's not okay," gasped Froggy. "Call me Charley."

"What's not okay?" asked George.

"They're taking everyone away."

"What do you mean, they are taking everyone away? Who is they? Who is everyone?"

"All those big city shitheads. The ones in the flannel shirts."

"What are you talking about?" asked Doc. "It's too hot for flannel shirts. I haven't seen—"

"Didn't you just see who got into that cruiser?"

"No," said Doc.

"The guy had a gun."

"Roger is a trooper. He always carries a gun when—"

"Not the trooper. The other man who got into the cruiser.

"What are they doing?" asked Doc.

"I think those men are picking up everyone who knows anything about the catamounts. They came after me, but I hid. I waited them out and they finally left. I heard them talking, though, and I am sure you are next. Where do you think that trooper just went?"

"We were supposed to talk to Roger, the state trooper, but he left," said Doc.

"He didn't leave on his own volition."

"In your opinion," said George.

"I saw the cop get into the cruiser and an armed man made the officer put his gun in the back seat."

"Do you know where they are taking him?" asked Doc.

"I heard them talking when they were at my place. Like I said, they didn't think I was there. Either that or they figured it didn't matter what I knew because they were going to get me anyway. They said that they were taking everyone out to Stillwater Lodge."

Doc looked at Froggy. "Really? Everyone? Why? For what?"

"Everyone that knows something about the catamount attacks, it looks like."

"Trying to cover things up again. But why take us all out there?" asked George. "What the hell are they going to do? Threaten us? Pay us to keep quiet? Why bother? They did a pretty good job of hiding everything last time. What they couldn't hide, they discredited. Worked, too. They pretty much ruined my credibility, not to mention my career."

"Look," said Froggy. "You probably think that I am full of shit, but I'm reasonably sober. Have been for a while. I ain't gone cold turkey, but I've cut down a lot. I've just been kind of playing the part. If everyone thinks I'm drunk, it's easier to observe things. And I have."

"Like what?" asked Doc.

"Like those catamounts didn't just appear. They were put there. I don't know why, but they were."

"By whom?" asked George.

"Who do you think? The same dickheads that want us all out at the lodge! Think about it."

"Those guys out at Schmidt's place?" asked Doc.

"Who else? Well maybe not those exact same individuals—the same types, though. Did you think those cats were some kind of natural phenomena? Why do you think they went to such lengths to cover everything up last time?"

"Well, I…" said George. "But I came around to accepting or trying believe they just didn't want people to think that something like a mountain lion attack could happen here. And they didn't want to admit that they weren't very good at handling it. I'm not sure who those people are. But why would the military or some government agency put mountain lions into the wilderness?"

"How the hell should I know? I'm the low life around here. At least I don't do much harm. They on the other hand…I don't know why. Something happened here and we know it. "They" can deny it all they want. We know what happened and that makes us problematic."

"Yes, problematic," agreed Doc.

"They want us out of the way," said Froggy. "I know a lot more than they think I know. I saw them release this last one. I was out hunting for turkeys. I saw them. Maybe not exactly all the same agent types, but our friend Mr. Smith was there, big as life. They opened the cage and the cat walked out. Just like that. It almost looked like it was responding to commands from Mr. Big Shot Smith himself. But you know what?"

"What?" asked George.

Froggy looked out the window at the parking lot. A Black SUV pulled up in front of the store and parked.

"They're back. We need to get the hell out of here."

"Aren't you being a bit paranoid?" asked George.

"No sir, I am not. See that car over there? Look at how those fellows are dressed. They're trying awful hard to pretend they ain't from away."

"You said that before, but I see you're right," said Doc. "It's not working very well, is it?"

"Nope," said Froggy. "Assholes!"

"If you're right—and I'm starting to believe you are, Charley—we can't go out there," said George.

"We can try behind the store," said Doc. "I parked behind the store," said Doc.

"That's probably why they didn't find you yet," said Froggy. "We can't use either one of your vehicles. I am sure they are looking for them. If they see your truck, they'll know we're around here somewhere. We won't get far in them."

"So what do we do?" asked George.

"Hope they haven't looked out back yet," said Froggy.

"What good is that going to do? We can't use my truck," said Doc.

"If we can get to the woods over by the river, maybe we would have chance," Charley suggested.

"If they see my truck, wouldn't they look there?" asked Doc.

"Maybe not first thing," said Charley. "I don't have a better idea, do you?"

Doc looked at George.

"I don't," said George. "We don't have a whole lot of choices."

The three men went to the back of the store. It was starting to get dark. Doc peeked out of one of the windows. A car pulled up next to Doc's truck.

"Shit!" he said.

*   *   *

Eli Hodge was sitting on the bed when the door opened. Mr. Smith entered the room.

"We're going for a ride," he said.

"I've rented a cabin in Greenville," said Jake.

"I'm going to visit my sister in California," said Mary Schmidt. "Peter's gone to Washington and it is time for us to go."

Jake kissed Mary and then got into his truck. Mary got into her Audi. Mr. Smith watched as they went their separate ways. Then he went into the barn. Moments later, he came out with Phil Ramsey.

Chapter 38

"Come on you guys. The fire's going good," yelled Josey. "It's going to be dark soon. Bring your flashlights."

On the other side of the small clearing, McKenzie straightened her sleeping bag. "We're coming," she said.

For a moment the steady breeze stopped. McKenzie swiped a swarm of black flies away from her face.

"Where do they come from?" The breeze returned. The hungry insects retreated.

"Thank goodness for the wind," said Josey.

Standing by the fire, Paul held up a bag of marshmallows.

"Has everyone got a stick?"

"Almost," yelled Cameron. "I just need to finish this one."

Using a pocketknife, Cameron whittled a point on a freshly cut branch. He passed it to his sister. Abbi took the stick and approached the fire. Kayla, Connor and Cindy followed behind her. They all carried long, thin roasting wands. Paul started to hand out marshmallows. McKenzie was the first to sit. She skewered one of the white squares onto the tip of her stick and extended it over the fire.

"I like mine nice and black," she said.

Paul sat down next to McKenzie. "Me too," he said.

The fire reflected in the youngsters faces as they all concentrated on toasting the white confection to suit their individual tastes. Some preferred burnt to a crisp, while others fancied something only slightly browned. Occasionally one would pull his or her stick out of the fire to inspect the progress.

Abbi brought the finished delicacy to her mouth. She blew on it.

"Careful, it's hot," Paul warned.

Abbi tried to bite into the blackened marshmallow again. "Ouch," she said. "It's really hot." She blew on it again.

"Give it a minute or two," said McKenzie.

"Does anyone know a good story?" asked Connor.

"I think I can come up with something," said Josey. "My Dad tells stories about Dangerous Dan McGrew. I could tell one of those."

"Don't tell one of the scary ones," said Cindy.

"I promise," said Josey.

"I'm up for a good story," said Paul.

"Me too," said Cameron.

"Does everyone want to hear about Dangerous Dan?" asked Josey. Everyone nodded.

McKenzie passed out another round of marshmallows. There was silence as the sticks were extended over the fire. A shifting wind sent smoke circling around the campfire.

"That hurts my eyes," said Kayla.

Josey stirred the fire a little with his poker. The fire brightened and the smoke diminished.

"A long time ago, a local sheriff named Dangerous Dan McGrew roamed these parts. He—"

Rob poured a small amount of Ardberg Whisky into Jade's glass, then his own.

"So are we okay?" he asked.

"I'm okay," said Jade. "You?"

"I'm okay."

"Do we need to talk?" asked Jade.

"I don't think so. Do you think we do?"

"No," said Jade.

"Any regrets?" asked Rob.

Jade grinned. "No. You?"

"No regrets," said Rob.

"And what about us?" asked Jade.

"Well, I was thinking it might be nice to go to bed early."

"Funny, I was thinking the same thing," said Jade. She leaned over and kissed Rob. He put both of his hands on her cheeks and kissed her back. He pulled back and then gave Jade another quick kiss. Jade grabbed Rob's hand.

"Let's go," she said. "It is definitely getting late, mister."

Chapter 39

The man with the Glock sat cross-legged on the carpet just behind the forward seats of the Class C RV. He pointed the gun at the woman in the passenger seat. The GPS on the dashboard, in a bossy female voice, occasionally barked instruction to turn left, right or continue on. For the woman, each direction change was a shot of aggravation that intensified her dread. Margret Hawkins was trembling. She heard her husband speak. For Chrissake, Hollis, she thought, don't piss the guy off.

"What's Stillwater Lodge? Why—"

"Sir," said the man in the back. "Just follow the GPS. Did I ask you to talk?"

"Have we done something—"

"Please sir, just drive."

Hollis Hawkins looked at his wife. In the dashboard light, he could see that Margret's hands were folded in her lap. She glanced at her husband. She gripped her fingers and pressed down on her crossed thumbs. She breathed in and then out. Had anything in her past prepared her for this? Things like this did not happen to people like her and Hollis. A man had climbed into the back of their RV, their home. The barrel of the pistol had been—and still was—aimed straight at her.

She imagined the projectile lodged in the chamber at the far end of the narrow black hole. The stark, steely-dark eye that stared right into the depth of her being. She imagined the pull of the finger, so easily initiated, that would instantaneously end her life. It was a chilling sensation. That's all it takes. Would she hear the shot? How many millions of people have died this way? Squeeze, don't jerk.

And Hollis? Margret felt Hollis' hand on her thigh. Her husband, the man she had chosen for better or worse. She put her hand on his and embraced it. Hollis and Margret. They had a thing called life together for over forty years: kids, the affair, the death of their parents, work, careers, travel, a family home and now a motor home. And suddenly... that intensely indifferent, severe steel eye that promised the end of it all. She looked at her husband. He looked back at her. He knew too. They had shared just about everything. Now they shared the horror. It was in his eyes.

Margret visualized the dark reaper. This was not how it was supposed to be. Where was the welcoming light? Where were their long lost loved ones? There was just the man with the gun who was indifferent to her and Hollis and to her profound sense of loss. She braced herself and looked back at the man. He offered nothing in the way of hope. This would not be the first time he had pulled that trigger. The man did not care and she knew it. He was trained not to care.

Then the GPS broke the silence. The RV turned left onto a dirt road. The headlights glanced over the old sign—Stillwater Lodge, 18 miles.

George, Doc, and Charley turned around and went back to the front of Morrison's. The outdoorsy-attired men waited next to their conspicuous vehicle. Charley checked the back door again.

"Still there," he said.

Mo and Chuck, Morrison's proprietors, both leaned against the checkout counter. Mo called out.

"What's going on, Doc? You act like you are afraid to go outside. Who are those guys?"

The three men walked over to the counter.

"That's a good question, Mo. We really don't know. We're just pretty sure that our well-being isn't the first thing on their minds"

Chuck looked out the window. "You know what," he said. "We've known you, Doc, pretty much all our lives. As to those guys, well, I don't know that I would give a plug nickel for them. How can we help?"

"Have you got a vehicle we could borrow?"

"I got that 1969 Camaro out back. She's a corker."

"Someday," said Doc. "But I don't think we would get far in that."

"She's fast," said Chuck.

"Yup, and she stands out like a sore thumb."

"Our pickup is parked on the side," said Mo. "It's loaded and ready to go to the dump. I could bring it around back."

"They're in both parking lots," said George.

"You could just go out that side door," said Mo. "Let me take a look-see. Maybe they weren't smart enough to watch that. Give me that wastebasket. I'll put it in the back of the truck. It'll give me a reason to be out there."

Mo opened the door and went outside. He came back in.

"Smarter than we thought. There are a couple of those guys hanging around out there. They ain't trying to hide. They're standing right under the light over there."

"How would we get into Mo's truck?" asked Doc. "Even in the dark, it would be kind of hard to get us all into that truck."

"There is that," said Mo.

"You know what?" asked Doc.

"What?" asked Charley.

"It's my truck out back. So, my guess is that they're waiting for me. They don't know about George or Charley. What if I walk outside, you know, innocent as you please—"

"And let them take you?" asked George.

"What are they going to do, kill me? I might as well find out what they have in mind. It would be good to know that you two were out there somewhere. You could take Mo's and Chuck's truck."

"Is that our only plan?" asked George. "I don't like it."

"We could try to get into the truck and all get caught," said Doc. "I'm going to get going before they decide to come in here to fetch me."

"Shouldn't we call the police?" asked Chuck.

"I am not sure whose side the cops are on," said Doc.

"Man, that's not good," said Chuck.

Doc nodded. "Give me a cup of coffee and a magazine or something."

Hands full, Doc walked out of the store.

Two of the men approached Doc and then escorted him to one of their vehicles.

Chapter 40

The Explorer pulled off into a large clearing that Northern Lumber had used to yard logs that they would later truck out to paper mills in Berlin, Lincoln or Groveton. On this night, there was no moon. The blackness was absolute except for the blaze of light exhaling from the parked vehicle. Various breeds of insects were attracted to the illumination, so Mr. Smith turned off the offending headlights. He stepped out of his vehicle. A steady breeze rustled the leaves in the endless expanse of trees. In the cities, who could really grasp the concept of pitch darkness? Here, it stymied the sense of sight. Hearing, on the other hand, was besieged by a not unpleasant cacophony of peepers, crickets and a persistent Whippoorwill.

He breathed the cool, crisp, clean night air. It was more than just smell, you could taste it—a sensation unknown in the urban environment where Mr. Smith had marked his territory. He waited. The door of the Explorer felt smooth against his back. Much like the catamounts, Mr. Smith was an animal of prey. He was conscious of everything around him, but it could not be said that he relished the smells, sounds, sights or textures that he so acutely perceived. To take a moment, to savor, could mean his demise. He was both a hunter and the hunted. He was a fixer and, when necessary, he was a killer. He did not enjoy taking a life. He certainly did not do it for pleasure or just for the sake of doing it. He always did what he had to do. It was that simple. He was always ready to spring.

He opened the door of the SUV. For a moment, the interior light blinded his eyes. Eli Hodge and Phil Ramsey were handcuffed and gagged in the back seat. Four eyes pleaded but Mr. Smith was not moved. He closed the door again. Better to be in the dark.

He figured that no one else would be out here at night, but who knew? That would complicate things. Mr. Smith did not like complications. He had been told that some of the loggers stayed overnight in their trucks. So far, he had not seen anyone, but there were many roads in this wilderness. Although some of the approaching vehicles would eventually be found at the lodge, it would be best if no one spotted any of his agency's rented cars and SUV's. That would be regrettable.

It would be unfortunate for anyone who happened to choose this night to be out in this part of the woods. Mr. Smith would be the hawk and the intruder would be the rabbit. It had nothing to do with right or wrong, just the right of the strong over the weak—a law of nature. Mr Smith had long ago constructed a moral code that justified his actions. He was a man of action. Anyone or anything that did not support his mission was simply a hindrance. Mr. Smith did not like hindrances.

He listened for the sound of the vehicles that he was expecting. They should have been here by now. The breeze stopped for a few moments and the night became animated with black flies. Mr. Smith let them bite. Why would anyone want to live here, he wondered?

Harry Huston often drove up to this place on the height of land just off the main road to the lodge. He could almost always pick up a couple of TV stations from New Hampshire, Maine or Vermont. Some nights, he might pick up something from Quebec but that was not of much interest since he did not speak French. Tonight, he would settle for reruns of "Hunter" and "Hill Street Blues". Maybe he should get a satellite TV. They were expensive though.

His microwave dinged. The aroma from beef macaroni his wife had cooked for him filled the cab of his logging truck. He especially enjoyed the food she cooked for his overnights. He liked to think he could sense the love that had been part of the preparation. Packaged meals from the supermarket lacked soul.

In her own way, his wife did indeed love Harry. She was content with her rather unimaginative husband, although she sometimes enjoyed her husband's nights away in the arms of someone she found on line. She was not looking for love. She just liked sex more than Harry did. Why would her husband need to know? Everything else in their marriage was fine. An occasional fling did not affect him. Men have always done this sort of thing. Why not women? That justification was enough for her.

Amazing the comforts of home his small cozy cab had: his DVD, a radio, a CD player, cell phone, his Glock G43 and CB radio right at his fingertips. His bed was warm and comfortable and the driver's side chair swiveled up to a small, retractable table. Harry loved to be in the woods but he also enjoyed his comforts. As usual, he was tired but it was a good tired. Logging was hard work but it sure beat sitting in an office all day. Harry felt safe and well. He pulled the tab on a Bud Light and picked up a fork.

Then, he heard engines. Intense light invaded his sleeper. He turned around. Headlights. How many? What are they doing out here at this time of night? Must be goddamned kids out partying. Harry held his right hand over his eyebrows and peered through his dusty windshield. The churning motors continued to violate the night. Not kids. He could make out a couple of SUVs and a camper. What the hell?

Two men approached the truck. Harry climbed into the driver's seat and opened the door.

"Get out of the truck, please," said one of the men.

"What's going on?" asked Harry.

"Just get down here, sir."

Harry climbed out of the truck. "What's—?"

The man who had spoken put his forefinger to his lip. He waved his hand in front of his face in a futile attempt to ward off the black flies. "Just be quiet."

"Now what?" asked the other man.

The first man took out his radio. "I'll ask Mr. Smith. I'll be right back."

The second man slapped the back of his neck.

"We usually don't spend much time outside at night this time of year," said Harry,

"Just shut up," said the man.

The first man returned.

"So?"

"He said to take care of it."

"You shouldn't have said Mr. Smith's name," said the second man.

"Nope, that was my mistake. Of course, there are a lot of Smiths in the world. Probably still best to err on the safe side. Bad luck for our friend here."

"Are we going to take him to the lodge?"

The first man took out his side arm and pointed it toward Harry. "No, there is no reason for him to be at Stillwater."

"What do you have in mind?"

"Keep an eye on him. I'm going to check out the truck."

The second man took out his gun.

George turned off the F100's lights and pulled over.

"Do you think they saw us?" asked Charley.

"No," said George. "We'd know it if they had. What are they doing?"

"Should we take a look?"

George nodded. He and Charley got out of the truck. They climbed a small hill that gave them enough cover to watch what was happening below. They remained quiet.

The first man climbed into the truck. He came back carrying a package of cotton clothesline rope.

"I checked the glove compartment. It seems our complication goes by the name of Harold Huston.

"Mr. Huston doesn't know it, but he has provided us with the solution to our problem. Accidents do happen. The inside of that truck has all the comforts of home."

"What are you...? Why? What have I...?" asked Harry.

"You haven't done a thing, you're just in the way, that's all. Bad luck. Wrong place at the wrong time. Come with me."

The first man pushed Harry toward the logging truck. He turned to the other man.

"Cover me," he said.

He pushed Harry again. "Get in," he said.

Harry tripped against the truck and then struggled into the driver's seat. The first man climbed up on the truck's step.

"Put your hands on the wheel," he said.

The logger did as he was told. The first man tied Harry's hands to the steering wheel. The second man kept his weapon trained on the truck driver.

The first man looked at Harry. "Really, it's nothing personal," he explained. "As I said, just bad luck."

"Are you just going to leave him?" asked the second man. "He could still get away."

"I don't think so. His microwave has a start delay. Somehow, some metal got into it. I don't know how that could happen. Our friend here must be a careless kind of guy. It should make quite a fire inside that sleeper cabin. The rope on his hands will disintegrate along with everything else. There're all kinds of flammable shit in there. You've got to love modern conveniences. They burn. It looks like this is going to be a night of horrible accidents. Mr. Huston has, when I hit the timer, exactly ten minutes to live. I wonder what got inside that microwave." The first man looked around. "Oh hey, he's even got that little gas grill. See that gas cylinder on the grill. That should make quite a bang."

He put the small container into the microwave, closed the door and pressed the timer button.

"They're leaving," said George. "It looks like they left the driver."

"He's not getting out," said Charley.

"I can't imagine they would just leave him here."

Charley looked out into the darkness. The light in the truck was still on.

"They seem to be gone. Should we go check on him? I'm afraid of what we are going to find"

"Me, too." said George. "Let's give it a couple of minutes to make sure they don't come back."

Harry worked the ropes. They held. The knots were the work of a professional. He knew he wasn't going to free himself in... in eight minutes. He could scream. Who would hear? He was alone. Should I just accept death? This is what it comes to, when the time comes. One minute I am here, the next gone. Poof! Forever! Just like that. I was bebopping along in my story, then no more. Not everyone gets ten minutes to think about the inevitable. He hadn't heard the microwave click on yet. Five more minutes maybe. He thought about his wife. The meal she had prepared. Why did he think about that? Because it mattered. In spite of everything, she cared. He had been fortunate enough to have someone who cared. His dinner was still waiting for him, but he would never eat it.

"Damn it," said Harry. "I'm not ready. Not goddamned ready!" He screamed out in defiance, "No!" Then he acquiesced to his fate. He no longer had the freedom to choose.

Mr. Smith heard the engines, then he saw the lights. The procession of vehicles pulled up, one by one.

The first man got out of one of the rental cars. Mr. Smith approached. He attempted to wave off the black flies.

"Goddamned place!"

"Well?" asked Mr. Smith.

"Unfortunately, there will be an accident in Mr. Huston's sleeper—a cooking accident."

"Will be?"

"Any minute now," said the first man.

"How far away?" asked Mr. Smith

"Not far."

"Will we hear it?"

"Oh yeah," said the first man. "We'll hear it."

Chapter 41

"Let's go!" said George.

George and Charley ran out of the woods across the defunct log yard. George opened the door to the truck. Harry stared at the apparition lit by the cab light. Someone was here. From where? How?

Harry realized he was still alive. Did he have a chance? It had to be too late.

"Get out! Get away!" he cried. "The microwave is going to....."

George looked into the sleeper. The timer started the two-minute countdown. He saw the metal inside the microwave.

"Shit! I can't get into the back. We got two minutes." Charley was standing in front of the truck. "Can you get inside through the other door and turn off that goddamned microwave? You got about a minute. I am going to try to untie him."

Charley climbed onto the passenger seat. "How do you turn it off?" he yelled.

"Hit cancel!" cried Harry.

"I can't find—"

George struggled trying to untie the logger's hands. "Unplug it."

"Where?"

"It's going to be too late. Hand me the knife on the table, then get the hell out. Now!"

George took the knife, cut through the rope wrapped around the steering wheel. He pulled Harry out of the driver's seat. Charley jumped to the ground. George and Harry fell onto their backs. Charley dragged first George and then Harry as far away from the truck as he could. George couldn't breathe. He gasped for air. Suddenly, the microwave blew and, in moments, the cab was engulfed in intense red, yellow, green and blue flames. The smell of melting plastic burned George's mouth and throat as he pressed on his diaphragm trying to regain control of his breathing.

"We need to get further away," yelled Harry. "At that temperature, the diesel could blow."

Charley grabbed George by the shoulder and under the armpit. George's lungs still refused to breath. Deep unrelenting grunts accompanied each attempt to inhale air. Running was torture, but necessary. Both Harry and Charley half-carried, half-dragged the stumbling veterinarian forward.

"Behind that hill," yelled Charley.

"Got him?" cried Harry.

"Got him."

Charley and Harry pushed George over the bank and dove to the ground.

The logging truck, its interior aglow, stood and then vanished into a brilliant inferno. The ground convulsed as in an earthquake.

"Well that's that," said the first man. "They must have heard that in Canada."

"Better be," said Smith. "More complications are not going to please our friends in higher places—or me."

"We took care of that problem, but this whole thing seems awful messy. The Catamount experiment seemed like a good idea but maybe we should have walked away after the first time. I hope this isn't an example of what things are going to be like under the new administration."

"Careful what you say, Mr. Jones. Decisions such as those are above our pay grade," said Mr. Smith. "We're soldiers. People like Schmidt do the thinking, not us. Our job is to do what we are told, even if we have to die doing it."

"An archaic kind of soldier, I would say. I don't plan on dying," Jones replied.

"Unfortunately, I'm afraid, there will be some dying but it won't be done by us," said Smith. "Actually, we are soldiers of the future. There's no battle field here."

"Are you comfortable with the killing?"

"Comfortable isn't the right word. I accept it. Isn't that what this experiment was all about—killing?"

"Our own people?"

"Can you think of another way? Democracy is not working. We need strong leaders. We are working for those who can lead this country into the future. Democracy is too messy. We need to be strong and devoted to our country as the greatest power on earth."

"I understand, sir. What about the cat?"

"First things first," said Smith. "We will have to deal with that, but not now. Have we got everybody?"

Jones hesitated. "That old drunk and the other vet from out West haven't been found."

"Damn it! Why the hell not?"

"We couldn't find either one of them. Believe me, we looked. We did our best."

"I guess your best wasn't good enough, was it?"

The man did not reply.

"Another goddamned complication," said Smith. "One more thing we'll have to take care before—"

"They shouldn't be too hard to deal with—once we find them, I mean."

"Oh, you will them find," said Smith. "They need to be here, too. Once we get all these goddamned people to Stillwater, you're going back out to get those two. You will find them, won't you?"

"Yes, sir!"

Chapter 42

Rob jumped out of bed. "What was that?"

Jade sat up. "It sounded like an explosion—not far away. Should we get up?"

Tristan put his cards down. "What the hell was that?"

"That sounded like it was nearby," said Pat. "Maybe, we should put our clothes back on and go down to the lodge."

"What's that?" cried Cindy. "Are we having an earthquake? I want to go back to Mommy."

"It's stopped," said Josey. "It sounded like an explosion, not an earthquake."

Kayla jumped up. "Did the lodge blow up? What about our parents?"

"It wasn't the lodge," said Paul. "The explosion was further away than that. I'm pretty—"

"We should go look," said McKenzie. "Why don't Josey and I go see? I'm sure everything is all right. Paul, you can stay here with the kids. We'll be right back."

Rob and Jade finished dressing. Rob started toward the window. He heard the sound of engines. A series of lights exposed the room and then disappeared. Finally, one beam remained. The engines stopped as if on some cue. Car doors opened. The light went out.

"Now what?" Rob looked out the window. He turned around "I don't know what's going on. It looks like half the county's out there."

Jade came over and looked. "Huh?"

George breathed in rapidly, holding his breath after each inhale. Even after his diaphragm returned to its normal cadence, George's lungs ached from the variety of toxic fumes that radiated from the remnants of the burning truck. Charley and Harry's lungs also wheezed as the three men climbed over the hill that had protected them from the impact of the explosion. In spite of the dense black smoke exhaling from the conflagration, flames and flares preserved the skeletal outline of the logging truck.

"Holy shit!" said Harry. "It's a damn good thing I didn't park any closer to the trees."

He turned to Charley and George. "I... You saved my life—both of you. I could have...I don't know what...How can I...? I don't know what to say. Just thank you. I mean no one ever had to save my life before. You guys don't even know me. You could have just driven away. You could have died trying to save me. Man! I don't know what I'm feeling. I'm sorry. Everything I say sounds stupid. Thirty seconds and I'd...I wouldn't be here."

George continued to try to control his breathing. He wrapped his arms around his shoulders in an attempt to control his trembling.

"It doesn't sound stupid. I can't explain anything. It wasn't a choice. I just knew—"

George looked at Charley. "We both did. I just need to sit down for a minute."

George found a suitable place to sit. Charley and Harry watched him. He clutched his hand at his waist. A gentle breeze filled with the acrid smell of molten or burning plastic continued to burn their eyes, nose and mouths. There were no black flies.

"Those men are not good guys," observed Charley.

George stood up as if he had just awaked from a deep sleep.

"That's a fucking understatement!" said George. "We're just the beginning. I think they plan to eliminate all those people they had with them. What they did here shows what they are capable of."

"Why?" asked Harry. "What did those people do?"

"Nothing, they didn't do a damned thing. It's not what they did. It's what they know. One way or another, they all know about the catamounts."

"What catamounts?" asked Harry.

"The mountain lions," said George.

"What's the big deal with that? Christ, I saw one a few years ago not far from where I was parked. A lot of us who work in the woods have caught a glimpse of them."

"Yes, but something else is going on. Charley saw some of those guys release one and they sure as hell don't want anyone to know about what they have been doing."

"What have they been doing?" asked Harry.

George started to walk back toward the pick-up truck.

"We don't know exactly, but some of the mountain lions around here have been a lot more aggressive than they ought to be. I have lived in mountain lion country all my life and I have never seen anything like the attacks we have seen here."

"I don't know how or why," said Charley. "But I'm betting that our Mr. Smith and his crew have had something to do with that. Just saying."

"So why are you two out here?" asked Harry.

"To try to avoid getting caught," said Charley, "and maybe to try to stop them."

Harry looked at Charley and Harry. "They're after you?

Charley nodded.

"How are you going to stop them?

"No idea," said George, "but we have to try."

"I have a pretty good reason to want a bit of revenge," Harry said.

"Yes, you do," said Charley. "Christ, I could use a drink!"

"Me too," said Harry. "So, what do we do now?"

George turned around. "There's some water in the truck.

"I don't need water," said Charley.

"All I got. Let's get out of here."

"Where?" asked Harry.

"Stillwater Lodge," said Charley. "Somehow, by following them, we managed to save you. I guess we'll just have to see what happens.

They don't know we are here and we know where they are going. We have that advantage. What do you want to do?"

"I'm not staying here," said Harry. "That guy, Mr. Gestapo, said that it was just bad luck that I was in the wrong place at the wrong time. He was almost right. You were there in the right place at the right time and I'm still alive. So fuck it, let's go. Besides, what else am I going to do?"

"Let's think about this. I'm thinking we don't have to go anywhere," said George. "They still want Charley and me. Someone is going to come back to try to find us. I'd bet my life on it."

"That's exactly what you'd be doing," said Charley.

"You have an idea?" asked Harry.

"What if something were to be in the road?" George looked around. "I'm not sure yet. A trap maybe."

The piercing yellow eyes observed as Smith and Jones got out of their vehicles. Both men carried their Heckler & Koch submachine guns.

Rob opened the office door. He and Ike stepped out on the deck.

"Hold it," said Josey. "Turn off the flashlight. Get down."

As if on cue, all of the engines stopped. Josey and McKenzie watched car and truck doors open. The first men to emerge from the vehicles carried what looked like assault rifles. Josey recognized one of the troopers, Roger Wright, and Doc. He also remembered the guide from Alaska. They had weapons trained on them. A man and a woman emerged from a camper, followed by a man with a pistol. Two Fish and Game officers and another trooper were pushed onto the ground.

Josey and McKenzie saw Ike and Rob come out onto the deck. The two men who had stepped out of the SUV pointed their machine guns at Rob and Ike. Another one of the armed men went to the SUV and pulled two handcuffed men out into the open. Both of the prisoners stumbled into Sergeant Wright. Roger fell backwards but kept his balance. He leaned forward to help the obviously weakened biologist, Phil Ramsey. The man pushed the barrel of his machine gun into Roger's abdomen.

"Get up," said the man. "Get away from him." He nudged his weapon higher. It fired. The retort echoed through the woods.

"Shit!" said the man. I didn't mean—"

Roger Wright grabbed his stomach and twisted into an embryo position onto the ground.

"It doesn't matter," said Smith. "Let's get them all inside. You two on the deck—bring him in."

The man with the assault rifle waited while Rob and Ike carried the dead trooper into the lodge.

An apparition disappeared into the night. Neither Josey nor McKenzie had seen it or the easy flip of its long tail.

Josey and McKenzie were stunned. They did not move.

"They just shot one of troopers," said McKenzie. "No! Look my parents and the Meurets are coming down to the lodge. We have to stop them."

McKenzie started forward. Josey pulled her back. The door to the lodge opened. A door shaped beam of light emanated onto the deck. The silhouette of a man with an assault rifle motioned the two couples to go inside. The man stood aside and the Nashes and the Meurets and Doc entered the lodge. The man looked around, closed the door, and remained standing as if at attention on the deck. The door opened. The man turned around, nodded consent and went inside.

"What do we do now?" asked McKenzie. "They have our parents."

"They don't have us," said Josey

"And the other kids? Do you think they know about—"

"If they don't, they will."

The lodge, silent, its windows illuminated by yellow light, appeared peaceful on the outside.

"What's going on?" asked McKenzie.

"I don't know. All I see is Mr. Wright lying there. I know him. He's a friend of my Dad's. They didn't seem to be concerned at all about shooting him. Did you hear what that guy said?"

"That it didn't matter?"

"Why do you think...? Why wouldn't it matter? Do you think they are planning to kill our... all of us?"

"I don't know," said Josey. "Why bring all of those people here and treat them like prisoners?"

"And kill a trooper? Who does that?"

"That's what I mean. Not the good guys. I wonder who they are. I would really like to find out."

"Even if we knew, what good would that do? What could we do?"

"I don't know, but as long as they don't know we're here, maybe we have a chance to—"

"To what?"

"I don't know, McKenzie, but I'm quite sure that we don't want them to find us. Maybe we can hide or get away. There's a lot of woods out here."

"We can't just run away. What about our parents and all those other people?"

"Shit! I know. I know. Fuck!"

"Do they really want to kill... all of us? Do you think... really?"

"They even have that guide from Alaska."

"And that older couple... Who are they? I mean what did they do?"

"It doesn't make sense," said Josey, "but whether it makes any sense or not, it's happening. Let me see if I can get close enough to the lodge to see what's going on inside. Do you have your cell phone? Maybe we can e-mail for help or something. The Wi-Fi signal might be strong enough to—"

"I left my phone in the cabin."

"Me, too," said Josey.

"We have all, kinda like, gotten used to not needing our phones here. What about the other kids?" asked McKenzie.

"They need to hide. We can't stay at the firepit. That's the first place they'll look. They'll make someone tell them where we are."

"In the woods?" asked McKenzie.

"Where else?"

"What are we going to do in the woods? I mean, I don't think I can just, like, wait."

"I wonder if we could hide somewhere in the lodge—or maybe in one of the cabins. Maybe they wouldn't look there," said Josey.

"And if they do?" asked McKenzie. "How can we hide all of us inside?"

"Do you have any better ideas?"

"What about the boathouse?"

"That might work. Okay, go get the kids. I'm going to see if I can see what's going on inside."

"So, the boathouse? What about the fire?"

"Yes, and add some wood to the fire. If they look for us, it'll draw them away from where we really are. I'll meet you in a couple of minutes," said Josey. "Then we'll figure out what to do next."

Josey crept up to the lodge and carefully peered into one of the dining room windows.

Chapter 43

Déjà vu, thought Rob. Murder at Stillwater Lodge. Hadn't they put that behind them? Was this place cursed?

This time, there were multiple men with menacing assault weapons. Maybe nine or ten of them—Rob hadn't had time to count. He and Ike carried in the body of their friend Roger Wright. Doc verified the death. This time, the intrusion on Stillwater Lodge was more threatening and organized. There seemed to be a chain of command. This felt like an invasion, but by whom? Rob, as a Fish and Game officer, had been trained in law enforcement and had worked with local, statewide and federal agencies. Whoever these people were, they were a different breed. They had already shot and killed Roger Wright. An accident maybe, but there was no apparent remorse.

Christ, thought Rob, if I had killed someone like that, I'd spend the rest of my life trying to get over it!

Through the window, Josey watched as Smith moved toward the center of the room.

"Everyone take a seat," he said, "If there aren't enough seats, sit on the floor. I want all of you sitting."

Except for the shuffling of people and chairs, the room was hushed. Ike refused to sit.

"What's—"

One of the invaders pointed his gun at Ike.

"Shut up, old man, and sit down! You saw what happened to that trooper. So, shut the fuck up!"

Ike mumbled something about Christly assholes.

"What did you say?" asked the man.

Rob tried to keep his friend from turning around. "Let it go."

"I said you were a Christly asshole."

The man walked up to Ike and rammed the butt of his gun into Ike's abdomen. Ike doubled over on the floor.

"Anyone else have any opinions they would like to share?" asked the man.

"That don't change nothin'," grumbled Ike.

"Okay enough!" said Smith. "Our number one priority before our party can begin is to find Mr. Mason and Froggy—or whatever his name is—the town drunk. In the meantime, let's all get comfortable. I could use a cup of coffee and something to eat. Who's responsible for the hospitality around here? Obviously, not that old bastard over there."

Jade and Marion stood up. "Can we go into the kitchen?" asked Jade.

"Please do," said Smith. "Jones, would you please accompany them? We'll all have something to eat. Afterwards, Madison, you and Johnson will go check all of the other buildings. Harper, Robbins, and Greene, you continue keeping an eye on our guests. We don't want any trouble. Hobbs, you will accompany Jones. Both of you will kindly find our two missing guests. While you're out there, check that lumber truck. Make sure the driver is toast. Take my vehicle."

"I'm not—" said Jones

"What?" asked Smith.

"Yes, sir!"

"Can I offer coffee to our guests?" asked Marion. "They have all eaten."

Smith turned toward the captives. "Sure, why not? What does it matter? Who's the owner?" Rob stood up. "Get me the guest register. Let's see if everyone is here."

"Hooper, you and Giles. Just in case, go watch the dock. We don't need anyone coming in by boat. Get some coffee and then go." Smith took out a radio. "I'm going outside for a moment."

Josey moved away from the window.

"Can I take a look at Ike?" asked Doc. "I'm a doctor."

Smith looked back. "A vet you mean. Be my guest. Seems appropriate enough to me."

"How about that other man? He looks like he could use some help."

"As I said, be my guest." Smith went outside.

Chapter 44

The man in a dark Brioni suit placed a sizable framed image of the German philosopher Nietzsche on the Rosewood conference table. He took a moment to admire it. He regarded the select group assembled in the room. He looked back at the painting before reciting a passage from Nietzsche's *The Will to Power:*

> A daring and ruler race is building itself up... The aim should be to prepare a transvaluation of values for a particulary strong kind of man, mostly highly gifted in intellect and will. This man and the elite around him will become the "lords of the earth"

"Ladies and gentlemen, we know why we are here," said the Vice President of the United States.

He looked at the men and women who were sitting around the table.

"You are the best and brightest from the most advanced countries in the world and God has spoken to all of us. Our mission is to make all our countries great. What is our mission?"

Every one of the ten men in the room replied in unison, "To make all of our countries great, to earn the right to be Lords of the Earth, and to save mankind from itself."

The Vice President continued.

"We stand united in purpose and in purity of heart. We will overcome all obstacles, at all costs, in the name of a better world. It is time to recreate an environment where our hard work and intelligence is rewarded. We will no longer have to support the weak at the expense of the adaptable. Natural selection provides the will to power. Democracy, socialism and communism are the Devil's work. Our governments are thwarting human development in the name of 'what's good for all.' Our purpose, indeed our duty, on this planet is to dismantle our over-reaching governments and support the industrious rather than rewarding lazy parasites."

"Our time is coming," said all in unison.

"Now down to the business at hand," said the Vice President. "Are we in control of the remaining mountain lion, Mr Schmidt? I can't believe we are still dealing with this when—"

Peter Schmidt leaned toward the table. "We are doing everything in our power to get the situation under control. Our men on the ground are bringing in everyone who could possibly—"

"Peter, that's not what I asked. Is the mountain lion under control? Yes or no?"

"We're trying—"

"Yes or no?"

"No," said Peter.

"So, we're still dealing with this colossal failure," said the Vice President."

"We heard from Smith. He doesn't know where the last one is."

The Vice President leaned onto the table. "Damn it! I want results."

"He knows that, sir."

"The experiment seemed to work so well at first," said a man sitting across from Peter. "The cats really did respond to our commands. We proved that cats could be trained. They would have been highly effective in culling certain parts of our populations. They would have been powerful weapons against our enemies. Not everyone in the lower classes can be trained to be useful workers. We've had success in our school reforms to begin to create a compliant working class. We don't want to create free thinkers. We are the thinkers. We have the advantage of data to track how are students are progressing toward our standards. It's already working."

"Why don't we just call them slaves?" asked another man.

"Never use that word!" warned the Vice President. "We're not racists but, historically, almost all of the great achievers have been white and have been men. We are for equal opportunity and we want our working class to be content. We don't want them to think of themselves as slaves. After all, robots will do most of the menial work. We'll provide enough entertainment to keep 'the people' happy. They won't have to work hard thanks to technology. We just need a class of complacent consumers for our vision to work. I hope we do a better job of training them than we did training those cats. Why didn't this operation work?"

"The cats were trainable," said the man across from Peter. "In captivity, they did exactly what we trained them to do. They were effective killers and they preyed upon quarries that we designated. Many assumed it isn't possible to train cats in the same way that dogs can be trained. We disproved that hypothesis."

"So what happened?" asked the Vice President.

"The three we released developed minds of their own once they were in the woods. We lost control. We're not sure that they acted randomly."

"What do you mean?" asked another man.

"It was almost as if they were obeying another set of commands. Maybe it was related to being in the wild—instinct, perhaps."

"Really?"

"We don't know. It just seemed—"

"That seems like happy horseshit," said the Vice President. "If these mountain lions are not in our control, they need to be eliminated. Is that being handled, Mr. Schmidt?"

Peter Schmidt nodded. "Yes, sir. Smith is working on it."

"Working on it!" mimicked the Vice President.

"Yes, sir. He is. He has almost all of the witnesses"

"Almost?"

"Smith is quite capable," said Peter.

The Vice President stood and raised his water glass.

"I certainly hope so. To the entrepreneurial class, the salvation of the world. All others will be trained for the good of the achievers. Parasites will be eliminated or reeducated. The end will justify the means."

He turned to Peter Schmidt. "Remind Mr. Smith to do whatever is necessary to bring Operation Catamount to a close. We are intelligent and reasonable men. We have to learn from our mistakes but I want this mistake fixed, now."

The man across from Peter Schmidt set down his glass.

"I still believe in the Catamount Project. A lot of money and time have been devoted—"

The Vice President was still standing. He put both of his hands on the cherry wood conference table. "We have other more expedient ways to eliminate those who would stand in our way. This was a noble experiment. Under our control, the catamounts would have been deadly weapons. But they weren't 100% under our control, were they, Mr. Schneider?"

"Perhaps with a little more time. We never tested them, as planned, in urban and suburban areas. The carnage would have been seen as an aberration of nature. We would have been the saviors."

"We are the saviors," said the Vice President. "We are doing God's will. Let's vote. How many are in favor of continuing the Catamount project."

Only one hand was raised.

"Opposed?"

The rest of the hands at the table went up.

"Democracy, Mr. Schneider. Democracy, if it means anything at all, is for those of us who have risen to the top through intelligence, good genes, education, dedication and through the efforts of our forefathers. However, it is not for the masses. History tells us that. Look at what mediocrity was wrought."

"I acquiesce," said Mr. Schneider. "As you know, my father was one of the original advocates for the Catamount Project. I have always felt that I was carrying on his work."

"And you were," said the Vice President. "We all appreciate your efforts and once we have consolidated our power, I will be the first to recommend that you continue this endeavor. In spite of our efforts to train the next generation to accept our authority, there will always be dissenters who will need to be dealt with. All options will be on the table.

"For now, the first priority is to remove any obstacle to my being made President. The majority are behind us. I'll be elected by the fools who believe in democracy. A free election will open the way for my... our power. The last thing we need is for this catamount thing to blow up in our faces. Evolution has selected us to lead and we'll pass on our superior genes to our progeny. We will provide the God-given leadership that the world needs.

"Power should not and shall not be left in the hands of the uninspired and the ignorant. We'll use this obsolete system of "democracy for all" to open the door. So many have shown their support for us. They have been persuaded that we care about them. We'll rescue them from themselves. Our time has come. Our prosperity has provided us with the means to mold the world to the benefit of the strongest and most deserving of our species. We are exceptional men and women. All others will serve for the benefit of those of us who have evolved. Our accumulation of wealth is the measure of our greatness. As Ayn Rand said, 'Wealth is the product of man's capacity to think'. We are the product of generations of human thought."

"And yes, we will add the power to manipulate nature to do our bidding. Fear not, Mr. Schneider, we value your contribution to our righteous cause.

"Are we all in agreement as to the next step in our ascent to our rightful place in this country and around the world?"

All of the men at the table nodded enthusiastically.

"What about the catamount that is still out there?" asked Mr. Schneider."

"It must be found," said the Vice President.

Mr. Schneider nodded.

The Vice President stood up. "Tell Smith I am not pleased. I want this problem fixed."

Chapter 45

Josey tapped on the boathouse door. McKenzie let him in. Abbi, Cameron, Paul, Kayla, Connor and Cindy sat in a semicircle. Cindy got up and hugged her brother.

"Is everyone all right?" she whispered.

Josey nodded. "I think so. It looks like it—for now, at least."

"Do they know about us?" asked McKenzie.

"Let's keep our voices down," said Josey. "I don't think so, but the head guy wanted to look at the guest register. I assume we're on it."

"What are we going to do?" asked Connor.

"I don't know exactly," said Josey. "We don't want to get caught. They shot a trooper and I saw them hit Ike in the stomach with an assault rifle."

"Mom and Dad?" cried Cindy.

Josey hugged Cindy. "Keep our voices down. We have to get out of here. Two of the men are coming to down to watch for boats. We need to go. Right now, they're drinking coffee but—"

"Where can we go?" asked Paul.

"Back to the fire."

"What do you mean when you said they are going to kill everyone?" asked Paul.

"Exactly what I said. They are here to get rid of all of us. I don't know how and I don't know why. I do know we do not want to get caught. We also might as well try to do something. Rather than, like, wait to die."

"What can we do?" whimpered Kayla.

"Did you ever see that old movie, 'Home Alone?'" asked Josey.

"That's the one where the kid outsmarts the bad guys," said Cameron.

"That was a comedy," said Connor. "These guys aren't funny. I mean what can we do? These guys don't look like idiots."

"Slow them down, maybe," said Josey. "See that board with the nails in it. They're sending two of the men to pick up someone else. They're looking for the other veterinarian and, for some reason, the town drunk. We all call him Froggy. Guess what? I know which car they are taking."

"So?" asked McKenzie.

"What if they were to get a flat tire?"

"It'd slow them down," said McKenzie.

"And piss them off," said Paul. "Is that—"

"There's a bunch of those boards," said Connor. "We could do it to all of their cars."

"How about all the cars except McKenzie's parent's SUV?" asked Paul. "I bet we could get out before they changed all those tires. We could get help."

"The keys are in our cabin," said McKenzie. "Nobody's there."

Josey went over to the lake end of the boathouse. He looked out the open window. "We could get away in a boat but—"

McKenzie joined Josey. "Not if they're guarding the dock

"I thought we agreed we don't want to leave without our parents. But what are we really going to do? We can't get them to drive all of their vehicles over the nails. I don't think they are that stupid."

Josey took a box of nails off the shelf next to the window. "There are a couple of hammers over there. I bet we could do some damage with those."

"We could," said Paul, "but I still worry that will make them really angry."

"If we do, they might take it out on our parents," said Kayla.

Josey crouched down. He still held the box of nails. "I think they are going to hurt our parents no matter what we do. I told you what I heard. They're going to hurt all of us. We have to try something."

"They are going to more than hurt us, aren't they," said Cameron. "Maybe we should go with Josey's plan."

Josey stood up. "How about this? McKenzie, you get the keys to your parent's car. You take Kayla and Cindy and see if you can get help. Abbi, Cameron, Connor—you can help Paul and I see if we can flatten as many tires are possible. At least two on each car. That should really mess them up. Every car except McKenzie's parent's."

"Even the RV, the cruisers and the Fish and Game truck?" asked Connor.

Josey spread his arms. "I think so. We want those men to be stuck here. Right now, we need to hide. Maybe we should split up. We can't come back here. We really need to get going. Remember when we played "capture the flag," that hide-and-seek game? We could use a couple of those hiding places. Abbi, you and Cameron stick with Paul. Connor, you stick with me."

"I want to stay," said Kayla. "Are you sending me away just because I'm a girl?"

"Me too," said Cindy. I want to stay with you. I'm scared but I would rather be scared with you."

"We're all scared," said Josey. "We don't have time...I just thought maybe someone could get out of here safely. Never mind, Cindy you come with Connor and me. Kayla you go with Paul, Abbi and Cameron.

"I'll stick with Cindy," said Kayla.

Josey started to respond and stopped. "Whatever."

"I have a good place up behind lodge," said Cameron.

"Good," said Josey. "Cindy, Kayla and Connor, we'll go over by that old rotten wooden boat down by the lake."

"Shouldn't we somehow meet up?" asked Paul.

Josey looked at his watch.

"It's a little after 8:00—8:09."

Paul reset his watch. "8:10 now. Where do we want to meet?"

"How about at that small beach? We'll meet in an hour and then we can figure out what to do next. They'll be looking for us and they'll be pissed," said Josey. "So...let's not get caught. McKenzie, wait in your car until we have punctured the tires. We'll give you time to get the keys. I'll let you know when to go. Then give us a couple of minutes to hide. Go get help. As soon as you get a signal, call the police."

"Boy, talk about poking a stick in a hornets' nest!" said McKenzie."

"I'm going to see what's happening inside while you get the keys. For now, everyone go back to the fire. Get the nails and find something to hammer with. I'll see you back there. Do it quickly. Get away from here before those guys come down to the dock."

Hank Harbor hated not being in control. He scrutinized the room. Experience had nurtured a faith that there was always a way out of a dangerous situation. There always had been. He would not still be here had it not been for "Plan B." Mostly though, those had been the result of planning, discipline and experience. He wasn't prepared for something like this. Surviving in the wilderness was a skill set that required an understanding of nature, problem solving, courage, preparation, alertness, adaptability, cunningness and daring.

He counted ten armed men, all of whom—notwithstanding the accidental shooting—appeared to be highly trained. The careless use of a weapon was amateurism. Maybe they were only recently trained? I'm betting none of them have actually seen any real action. Smith? Maybe. The lack of concern for the victim was disturbing. In the midst of battle, a soldier will dehumanize his or her enemy but upon reflection he or she will also have developed a certain sense of empathy for a fallen foe. No evidence of that among these men. No visible expression of humanity. Probably not military, FBI, CIA, Navy Seals.... Who had trained—or brainwashed—these soldiers of... Soldiers of what?

All that mattered, really, was that he every man and woman in this room, except these ill-mannered enforcers, was in mortal danger. Unless somehow the tables could be turned? Somehow, but how? The dining room was quiet. Some of the guests were tentatively drinking coffee. The men with the weapons took turns eating and standing watch. Nothing was said. These men knew what was required of them. Very mechanical, Hank thought. Could that be used against them?

Rob sat next to Jade and was holding her hand. Hank felt something like jealousy. Not jealousy really. He didn't own this woman. Envy rather. Harbor was quite sure that it would be a long while before he met another lady like Jade. How many chances does a man get in his lifetime? Rob was a lucky man.

Could the retired Fish and Game officer be counted on in a fight? Hank thought so. Rob had law enforcement training and he had survived a mountain lion attack. The other trooper and the two Fish and Game officers had attended the law enforcement academy as well. Doc looked capable. He couldn't do anything for the dead trooper but the biologist and Ike had benefited from the vet's attention.

What about the rest? The man with the dog was also holding a woman's hand. Hank was good with names—Ed and Marty. Weren't they divorced? The other couples were Pat and Holly plus Karley and Tristan. He had talked to all of them but he did not have a feel for how they would respond under stress. He did not know the older couple or the other two men. There were too many unknowns. For the moment at least, Hank was atypically confounded as to how he was going to turn the tables on these intruders. Then he realized that not everyone was there. Where were the kids?

Chapter 46

"Where are the kids?" asked Smith. "Who are the parents?" Smith looked around the room. "As if I couldn't guess. Over here please."

Smith pointed toward the table next to the sidewall window. Back at the window, Josey watched the Meurets, the Nashes, and his Mom and Dad approach the table.

"Please take a chair and sit down."

The parents complied.

"Mr. and Mrs. Nash and Mr. and Mrs. Meuret, you're on vacation. So, I'm guessing it is a bit too early for your kids to be in bed? I'm also assuming, I think correctly, that there is no movie theater nearby."

Smith looked at Ed and Marty. "I'm not sure who you are. You're not on the guest list."

Ed hesitated. "We're friends of the owners. Just visiting."

"Well, what about you? Do you have kids?"

"We're divorced," said Ed.

"That's not what I asked."

No one spoke.

"Look," said Smith. "this is a messy business. I don't like it but it's my job to assure the destiny of our country. Properly educated children are the future. If they can be spared, I wish to do them no harm.

"Where are they?"

Ed looked away from Smith. Something moved behind the screen in the window and then disappeared. Ed looked back at Mr. Smith. He took Marty's hand. He put his head down as if he needed a moment to think. He scanned the table. Smith was standing next to the window with his back to the wall. He had not seen Josey, but Ed and Marty did. Marty squeezed Ed's hand. Josey ducked down. Ed leaned into the table.

"They're having a campfire," said Ed. "roasting marshmallows and s'mores. Sleeping outdoors overnight."

"Overnight?" confirmed Smith.

Josey nodded in the window.

"Yes," said Ed.

"One more question," said Mr. Smith. "Have any of your kids seen the mountain lion?"

Karley started.

"No," said Tristan.

"Even after it was shot?"

"We didn't want to upset them," said Karley

"I hope you're telling me the truth."

Smith motioned to one of his men. He pointed to Marty and Ed.

"Go with my colleague and wish them good night. Make sure, for their own good, they stay at the campsite."

"Can we finish our coffee?" asked Ed

Josey disappeared.

"Be my guest. I assume the kids aren't going anywhere."

Smith got up and went over to Jones and Hobbs. "Are you men about ready? We haven't got all the time in the world."

Everyone at the table was silent. Holly took Pat's hand. The coffee she had drunk was not sitting well. She was not allowed to go out to her daughter and two sons. She was a prisoner. These men, fellow human beings, were exercising the power their guns afforded them to deprive her of authority over her own life. She looked around the room. It was not just her freedom. Some of the hostages looked, as she imagined she did, stunned and subdued. A few, especially the hunter from Alaska, the other trooper, the owner and his girlfriend Jade appeared to be assessing their situation. Jade and the cook had helped the other owner, Ike, into a chair. The old man was obviously in pain but he did not look defeated.

While she admired their composure, she was not optimistic about the prospects of escape or even survival. No one had come right out and said so, but Holly was sure that these men were not here to collect ransom. They had come on a mission to eliminate everyone they had brought with them. Moreover, it seemed, the adults at the lodge would have to die as well. That's why the dead trooper didn't matter to them.

Holly was also disturbed by the suggestion that these men might spare the children so that they could be "properly educated" for the good of the country. What country? That did not sound like the country she lived in.

This, she thought, is what it feels like to know for certain that you can die. We all accept that in some kind of abstract way. People on their deathbed eventually come to the realization that their time has come. Some fight against that inevitability. Others yield. It must be like that for the soldier. The warrior on the ground may be cannon fodder but he has to move toward the enemy and the bloodshed. There is no escape. Some will miraculously survive. Others will not. The experience will scar a few for the rest of their lives. They will wish they had died on that battlefield. What about the death row prisoner? He or she can only wait.

These men are our executioners. I know it. We can't just wait. I am not ready to resign myself to that. There must be a way to stop this. I will not let them take my children or kill my husband or just watch while they murder everyone in this room. We must think of ourselves as soldiers, not prisoners.

"What are you thinking about?" asked Karley. "You look like you you were far, far away."

"Oh, don't I wish we were all far away from here. Believe me, I was right here."

"Thinking about what could happen to all of us?" asked Marty.

"Yes, and what we can do about it."

"Yup," said Tristan. "I think we are all thinking the same thing. Probably every one of us in the room except those goddamn replicants."

"What?" asked Holly.

"Oh, advanced robots with human traits—from the film 'Blade Runner.' These thugs remind me of the replicants in that story. Actually, those replicants seemed more human than these goons. It doesn't matter, you get my point."

Ed leaned into the table. "I do. But look, these bastards aren't robots. They are human and they are making mistakes. Josey has been listening outside this window."

"Really?" asked Pat.

"Right outside this window. Kind of careless. I can't believe Smith doesn't have someone outside. He probably thinks that because we are in the woods, there can't be anyone out there. He also doesn't know kids very well."

"What can the kids do?" asked Karley.

"Not sure," said Ed. "Knowing my son, I'd guess we'll find out soon."

"Knowing our kids," said Pat. "you just might be right."

Karley and Tristan nodded. "I just hope they are careful."

"Here they come," said Paul. "McKenzie's not back."

Josey picked up a freshly cut stick. "Pretend everything is—"

Ed, Marty and another man walked into the clearing. The flames from a well-established fire flickered on the boy's and girl's faces. They were all intent on roasting the ivory, mushy marshmallows. Some of the small white squares were engulfed in flames; others were being carefully browned. Josey stood up.

"Hi, Mom and Dad."

Ed and Marty stepped into the illuminated corona that surrounded the fire. A breeze blew smoke toward the approaching adults. Their companion hung back in the darkness.

"You guys all set for the night?" asked Ed. "How about you, Cindy?"

Cindy got up and hugged both of her parents. "I'm all set."

"Are you scared?" asked Marty.

"A little bit, but I have Josey."

"Everyone else ready? You should be hitting the hay before too long. You're lucky, the breeze from the lake should help with the black flies."

"Thank you, Mrs. Rollins. We'll get in our sleeping bags after we finish roasting the marshmallows," said Cameron. "Who's that with you?"

"A new guest," said Ed. "Mister—"

"Greene," said the man. "Have a good night camping."

"We definitely will," said Josey.

Cindy let go of her parents. "I love you Mom and Dad."

Both Marty and Ed responded as they let go of Cindy's hand. "We love you."

"I love you Mom and Dad," said Josey.

"We love you too. Have a good night."

Marty turned away from her children and did her best to keep from breaking down. "We'll see you in the morning. Sleep tight."

"Say good night to our parents," said Kayla.

"Tell them we love them," shouted Abbi, Cameron, Paul, Kayla, McKenzie and Connor.

"We will," said Ed. He held Marty's arm to keep her from collapsing.

"Keep moving!" whispered Greene.

Chapter 47

McKenzie stood up.

"I have the key but I can't find any of the phones. They must have taken them all. So we can't call for help."

"Do we still want to give them flat tires?" asked Josey.

McKenzie approached the fire. "I'm not sure. If we do that won't they retaliate? They might kill our parents. They'll come after us. Right now, they are letting us alone."

"Aren't they going to do that anyway?" asked Paul.

"Josey said that they were waiting to get two more people. I don't think they want to do anything until they have them," said McKenzie.

"They're waiting to get Mr. Mason and Froggy," said Josey.

"The drunk you told us about?" said Kayla.

"What the heck do they want with him?" asked Paul.

McKenzie continued to play with the fire. "I don't understand any of this."

"It's because of the mountain lion," said Josey. "I'm pretty sure."

"What do you mean?" asked McKenzie.

"They asked if we had seen it. Your Dad told them we hadn't."

"I still don't—"

"I think they want to get rid of anybody who saw the mountain lion."

"You guys saw it," said Abbi. "We all saw it when it was dead. What's the big deal about... They want to get rid of us just because we saw the mountain lion?"

"It sounds crazy," said Josey, "but once they find Mr. Mason and Froggy, we're all screwed. They seemed to believe our parents when they said we hadn't seen the mountain lion but—"

"Get rid of us?" asked Cindy. "What does that mean?"

"Never mind. It doesn't matter," said Josey.

Cindy wanted to cry. She held back. "It does too matter, Josey. Why do they care about that stupid mountain lion?"

Cindy sprang to her brother's side and locked her arms around his waist. "We have to stop them, Josey."

Josey returned his sisters hug.

"Yes, we do," said McKenzie.

"Are we going to flatten their tires?" asked Paul.

Josey picked up a stick and poked the fire. "No, it was my idea but I agree with McKenzie. It's kind of stupid. That'll just piss them off. Then they'll come after us and we won't be able to do anything."

"What can we do?" asked Paul.

Josey stared at the fire.

"Not sure," said McKenzie. "But I like the *Home Alone* idea. We only do one thing at a time. Kind of like the early Americans fighting against the British or like terrorists."

"Yeah, but what can we do?" asked Paul.

The headlights lurched and swayed as the shiny black Explorer worked its way along the seemingly endless dirt road. Jones clutched the steering wheel. Hobbs attempted to hold himself steady by grasping the handgrip over the passenger's side door. The vehicle swung around a sharp corner and then entered a long, straight stretch.

From a distance Charley, Harry and George watched. Two lights appeared at first to be silent tiny bobbing eyes. As the two lights grew larger, the sound of the powerful V-8 engine invaded the insect, bird and occasional animal chatter coming from the aboriginal inhabitants of the Maine woods.

"Here they come," said Charley. "Get ready."

George started the engine. The lights from the SUV became wider and wider. Then they flooded the truck.

"Now!" yelled Charley.

The old truck's headlights appeared virtually out of nowhere and George hit the gas pedal.

"What the hell is that?" cried Hobbs. "It's going to hit us."

Instinctively, Jones swerved to the right. The Explorer's front wheels spun, looking for traction. There was none. The left rear wheel hit the edge of a deep ditch with just enough force to tip the SUV onto its side. It slid into its resting place. One headlight continued to perform as if looking for a way out. A wall of sand blocked the other. The old truck stopped, pulled back just enough to illuminate the distressed vehicle fully. Doors opened and closed. Charley and Harry stepped out of the pick-up and moved into the darkness. Each stood by a pile of substantial, yet manageable, rocks. Both men waited, each with a rock in their dominant hand—right for Harry, left for Charley. George waited in the truck. He left the motor running.

The fire illuminated eight silent campers who still held their roasting sticks. Each one randomly poked the fire. Connor got up, grabbed a split piece of pine and threw it on the fire. Once the newly added wood caught fire, intermittent sparks popped out into the clearing. Most fell harmlessly to the ground but Kayla, Cameron, and Abbi flicked the tiny embers off their shirts before they had a chance to burn into the fabric. Momentarily, the white smoke rose straight up from the fire until a breeze off the lake sent it into McKenzie's, Paul's, Cindy's and Josey's faces. All four lifted their arms to cover their eyes. Then the smoke swirled around to attack Abbi, Kayla and Connor.

Josey stood up. "So we all agree the tire idea was kind of dumb?"

McKenzie pushed herself up and stood next Josey. "Perhaps not completely stupid. Now that those two guys are gone, I'm guessing no one is going to need their car until they have done what they came here for."

"Killing us," said Cameron.

"Well it would be kind of sweet if they couldn't go anywhere after they killed us," said Connor.

"How about we make that like plan Z," said McKenzie.

"So, what's plan A?" asked Josey.

"Well, at the moment there are eight of them. Two are down by the dock. Two have left to go find the veterinarian and the drunk. I think the ones who checked the cabins are back inside. They probably took our phones. There are eight of us outside. They think we're just a bunch of dumb kids. That has to be good for us. Our parents, the guide from Alaska and the people from the lodge are all inside. There are more of us than there are of them."

"Yeah right," said Kayla. "But we don't have really big guns like those guys do."

"Just like the kid in *Home Alone*, we have surprise."

McKenzie picked up one of the boards from the boathouse. She held it up and put her index finger on the tip of exposed nail.

"We have these."

"That would hurt," said Paul. "But how do we get close enough?"

Cindy shuddered. Josey took her hand.

"Yeah, it would," said Cameron.

"Maybe we could think up some booby traps just like in the movie," said Connor.

"The old guy in the film used a shovel," said Abbi. "I saw a couple of those in the boathouse."

"That would hurt, too," said Paul. "But we can't go there with those two men on the dock."

Josey picked up another board. "These are all we need."

"Kill them?" asked Abbi.

MacKenzie tapped the blunt side of the board against her thigh. "If we have to. It's kinda like us or them."

"Not kinda" said Cameron.

The light that emitted from two flashlights criss-crossed over the dock and reflected intermittently on the water. Hooper and Giles approached the shore and stepped onto the sand.

"All clear," said Giles.

Hooper nodded. "Roger that."

The large feline figure crept around the front of the boathouse. Light briefly reflected in its piercing yellow eyes. Then the beast sprang. Two flashlights flew into the air and then bounced on the ground pointing randomly in different directions. There was a gurgling sound—something being pulled apart. Then there was silence.

*   *   *

The door of the SUV opened. Jones peered out. One lone headlight illuminated the Explorer. Two other lights momentarily blinded him. He heard the sound of an engine. He ducked back down and reappeared with a pistol in his hand. He pointed the weapon towards where the two small lights had been. Nothing. Then he turned in the direction of the sound. His eyes adjusted to the stronger beam. It looked like a truck. What was it doing here? "That's what—" He re-aimed the pistol at the truck. Both Charley and Harry stood up. Each held a fist-sized rock.

"Me first," whispered Harry.

"Right behind you," said Charley.

Both rocks hit their mark—one in the head, the other on the chest. Jones sank back into the vehicle. His gun slid down to the ground. The door remained open.

"Not bad," said Charley.

Charley held up his left hand, Harry his right, for a quick high-five.

Harry picked up another rock.

"All set?" asked Smith.

Madison nodded. "The point of origin should be impossible to detect."

"Should be?"

"Sorry sir, will be. I know what I'm doing. An old building like this. Kaboom! And everything in it."

"Speaking of that, how are our guests doing?"

"Subdued, but that old codger—if looks could kill!"

"Well, they can't but we have our methods, don't we, Madison.

"We do."

"I'm not happy with how long this is taking. Time isn't on our side and we have another loose end."

"What?"

"They want us to find the cat."

"And?"

"Eliminate it, bring it back, stop it, whatever it takes."

"Do we know where it is?"

"Of course not. If we could control the goddamned thing, we wouldn't have to be here. This whole thing has been a colossal fuck up right from the get go. I told them so."

"Who's them?"

"Who is always them? The ones with power, money and big ideas."

"You're not questioning—"

"Oh Christ, no. I'm just saying that—between you and me—maybe now and then they should listen to those of us who have to deal with things out in the field."

"We're heading for better times," said Madison.

"Better times," agreed Smith. "It won't be long now. As long as we learn from our mistakes."

"At least the country won't be run by elected politicians anymore. We need to give the Vice President a chance once he's in."

"Well Madison, are you up for a challenge? Why don't you take Greene. Maybe the two of you can convince the great white hunter from Alaska to help you find the cat."

"How am I going to do that?"

"Don't know. You'll think of something. Perhaps, point out that it would beneficial to all of us, if that cat were to be eliminated once and for all goddamned time."

Chapter 48

Virgil growled and then rose awkwardly to his feet, barking. In spite of his limp, he rushed to the door. His hindquarters pivoted back and forth but he appeared to ignore the pain he normally experienced when moving. He continued snarling. He stood at the door and turned his head, pleading to go outside. Ed looked around the room and walked cautiously to his distressed dog. Smith picked up his pistol.

"Shut that damned dog up, or I'll do it for you."

"Can I take him outside?" asked Ed.

"I'll shoot him, if you don't," said Smith. "My men are out there. Don't try anything stupid."

Ed opened the door. The old dog bolted out of the door. Ed turned back. Using his gun hand, Smith motioned for him to go. The door slammed shut as Ed walked down the porch stairs. The barking stopped. Ed's eyes adjusted to the darkness. He could make out Virgil sniffing wildly down by the beach. Then, the dog returned to where Ed was standing. He looked at his master and then started back down to where he had been feverishly following the scent of something very interesting and or extremely disturbing.

Virgil looked back. Ed's stomach turned. The breeze carried a sickening, gaseous, metallic mixture of feces, urine, blood and exploded guts up his nose. Once there, the smell was impossible to lose and Ed knew that Virgil was sniffing around violent death. Only once, in all of his years of hunting, had he gut-shot a deer. The stench was similar but somehow unique. He knew exactly what it was. You never forget the bodies left behind by a mountain lion. What he smelled was human.

He choked back the contents of his stomach and hesitated. Virgil stopped and waited, started to move, then waited. Ed did not want to go. He did not want to see what, no not what, who was on the beach. Just go back inside and forget... Ed looked at his dog. Virgil turned. Ed followed. The offensive smell grew stronger. Two beams of light crossed like engaged swords. In spite of the carnage, Ed exhaled a breath of relief. He recognized the new, conspicuous, but now torn, flannel shirts worn by his captors. The bodies were, thank God, adults, not children. The kids were safe. Or were they, if the cat was here? Oddly, Ed's original repulsion to the smell of death had settled into a calm acceptance. For a moment, he considered kicking one of the bodies, then he thought better of it.

This disrespectful gesture would be lost on the recipients. Instead, he knelt near one of the assault rifles. Could he figure out how to use it? Ed liked to shoot and he loved to hunt but he had never been drawn to weapons whose only purpose was to kill other human beings. However, the goons inside the lodge would benefit from an attitude adjustment. Would he be able to use this weapon effectively without doing more damage than good?

"Pick that up and you're a dead man," said Smith.

Greene and Madison approached Hank Harbor.

"Come with us, we need to talk."

The door to the porch opened. Virgil walked into the room. Ed came through the door, followed by Smith.

"Mr. Harbor, come with me. Madison and Greene, I have a new job for you. Hobbs and Giles need your help down by the dock. It's a fucking mess.

"What do you—" asked Madison.

"They're both dead."

"How?"

"Probably by our secret weapon. Just go clean it up. We can't have bodies everywhere, at least not outside. Find a place to bury what's left of them. No trace. Understand? No one can know that we were here."

"Yes, sir," answered Madison.

"What others?" asked Hank.

"Not your concern, Mr. Harbor. What I want you to do is find that mountain lion and bring it back to me. Dead. It's the last one. We're not negotiating here. Don't even think about refusing. Remember that these people's kids are camping outdoors not far from where that cursed beast just slaughtered two of my men."

"I'll need my guns," said Hank. "How do you know it's the last one?"

"Doesn't matter. No guns. You'll be using that bow I saw in your truck. I assume you are pretty handy with that. You're probably a one arrow wonder. That's what you're going to get—one arrow."

"What about my handgun?"

"No."

"Two arrows?"

"Really, Mr. Harbor? You need two arrows?"

"Best to be sure."

"Okay, two. Try anything and people in here will suffer for it. I might start with the kids. Got it? Do I need to send one of my men with you?"

"Yeah right. Your men would just get in the way. Besides, it looks like you're starting to get a little short-handed. I usually work alone, but I will take Mr. Schurman with me. He knows the area better than I do."

Mr. Smith hesitated before agreeing.

"I guess I can live with that but I'm very serious, Mr. Harbor. If you try to escape or any other horseshit, someone will pay the price. Do you understand what I am saying, Mr. Harbor?"

Hank looked at Smith. "Yes, I get it. I have no intention of putting anyone at risk. Each and every one of these people you are holding against their will is worth a hundred time the likes of you and your gofers. So, get my bow and my two arrows. And I need my dogs. Don't fuck with any of these people and I won't fuck with you, at least for the time being. You have my word on that."

"I know I do," said Smith.

"After I return the bow, all bets are off. You have my word on that, too."

Smith smiled. "Of course, Mr. Harbor, but sometimes life is a bitch and it looks to me like I'm holding all of the cards—I mean every last one of them."

Jones lay on the passenger door where he had fallen. Hobbs had taken off his shirt and rigged a makeshift bandage around Jones's head. The flannel didn't do all that much to stop the flow of blood oozing from the wound. Hobbs had other concerns. There was hardly enough room to maintain his footing around Jones's motionless torso. Hobb's muscles were starting to stiffen from crouching. He gripped his pistol as he looked up at the open window just above his head. Could he get a couple of shots off before a rock hit him? He could not let them get the gun that must be lying just outside. Damn, this shit is not what I signed up for.

Outside the SUV, George got out of the truck. Charley and Harry still held rocks.

"What do you think?" asked George. "Can one of us get that gun?"

"I've got a whole arsenal of rocks," said Harry. "I see a head pop out of that car and—smack!"

"You do seem to have talent with those rocks, my friend, but the next guy will probably be a lot more cautious. He might just come out shooting. I think that's what I would do," said George.

Harry looked at the truck. "We could ram him."

"Do we want to risk damaging our truck?" said George.

Charley put down his unused rock. "No? Okay then, cover me. I'm going after the gun."

George appraised the two rock piles. He chose a missile that looked like it could serve his purpose. Both he and Harry moved closer to the SUV.

"You sure?"

"Yup, no way they can see me from in there. It'll take two seconds. I can see the gun. It's right there by the wheel."

Charley bolted to the overturned vehicle. He pressed his back against the still-warm undercarriage, caught his breath and then crouched down to pick up the gun. With the pistol in his hands, he started back. He heard something. Then two shots. Charley hit the ground. Two rocks flew over the Explorer.

Josey picked up a plank with two nails protruding through the top end.

"Add just enough wood to the fire to keep it from burning out. McKenzie and I are going to see if anything has changed. Maybe we can get some more boards and nails—or something else we can use. Don't leave the campsite. Pretend you're asleep just in case they check on us."

McKenzie and Paul clutched weapons similar to Josey's.

"All set Paul?" asked Josey.

"Yes."

Josey looked back toward the campsite. "Do what Paul says, okay?"

The remaining campers replied with a muffled "Okay".

McKenzie and Josey held close to the edge of the forest surrounding the lodge.

"What's going on down there?" asked McKenzie. "It looks like they're picking something up. What's that smell?"

"I don't know but what they are picking up isn't alive."

"Some kind of animal?"

"Or not."

"Dead people? Not our—"

"The men with the shovels aren't. We need to look."

Josey held up his board. "Do you think you could use yours?"

McKenzie shuddered. "Honest answer?"

"Yes."

"I don't know. Do you?"

"No."

Harry picked up a second rock. George did the same. The man emerging from the Explorer's aimed and fired two more rounds. Both rocks struck the man midbody. He disappeared back into the vehicle.

"Now!" cried George.

Both men ran toward Charley. The old alcoholic was on his back. He tried to push himself up but failed. He managed to toss the pistol to his side. Harry picked it up. Harry looked at George. The veterinarian nodded. Harry ran to the front of the SUV and fired four shots into the windshield. It shattered. Harry backed up and hid behind a rock. Nothing. He arose and fired two more random shots into the vehicle. Silence. He waited again for what seemed like hours.

George knelt down next to Charley. He couldn't avoid the blood that was pooling around the wounded man's body. Charley looked up. Blood seeped out of his mouth.

"It's okay," he whispered. "I was already a dead man." Charley managed a smile. "The liver, you know... better to go out in a blaze of glory."

Charley exhaled and was gone.

Harry ran to the side of the tipped vehicle. Still nothing. He peered around the open space that had once held a windshield. He saw two men. Neither one moved. Holding the pistol, he leaned over the pile of glass into the driver's side. Four blank eyes stared back at him. Blood dripped onto the ground under the driver's side door. Harry stepped back and went over to where George stood over Charley.

"He's gone," said George. "He appeared to be happy. He said something about going out in a blaze of glory."

"He seemed like a good man," said Harry.

"I think so," said George. "Hopefully, we can come back and make sure he gets treated right."

"What do we do now?"

George nodded over to the Explorer. "I think a couple of assault rifles and pistols might even the odds a bit."

"You know how to shoot those big ones?" asked Harry.

"I don't know what they use now, but I fired a M16 a few times in the Air Force way back when."

"I'll stick with a handgun," said Harry.

"Okay. Let's throw the rifles in the truck just in case."

"Christ, if I used one of those, I'd probably kill everybody, us included."

George looked at the over turned SUV. "You want to go get their guns, or me?"

"Be my guest," said Harry. "but maybe we should get help."

"Who? How?"

"Police?"

"What police? They're miles away. Who's going to believe us?"

"There's probably a radio in the Explorer."

George approached the blown out windshield. "I'm sure there is but I'm afraid if we use it we might alert Smith that we are coming. I'll grab their handsets, though. They might come in handy. I'm going to crawl in. I'll pass the stuff out."

Chapter 49

McKenzie and Josey approached the clearing below the parking lot. They moved from tree to tree until they reached the boathouse. Josey went first. He looked in every direction. He saw two figures come out of the lodge. They seemed occupied so he bolted across the open space and threw his back against the boathouse wall. He slid to the left and peered around the corner.

A man shoveled something into a wheelbarrow.

"What a goddamned mess!" said Greene. "Is this what you thought we'd be doing?"

"Just shut up!" said Madison. "I'm sick of your bitching. Let's just get this done."

Josey pulled back. Whoever had been up by the lodge appeared to be gone. Josey extended his right hand and flipped his fingers. He pointed to the space next to where he was standing. McKenzie joined him. Josey again inched toward the corner of the boathouse.

Madison lifted the wheelbarrow handles.

"Where' you going to take that?" asked Greene.

"There's a path over on the other side of the boathouse. I figure we can move all of this over there and then find a place to bury it."

"It? Christ, these were friends of ours. And isn't that where—"

"Look, John, I don't like this any better than you do. We have orders. You stay here and I'm going to find a place. Okay?"

Greene turned away. "But?"

"But what?"

"The kids are camping over there."

"It's a big forest. I'll find a place. Okay?"

"Okay."

Madison started toward the boathouse.

Josey moved back. He pointed in a circular motion to the far end of the wall. McKenzie nodded and slid around the corner. Josey followed. He lifted his makeshift weapon higher.

"He's planning on going over there," he whispered.

Madison struggled with the heavy wheelbarrow in the soft, sandy soil.

"Fucking A!" he mumbled.

He continued to push. Then he saw something. Josey lifted his board and the nails hit their mark. That something was the last thing Madison ever saw.

Trembling, Josey pulled the lethal weapon away from the man's head.

"Shit!" said Josey. "Shit!"

Josey started to pull the body—

"What was that?" cried Greene.

McKenzie raised her weapon. Oh God, the other one is coming, she thought! She jumped out just as the man approached the end of the wall.

Her board also hit home.

The kitchen door opened. Marion appeared carrying a tray of sandwiches. She avoided the four armed men. She set the food on a table near the wood stove. She turned back toward the dining room.

"I'll get more coffee."

"Thank you, Marion," said Margret Hawkins. "You have been wonderful."

"It's the least we can do."

"Why don't you offer them highfalutin shitheads with big guns and small penises some sandwiches filled with a heavy dose of rat poison?" mumbled Ike. "There's more than enough in the back room."

Marion stopped. "Ike, for—"

Smith turned around. "Would one of you please make that old geezer shut up," he growled. "He's developed a habit of getting on my nerves. We're not eating anything that he doesn't eat first."

"Christ, I'd gladly eat a pound of poison iffin it meant you'd eat it too. I'd be dyin' for my country. I'd be a hero."

Smith turned to Harper. "If that woman can't control the old fart, you want to encourage him to—"

"No need. I said my piece. I'm keepin' my opinions to myself, leastwise for now. I'm goin' to have a sandwich. You care to join me?"

"Fuck you!" said Smith. "You're a dead man anyway."

Marion came back with a container of coffee.

Robbins watched her. "She seems like a nice sort. She kind of reminds me of my grandmother."

"Don't get too sentimental over her," said Smith.

Marion set the coffee on the table and then sat on the arm of Ike's easy chair. She looked at her husband and cracked a smile.

"Are you all right, old man?"

"Christ no, I'm not all right! My stomach hurts. I'm sick of bein' cooped up in here and I don't want any more Christly coffee. I want some goddamned whiskey."

Marion produced a small flask. "I figured you might. Medicinal purposes."

"You planning on sharing some of that?" asked Ed.

Ike took a swig. "Course, I ain't."

Ike passed the flask to Ed.

Ed sipped a small amount of the dark liquid and passed the container back to Ike.

Ike held the whiskey up. "Anyone else?"

There were no takers.

Ed sat back down on the couch next to Marty.

Jade sat on a stool next to where Ike tied and sold his flies. She looked at her fellow captives. Ed and Marty seemed to be drawn back together. She hoped the Rollins would have the chance to be a family again. She liked Ed and Marty and their kids. She had not gotten all of the names of the people in the room. She wished she knew them. The couple with the camper sat in the corner holding hands—I think Margret is her name. Seem like nice people. All they did to get here was to be in the wrong place at the wrong time.

The Meurets and the Nashes sat around one of the dining room tables. Amazing, in spite of everything, how those two families have held up! She had met Phil Ramsey earlier. The biologist stared at his surroundings like a cornered animal and then would nod off. The fisherman sat on the floor in the corner to the right. She knew the trooper and the two Fish and Game officers. Alex, Doc, Bruce, and Al sat together, their arms folded on the table. Jade wondered why Bruce and Al were together. Game wardens usually traveled alone. Collecting the mountain lion must have been considered important. That's why we're all here.

There are only four of them in this room now holding all of us. Two are dead down by the dock. Two have gone to who knows where looking for George and Froggy. There's a lot of places to look and they don't know the area. Who knows how long it will take those other two to do what they have to do to make those bodies disappear? Only four left in here, but they're armed and we're not. And Rob and Hank? Please come back both of you. I hope I'm lucky enough to someday be like Marion. Old age with Rob. Maybe I can be at least half the person that she is with Ike.

McKenzie and Josey clutched their boards. They looked at the two men lying on the ground. The wheelbarrow had tipped over spilling its contents next to Madison. Josey swallowed hard trying holding back the contents of his stomach. His mouth tasted like acidic marshmallows. He stepped back, turned around and puked.

"Jesus!"

McKenzie dropped her weapon and emptied the contents of her stomach. She turned to Josey.

"Hold me." Josey did. "Are they—"

"Yes, I think so," he whispered.

"That was so, I mean, too easy."

"Doing it was. Now, not so much."

McKenzie pulled back. She looked at Josey. "No, now not so much. One of them was the guy that came to the campfire. Little did he—"

Josey held McKenzie's hand. "Be dead? God! What's that?"

"Coyotes? They sound awful close," said McKenzie.

"It sounds more like—"

Three howling dark figures raced toward the two teenagers.

McKenzie stepped toward the boathouse.

"Dogs? Are they dangerous?"

Tails high and wagging, the three medium-sized Black and Tans nuzzled McKenzie and then Josey. Then they returned to the job at hand, sniffing.

Hank and Rob approached the carnage.

"Apache, Summer, Zigi. Stop! Lie down!" Hank commanded.

Breathing heavily, with small amounts of drool dripping out of their mouths, the dogs obeyed.

"Are you two all right?" asked Rob. "What happened?" He looked at the discarded makeshift weapons. "You—"

Josey nodded. "We both did. We had to, Uncle Rob. We had to."

"Jesus!" said Rob. He walked over to his godson and held him. McKenzie, shaking, joined the hug.

"We had to," Josey repeated. He shivered but succeeded in regaining his composure.

The dogs were anxious to move.

"Stay!" ordered Hank.

One of the dogs yipped his desire to continue to explore the close by carnage.

"Quiet!"

Hank contemplated the death that lay before him. He approached the young woman and man. He held out his hand.

"You two are something. Not everybody... All I can say is you two are something."

Josey and McKenzie hesitated but then shook the guide's hand. They looked at Hank and waited.

"We have to move fast," responded Hank. "These two bodies need to disappear. Someone will be down at some point to check on them. Let them. I don't want Smith to think Rob and I did this and we sure as hell don't want him to know what really happened. We'll leave the other mess. That's not our problem."

Hank looked at McKenzie and Josey again. He looked at the boards lying on the ground. "Do you think you could do it again, if you had to?"

"If we have to," said Josey. "I think we can."

McKenzie nodded. "But, I hope—"

"I know," said Hank.

"What about the bodies, then?" asked Rob.

Hank pointed toward the dock. "Over in those boats. Hopefully they won't look there, at first anyway."

Rob started toward the two men that Josey had killed. "I'll take care of that."

"What about their guns?" asked Josey.

"Do you know how to shoot?" asked Hank.

"He does," said Rob. "A handgun, anyway."

"Okay, keep them. Don't use them unless you really have to. I don't know what Smith will do if he hears a gunshot. We'll hide the rifles in the boathouse. After that, Rob and I need to do what we need to do."

"What's that?" asked Josey.

"Kill the catamount. Orders from Smith himself. Right now, it's the best for all of us if we eliminate that threat. Four dead here, two out driving around East Bejesus. That leaves Smith and three of his bozos. The odds are getting better.

Hank glanced at his dogs. "These fellas are ready."

He looked at the slaughter on the ground. "I need to get the dogs away from this. If the cat is anywhere near, it has heard the dogs. I wish I didn't have to use them. I don't want that damned thing to panic. There is something unusual about these mountain lions. This one might attack us rather than run."

Hank held up his bow. "This against whatever did that. I hope I'm not having an off day."

"Me, too," agreed Josey

"Are you good, McKenzie? Josey?" asked Rob. "Really?"

"We'll be okay," said Josey.

McKenzie nodded.

"You are sure?" asked Rob.

Josey picked up his board. He looked at McKenzie. "We're sure. What else are we going to do?"

"You could go back with the other kids," said Rob.

"No, I don't think so," said McKenzie. "I don't want them to—"

"If Smith sends someone else down, we'll be ready," said Josey. "Uncle Rob?"

"Yes, Josey."

"I guess I'm not—"

"A kid anymore?"

"Something like that, I guess."

Rob hugged Josey again. "I wish you were."

"Me, too," said Josey.

Hank walked over to the dogs. "We'll check on the campfire before we go into the woods."

Josey and McKenzie watched the two men walk after the dogs.

"I hope they'll be all right," said McKenzie.

"They will be," Josey assured her.

***

"Isn't that Stillwater Lodge down there?" asked Harry.

"I think we ought to park the truck up beyond the entrance. If anybody leaves, they will most likely go the way we just came from."

"Can you see any place to park? It's hard to see without the headlights."

George drove by the driveway to the lodge. Further up the road, he turned on the headlights

"I remember a place right up there."

He turned right into an old logging road and switched off the lights.

"Grab the pistols and the clips. Let's go!"

"What are we going to do?"

"No idea," said George.

Chapter 50

Hollis Hawkins had progressed from resigned fear to resolved anger. There's four of them and sixteen of us. There must be some way to get at least one of those damned guns. If they're going to kill us anyway, we could— If I die trying, at least Margret might live. I wouldn't want to be one of them if Margret had a shot at revenge. We've always said, "Don't piss off Margret." Hollis squeezed his wife's hand. "How are you feeling?"

"Pissed off."

"You know what?" said Pat. "I'm sick of Smith."

"Join the club," said Holly, "but what—"

"We have to risk our lives to save them," said Tristan. "I don't see any other way."

"What do you mean?" asked Karley.

Tristan leaned into the table. "We outnumber them. If we could somehow distract one of them long enough to—"

"To what?" asked Karley.

***

"Are we going to die together?" asked Marty.

"There's some irony to that," said Ed. "Is that okay with you?"

"Maybe someday, but not yet. I'd like to try living together again first."

"So would I."

Eli Hodge stood up.

"Sit down," yelled Harper.

"I need to stretch my legs. My back is killing me."

"One minute and then sit back down."

Eli saluted. "Yes, sir."

Harper aimed his rifle at Eli. "Are you making—"

Phil Ramsey pulled himself up off the floor. "Leave him alone."

"You don't look like you could stop me," sneered Harper. He walked over and pushed Phil back down.

Jade and Marion stood up.

"Enough!" yelled Smith. "Everyone shut up! You over there, sit back down and I don't want to hear any more talking. Got it? Harper, would you please do me a favor and go see what is keeping Madison and Greene?"

The room reminded Hawkins of a classroom full of unruly students. The difference is that an ineffective teacher doesn't have an assault rifle to keep everyone in submission. What Smith and his ilk don't get is that force only works short term. Eventually, there's always somebody who rebels. All it takes is one. Then it spreads. Like a virus. It's a law of nature.

Ike Roberts stood up.

"What now?" asked Smith.

"I need to go potty."

Trooper Hall raised his eyebrows to the two Fish and Game officers sitting with him at the table. "What do you think? What if we all rushed at them at once? How many of us would they get?"

"Oh, probably all of us," said Bruce. "You ever shoot one those things they're carrying?"

"A few times in training, but aren't they going to get rid of us anyway?" asked Alex.

"Yes," said Bruce, "but I don't think they want to do it by shooting us. If that was the plan, we'd be dead by now."

"What do you think they're going to do with us?" asked Alex.

"I'm not sure," said Bruce.

"Is it just me or do you sense a change in the mood of this room?" asked Al.

"May I go, sir?" asked Ike.

"I need to go, too," said Pat

"Me, too," said Tristan.

"Me—"

Smith's lip started to quiver. "One at a time!" he barked. "Everyone else stay put and shut up. "

Paul put another log on the fire and then wriggled back into his sleeping back. Using his elbows, he remained sitting. Abbi, Cindy, Cameron, Kayla and Cameron were all, eyes open, lying down.

"I hear something," whispered Cindy.

"Me too," said Abby.

Paul whispered, "Pretend you're asleep."

Rob and Hank approached the campsite. The dogs remained behind, waiting for their next command.

Rob knelt down next to the fire. "Cindy, are you awake? It's Uncle Rob."

"Over here!" said Cindy. "We're all awake. We can't sleep."

All of the campers sat up.

"You all okay?" asked Rob.

"We're okay," said Paul.

"I'm scared," said Cindy.

"Me, too, said Abbi.

"We all are," said Paul, "but we're also tired of doing nothing. Isn't there anything we can do?"

"The best thing you can do is stay here. Mr. Harbor and I'll be back."

"Where are you going?" asked Cameron.

"I know where they're going," said Cindy. "Mr. Harbor is the mountain lion hunter. There's another catamount, isn't there?"

Rob looked at Hank. "Yes, but we're going to take care of it."

"Can't we go back to the lodge?" asked Connor.

"You're safer here," said Rob.

"Uncle Rob?" asked Cindy. "Is everything going to be all right?"

"Yes, it will be."

"That's what my Dad said last time and it wasn't."

Rob stood up. "Guys, we're going to get through this. Let the adults handle it. Please, just stay here. Okay?"

The boys and girls nodded. "Okay Mr. Schurman."

Rob and Hank disappeared into the woods. The dogs led the way.
"Do you want to stay here?" asked Kayla.
"No," said Paul.

Gun drawn, Harper walked toward the boathouse. He saw Gile's and Hooper's remains, the wheelbarrow... and then something moved.

"Don? John? Where are you? Is that—"

He saw something above him. Then he felt the pain in his left shoulder. He rolled away as two shadow-like figures emerged from the side of the boathouse. He sprang to a crouched position and took aim.

"Stop or I'll shoot!" he yelled. "Throw down those things in your hands."

Harper glanced at his shoulder wound. It hurt but he would not die from it. Josey and McKenzie dropped their make-shift weapons. Harper looked at the two boards and the protruding nails.

"Shit!" he said. "Goddamned kids. Get over here. I knew we should have done something about you. We will now."

Still pointing the gun with his right hand, Harper knelt down to pick up one of the boards. It was painful but manageable. He placed it back on the ground.

"How about we give you a piece of your own medicine?"

He spoke into his body microphone. "Harper here. I don't know where Madison and Greene are but—"

A tiny speaker responded. "What do you mean you don't know," said Smith. "Aren't they there?"

"No, but we—"

"Just find them."

"But—"

"Just find them."

"Yes, sir. Could you send Robbins or Johnson down?"

"What for?"

"I need some help dealing with—"

"What?"

"Two of the kids attacked me?"

"Jesus! What—"

"Look, I'm hurt and I could use some help."

"You couldn't handle a couple of kids?"

"They made clubs out of boards and nails."

"What? What about Greene and Madison? What about the other kids?"

"That's what I'm trying to... I haven't' seen the other kids. Greene and Madison aren't here."

"Really? Where the fuck are they?

"I told you I don't know."

"What do you mean you don't know? Where—

"I think the kids might have gotten them," said Harper.

"Two goddamned kids? Christ! All right, I'm sending Robbins. Find Greene and Madison and then I want you to bring all of the kids back inside. Think you and Robbins can you handle that?"

"Yes, sir. We will handle it."

George and Harry started walking down the hill toward Stillwater Lodge. The yellow interior lights glowed out of the side windows. Reflections from the front windows rippled on the lake. They could make out three figures standing down by the boathouse.

"I wonder what they are doing?" whispered Harry. "What do you think?"

George pushed Harry. "Get back."

The side door opened and a man, armed, appeared in the entranceway and then walked out and blended into the darkness. George and Harry watched his progress as he repeatedly appeared in the light from the windows and then disappeared again into the shadow areas of night. Finally, they could make out the figures down by the shore.

"This way," said George. "Let's see what's going on inside."

"Did you hear that?" asked Harry. "Coyotes?"

"I'd say dogs," said George.

Rob's and Hank's headlamps scanned an abandoned logging yard.

"How about here?" asked Rob. "What now? I've never done this kind of hunting."

"Looks good. The dogs are ready. I wish I had a couple more. This cat is predictable in some ways but odd in other ways. The more dogs, the harder it is for the cougar to zero in on one dog. If that happens, one swipe can kill the dog. That usually happens if the cat is cornered in an open space with no trees. If there are trees, they will usually look to go high. That's when I come in."

"Well, we got trees," said Rob.

Hank checked the GPS tracking collars on the dogs and then looked at his handheld receiver.

"Yup, we got trees. The GPS can track the dogs for up to ten miles."

"I hope the cat hasn't gone that far."

"Mountain lions can cover a lot of territory, but I'm betting that this one is still nearby. It's as if it has been trained to be. I'm counting on it. We don't want to go back empty handed."

Hank released the dogs.

Robbins trained his pistol on Josey and McKenzie.

Using his good arm, Harper held up one of the makeshift weapons. His pistol hung limply from his other hand.

"Look at this. These fucking delinquents—"

"For Christ's sake, Greg, they could have killed you!"

"They tried. And I'm wondering what happened to John and Don. I don't think they just decided to go for a stroll."

"You think?"

"I know one way to find out. I'm going to cuff them to that railing over there."

Harper put the board down and passed his gun to his right hand. He motioned to the two teenagers. "Move."

Josey and McKenzie did as ordered.

"Keep me covered, Dan," said Harper as he pulled out two sets of handcuffs.

He cuffed Josey and McKenzie to the railing and then picked up one of the boards. "There's another one over there, if you would like to join the fun."

Mr. Robbins declined the offer. "I'll keep watch."

Mr. Harper approached McKenzie. "Now young lady, would you like to tell me what happened to our colleagues?"

Josey slid over and attempted to throw himself in front of McKenzie. Mr. Harper shoved him aside.

"Shoot him, if he moves again. Just don't kill him. I want a crack at him too."

"But we're not supposed to—"

"I don't give a shit!" growled Harper.

George peered into the window. "They got quite a crowd in there but I only see two guys with guns. Nobody looks very happy. Take a look."

George moved aside. "What do you think? There were more than that when they were looking for Charley and I."

Harry stepped away from the window. "If there are more, I wonder where they are. Maybe we just can't see them."

Harry peeked into the window again. "Some old guy just came back into the room. Other than that, looks the same."

George took a look. "That's Ike Roberts. He looks pissed off. He's standing by Ed Rollins."

George watched as Smith walked across the room, spoke to Ike and then shoved him onto the floor. "Things are looking kind of tense in there."

"Okay so, we have two in here," said Harry. "We had two back there in the Explorer. I know there were more than four."

George turned towards the lake. "Someone's down by the dock. It looks like three or four."

"It must them," said Harry.

"Probably, but it could be the kids."

"What kids?"

"Some of the guests have kids—mostly teenagers."

"Jesus!" said Harry. "So what do we do?

George turned back to the window. "I think we go in."

"What if there are more—"

"You've got a full clip."

"So do they," said Harry.

"Let's try the kitchen door," said George..

— 222 —

Chapter 51

Paul motioned for Cameron, Abbi, Connor, Kayla and Cindy to stop.

"Holy shit! What was that?"

"It sounded like my sister," said Kayla.

"Over there," said Connor. "By the dock. What are they—"

"One of them is smashing McKenzie using one of our boards," said Paul. "We have to do something."

"What?" asked Abbi. "The other one has a gun."

McKenzie screamed again.

Paul held up his board. "We have these. Cameron and Abbi, can you do it?"

"What?" asked Abbi.

"Use these?" said Paul.

Cameron and Abbi nodded.

"Okay, you get behind the guy with the gun. Don't think about it. Just hit him as hard as you can from behind—both of you. You go first. We'll be right behind you. Try to hit him so he'll drop the gun."

McKenzie sobbed.

"Connor, you and I are going to get the guy who is doing that to McKenzie. You okay?"

"Yes, I'm good. Let's go," said Connor.

"Kayla, you and Cindy stay here. Let us know if anyone else comes."

Smith spoke into his body mic. "What's going on, Harper?"

"Just taking care of some business. A couple of the kids have been very naughty. I'm giving them a taste of their own medicine."

Karley and Tristan stood up. "That sounded like my daughter," screamed Tristan.

"What are they—"

Mr. Smith pointed his rifle at the Nashes. "Shut up and sit the fuck down!"

Then into the mic. "Quit fooling around. Clean up the mess. Bring those damned kids up here. It's getting fucking late. I don't want to spend another goddamned day here. Where are Giles and Hooper?"

"That's what I'm trying to find out."

The microphone went dead.

"What are they doing to our daughter?" screamed Tristan and Karley.

Smith turned to Johnson. "Would you please shut them up!"

"They're taking us up some rugged terrain," said Rob. "Do the dogs ever get tired?"

"They're in better shape than you and I will ever be. They can go for hours. Even once they have treed the cougar, they don't quit. Even without the GPS, the barking would lead you to the tree. Ever heard of the word 'dogged'? I'm guessing that's where the word came from."

"I can hear them. How far do you think they are?"

"Not far, a mile or so. Just as I thought, it looks like the cat is still in the area. If it weren't, this would take a while. It's easier in the winter. You can see the tracks. Finding one and then getting it into a tree is the hard part. Most mountain lions don't like to show themselves. Most of the time when they are around, you'd never know it. Dogs pick up the scent, so they know where to go. If they do their job, one arrow should be all I need. That's the easy part. You ready to do some hiking? You can stay here if you want. It's up to you."

"Nope, in for a penny, in for a pound."

Harper held the board high and to his right side. He was ready to hit McKenzie again.

"No please," sobbed McKenzie.

"You ready to tell me what you did with Greene and Madison?"

Slouching down with her hand held above her head by the handcuff, McKenzie looked up. Four figures approached the two men who were holding her and Josey captive. Josey saw them simultaneously.

"Why don't you hit me? You pathetic, sadistic coward."

"Shut up, you... You'll get yours."

Cameron and Abbi walked right up behind Robbins, lifted their weapons and Robbins doubled over and fell to the ground. He dropped his rifle. Cameron pulled the injured man's handgun out of the holster. Abbi threw the assault rifle into the woods.

Harper turned around, "What the—"

He saw Connor and Paul and then his world went black. Paul grabbed Harper's pistol.

"The keys are in a holder on his belt!" yelled Josey.

"Where?"

"Right next to where the cuffs were."

"Got em!" said Paul.

He released McKenzie and then Josey.

Paul and Josey went over to the wounded girl.

"Are you okay?" asked Paul. "Can you get up?"

McKenzie started to push herself up. Josey leaned over to help her.

"Ouch! Careful, he hit me on that shoulder."

With support from Josey and Paul, McKenzie stood up. She grabbed the railing with one hand and held on to Josey's hand with the other.

"It hurts but I think I'm okay. For some reason, he hit me with the flat side on my shoulder and shins. It really hurts."

"I can see the black and blue. Nice tattoo," said Paul.

"Probably saving the nails for later," said Josey.

"He wanted me to tell him what we did with those two men. If he'd used the nails, he would have killed me. Is he dead?"

Josey knelt down. "Nope, not yet. Paul, help me drag him over to the railing. Let's see how he enjoys being shackled by his own handcuffs. That is, if he ever wakes up."

Robbins was still doubled over on the ground. He looked up at Connor.

"You know how to use that, you little pip squeak?" The wounded man tried to get up but slid back down onto the ground. "I'll break every bone in your body," he snarled.

Paul, Josey and McKenzie came over and looked at the man. Josey looked over at Connor. "Keep the gun on him. Paul and I will drag him over to the railing. Let's see how he likes the handcuffs."

"Fuck you!" said Robbins. He tried to kick Connor.

Paul and Josey dragged Robbins toward the railing. The angry man continued kicking and mumbling profanities.

Connor looked over at Abbi. "Go get Kayla and Cindy. And go into the boathouse and grab some duct tape. I'm tired of listening to this guy."

Harry started to open the kitchen door. He turned around. "What the hell is going on down there?"

"Don't know," said George. "Maybe we should go see. What do you think?"

"Let's take a look."

"Very carefully," said George.

The two men moved away from the lodge. They crouched as they made their way between the vehicles in the parking area and then moved to an island of trees next to the boathouse.

George and Harry watched as two boys dragged a man to a railing. Another unconscious man was already bound to the same railing. Three young girls came out of the boathouse. One was carrying a roll of duct tape. One of the older boys tore off a foot or so of tape. The conscious man kicked and cursed but the boy avoided the assault and applied the tape.

"I know who that is," said George. "That's Ed Rollins' kid. Boy, has he gotten older."

The boy looked at the slouched figure next to Robbins. He shrugged, tore off another piece of tape and stuck it over the unconscious man's mouth."

One of the girls approached Josey. She whispered in his ear.

Josey motioned to Paul. "Abbi says there's somebody in those trees."

"Who?"

"No idea."

Josey put his hand down to his belt and reached for Harper's gun. "You ready?"

"Yeah."

Josey moved over to the side of the boathouse. Paul followed. Josey motioned for the others to move toward the back of the small building.

"Who are you," called Josey. "We know you're there. We have guns."

George stepped into the open. "You don't need the guns. I'm George Mason. I'm Doc's friend. Do you remember me?"

Josey and Paul showed themselves. "Mr. Mason? What... I mean, how did you get here?"

"It's a long story." Harry emerged from the trees. "This is Harry. He's on our side. What happened here?"

"That's another long story. This is Paul." Paul shook hands with the two men. Josey motioned for the other kids to come over.

"We best share our stories. After that, if we do the math, I think we're going to find that there are only two of these ass... —I mean jerks—left," said George.

"No, they're assholes," said Paul. "So what are we going to do?"

Rob and Hank bushwhacked their way up the steep incline.

"Jesus, I thought I was in better shape than this," said Rob.

"Rough going," agreed Hank. "I've gotten a little out of shape since I came here."

"How do you mean?"

"At home, I pretty much provide for myself. I hunt, fish and trap. I guide sportsmen on outings sometimes, but to tell you the truth, I don't need to. I've always liked this lifestyle. Making it in the bush keeps you fit, physically and mentally. I don't need to go to the gym or anything like that. I'm more alive in the backwoods. I hate supermarkets, malls and places like that. I know my lifestyle isn't for everybody, probably not for most. Didn't know any better when I was younger. Back then, I made some money when working in technology."

"Really?"

"That helped me get into flying, buying tools and purchasing dogs for hunting and sledding. I like the company of dogs—better than humans mostly. On a day-to-day basis I live off what the Alaskan Wilderness provides me the opportunity to obtain. Guiding pays pretty well but I have more money than I need. Once in a while, I get the urge to get out of the woods, but not often. I'm really not a people person. I like being alone. At least, I always thought I did."

"Are you having second thoughts?"

"No, I don't think so."

"So what do you do if you get sick? Or what will you do when you get too old?"

Hank smiled. "Probably die. That's a first world question," he answered. "Millions of people in the world don't have any kind of safety net. Actually, nobody really does. I usually have radio contact and we do have helicopters. As to getting old, I don't see the advantage to getting too old. Maybe I take a different position in the food chain. That would be fair enough, in my mind.

"On the other hand, if I lived your life, I'd probably be more of a socialist. When you live in groups large or small, you have an obligation to take care of each other. If someone needs my help, they will get it. It's harder for me to accept help, but I'm beginning to see that there's value in that. We can't all just live for ourselves.

"In spite of what I said before about preferring dogs to humans, we are all in this together. I just choose to take advantage of one of the places in the world where you can still get away with surviving by using basic skills. Actually, it's not surviving—it's living. It also happens to be indescribably beautiful there, even if it can be dangerous. I would rather face a grizzly than drive on that highway coming out of Boston. What's it called? Route 128?

"There's a big difference between living to benefit yourself as opposed to choosing to live a solitary life. I hate it when self-serving politicians use my way of life as a rational for grabbing all they can get at the expense of everyone else. That's not what I'm about."

"I get that. All of us here at the lodge are looking for something we couldn't find in other places—even Ike and Marion. Marion went to Auburn, Maine for a while. Ike tried Berlin. That was a disaster. Jade left a career as a teacher and Lord knows I tried to fit in to the so-called normal world. I never felt like I belonged. Once I figured things out, I discovered that I felt just fine right here."

"Hey, my friend, I think you are doing just fine. You got a good thing going. Stillwater Lodge is its own little paradise. You know, I envy you because you found the right people to share it with—and the guests add something too. Until I came here, I didn't realize that I might be missing something."

"You're not married, right? I have it on good authority that you're not gay. Jade said you have a girlfriend."

"Yeah, Elizabeth, and she looks at things the same way I do. We get together when the spirit moves us and we want to make the effort to travel. Having a plane helps, but it is still quite a trek. She runs an outpost camp. We tend to see each other mostly in the summer. It's hard to get in where she is in the winter. I do enjoy her company. I like to think she enjoys mine."

"I suspect she does. You don't seem to have a problem attracting women. So, is coming here getting out of the woods?"

Hank smiled again. "Kind of. You guys have been feeding me, providing everything I could ask for. I'm getting a bit soft."

"Literally everything," said Rob, "I guess."

"Rob, I can't really apologize. There are certain moments in life that—"

"Hank, I'm sorry. I'm the one who needs to apologize—for the sarcasm, I mean. Not one of my best traits. Jade, by the way, has no regrets—in fact, quite the opposite. I think she got something that she wanted and perhaps even needed and I think you did too. She'll have a place for you in her heart for the rest of her life. It's kind of a surprise to me, but I can live with that."

"Yes, I'll have a place for her as well."

"We seem to be finding something in each other," said Rob, "A few years ago, I would have felt threatened by you, but I have no right to prevent her from making her own decisions. I think she may love me more for realizing that. We don't own each other. We're too old to still believe in that kind of bullshit. I want us to be together because we choose to be, but I do hope we can make the most of whatever time we have left. Life is better with Jade. It's that simple."

"I'm no threat to you. You're a lucky man and Jade is a lucky woman. I think you and she, all of you, have something good here. Keep it going. It might be hard after what's happened. Here's hoping you can get it all back. Let's take care of this cat. Then let's see what we can do about those assholes back at the lodge. Time to live free or die and it's time for me to go see Elizabeth.

It was Rob's turn to smile. "Live free or die?"

"Yup."

"Going back to the woman?"

"We both are and here I was looking to just turn into a curmudgeon in my old age," said Hank."

"I thought you were going to donate your body to the food chain. By the way, I have a lot of experience with curmudgeons. You have a ways to go."

"You mean Ike? He is a character, but you gotta love him."

"For God's sake, don't ever tell him that. We'd never hear the end of it."

Ahead, the dogs barked and yapped like a pack of wolves. Hank looked at his GPS. "I'll keep it to myself. The dogs have stopped climbing. My turn."

Moving around heavy underbrush, then over and about more than a few blowdowns, the two men at last reached the top of a partially open ridge. To the right, the dogs assaulted an old white pine tree, occasionally jumping on its side in a vain attempt to reach the mountain lion that had wrapped itself around a large limb twenty feet above the ground. With a low growl, the catamount surveyed the surrounding area, occasionally baring its formidable teeth.

"I see it," whispered Hank.

He pulled the bow off his shoulder, loaded the arrow, aimed upward and took his shot. The dogs continued baying. Hank lowered the bow. He waited. A moment later, the cat came crashing down through the lower branches of the tree.

"You didn't load your second arrow," said Rob.

"Didn't need to," said Hank.

He knelt down and looked at the dead cat. He ordered the three excited dogs to stop. Apache, Summer and Zigi laid down and waited.

"She's beautiful. Odd! The darkest color I have ever seen. Just like the other one. Good size. I wonder if this is the result of cross breeding. I'm guessing around 160 pound. I usually gut the animal right after I kill it. I don't have the tools."

"I wonder what they're going to do with it," said Rob.

"Get rid of it and probably us, too. Isn't that what this is all about?"

Tristan pushed himself off the floor and headed for the restrooms. Everyone else in the room, one at a time, followed Tristan's lead.

Johnson glared at the losers he saw disrespecting his power. His stomach churned. He could feel his heart pound and the heat in his cheeks. The story of my life, he thought. These people got all the breaks. I've had it. Me, I never got any help from nobody. That's why I'm here. It's my turn. Johnson's lower lip trembled.

"Sit the hell down!" he yelled. "I'm in charge here. I'll kill you all."

Everyone in the room stopped. Smith spun around. "The hell you are. We don't want bullets... Sit down."

Tristan started to move. Smith crossed the room. He pulled out a Ka-Bar Mark 2 knife, grabbed Karley and held the knife to her throat.

"So who does it look like is in charge here? As far as I am concerned, you can all shit and pee in your pants. Sit down. All of you. Any bullshit and she's dead."

Tristan started to speak.

"I said any bullshit. Sit down."

Everyone returned to where he or she had been sitting.

Smith turned to Johnson. "Lock her to that post over there. If you need to hurt somebody, do it with your knife," he ordered.

Johnson did as he was told, backed off just behind Karley, unsheathed his knife and stared across the room. He tried to swallow but his mouth was too dry.

— 231 —

"Goddamn it, I thought you said Mr. Smith was one of the best," said the Vice President."

"Just minor obstacles," said Mr. Schmidt.

"Minor obstacles? They can't account for all of their men. The cat is still running loose, capable of God knows what and they haven't found everyone who knows the damn thing exists. Those don't sound like minor obstacles. Christ, the election is a month from now. This whole thing was a harebrained idea in the first place. I shouldn't have let you—"

"Dan, calm down."

"Don't tell me to calm down. Not ever. I asked you to take care of this and you haven't done it. I was counting on you. You let me down."

"Look, one of missing witnesses is a drunk and the other is already considered to be wacko because of his catamount ravings. I don't think—"

"I don't care what you think. Fix this and don't bore me with the details. That will be all, Mr. Schmidt."

"Yes, sir, Mr. Vice President," said Peter Schmidt.

Chapter 52

Except for the occasional scratch of a table or chair on the aged wooden floor, the dining room was deathly still. Only the infrequent clearing of a throat or the rustle of clothing signaled the presence of life. The door leading to the back of the lodge was thankfully ajar.

George tried to determine the location of the two remaining kidnappers. To his right, he saw a woman handcuffed to a post. There was one of the men. He stood behind the woman. He held an intimidating knife stiffly in his right hand. George noticed that the man's lips twitched, inducing a tic in his left cheek. The man stared right by the restrained woman to something across the room. George could not make out what the man was focused on. It was just too far to the left.

Loose cannon, thought George. The others that George could see all sat on the floor looking to the left at the man with the knife. Then they looked towards the right at something else. Sometimes they would regard each other, glance away, and then their eyes would stare at the floor. George assumed that the apparent leader, Smith, was the object of everyone's attention on the right.

Trooper Alex Hall had not given up on hope that one or both of the men would let down their guard. It had not happened. Not yet. The development with the woman was not good. He had not foreseen that happening. It was apparent that Smith did not want to shoot anybody. Killing was going to be okay though. I wonder what he has in mind. Whatever it is, left over ammunition rounds do not seem to be part of the plan. He thought about his friend, Roger Wright. He'd been shot—accidentally. What did they do with his body? As he scanned the room, he noticed someone looking through the doorway at the back of the room. Maybe—

"There's someone at the doorway over there," cried Johnson.

Alex folded his hands on the table. "Damn," he said to himself.

"Talk about dead weight," said Rob. He let go of the dead catamount. It flopped to the ground. Hank took the bow and his one remaining arrow off his shoulder and laid them on the ground.

"That was a hike."

"I guess we should bring this to Smith," said Rob.

"I guess," said Hank.

Cameron and Abbi came out of the woods. He motioned for Cindy, Connor, and Kayla to hold back.

"Where are the others?" asked Rob.

"Mr. Mason, the vet, and some other guy are here. They've gone inside," said Cameron. "Josey, McKenzie and Paul went with them."

Rob turned toward the lodge. "What are they going to do?"

"We don't know. They told us to stay here," said Abbi. "They have some guns they took from those guys."

Robbins was no longer unconscious. He and Harper glared at Rob, Hank and the kids.

"Do any of us have the keys to one of the vehicles parked over there?" asked Hank.

Rob reached into his pocket. "I have the keys to Ike's Jeep. It's up by the kitchen."

"Can any of you drive?" asked Hank.

"I can, kind of," said Connor.

"Actually, I can," said Abbi. "I've been driving my Dad's old tractor. Cameron can too."

"Is the tractor a standard," asked Rob.

Abbi nodded.

Hank took the keys and handed them to Abbi. He motioned to Cameron. He looked at Rob.

"Does the Jeep's emergency brake work?"

"Yes, hard to believe, but it does."

"Okay," said Hank. He turned to Abbi and Cameron. "I have an idea. When I whistle, start the Jeep. Leave it in neutral and run into the woods."

Hank motioned to Connor. "You guys wait over there." He pointed toward the mountain lion. "You don't need to be right next to it, but keep an eye on it for me."

Hank took out his bow.

George and Harry walked into the room.

"I hear you've been looking for me," said George. "I'm George Mason."

Smith walked over to the two men.

"Really? What are you—"

"I heard you were looking for me."

"From whom?"

"Two dead guys."

"What two dead guys?"

"Friends of yours, I think. They looked like they came out of an L.L. Bean Catalog and they were driving a ridiculously pretentious excuse for a SUV."

A motor coughed twice and then revved before settling into a steady gurgling idle. Smith took out his pistol.

"What's that? It sounds like a motorcycle."

"I'd say that's my Jeep," said Ike. "Needs a new muffler."

"Who would be—"

"How the hell should I know?" snarled Ike.

"Johnson, explain the situation to our new friends. Anybody tries to be a hero, that woman dies. On second thought, Johnson, feel free to shoot. We can dig the bullets out later, just like we did with Mr. Wright. It's kind of messy but I don't care anymore. I am a patient man, but... it's time for this to end."

"Amen to that," mumbled Ike.

Pistol and weapon light ready, Smith moved toward the front door.

"I am also very sick of you, old man. I'll be back."

"I can't hardly wait," said Ike.

Smith glared at Ike and then turned his back to the wall just to the right of the door. He assumed a crouch position, opened the screen door and scanned the area with his weapon light. The Jeep's engine continued to grumble. Smith slid back into the room and resumed his standing position against the wall. He turned off his light, swung onto the porch, knelt and then crawled directly to the porch door. He kicked the door open and slid down the steps. With his back to the wall, he crept to the end of the building. He surveyed the vehicles. Nothing moved. He could just make out the Jeep, dimly illuminated by the lodge's window lights. There didn't appear to be anyone in the old vehicle.

"Who's there?"

Out of the darkness. "It's me."

"Who's me?"

"Hank Harbor. I have the mountain lion."

"Where's—"

Smith turned on his light. He pointed the brilliant beam toward the Jeep. There was no one inside. How? Then he turned the light to the right.

This was to be the last of many mistakes that Smith had made in his life. He saw Hank Harbor with his bow raised. The arrow hit Smith before he could pull the trigger.

Chapter 53

Everyone in the room watched as George and Harry sat down next to Ed and Marty. The uncomfortable silence returned.

"What's happening?" whispered Ed. "Are the kids—

George leaned forward. "Everybody's okay."

"What now?" asked Ed.

"Shut up!" yelled Johnson.

Holding his hands up, George acquiesced. Then he scanned the room. He looked at the kitchen door and lowered his head. The door opened. McKenzie walked in.

"Can we get some more marshmallows?" she asked.

Everyone in the room looked at the girl.

"McKenzie," cried Tristan, "get out of here!"

McKenzie smiled. She watched Josey walk unnoticed up to the man with the knife. He stood behind him. Johnson waved his blade in the air toward McKenzie.

"Stay right there or I'll kill this woman. Do not... What the hell?"

Josey held a pistol against Johnson's head. "Drop the knife."

"You're just a kid. You wouldn't have the guts."

Johnson started to bring the knife back up to Karley's throat. Everyone watched. Paul, armed with a pistol entered the room from the kitchen. He looked around. He didn't see Smith, so he trained his weapon toward the man threatening Mrs. Nash. Johnson held the knife to Karley's throat.

"You haven't got the guts either. Drop the guns or this woman dies."

Josey continued to hold the gun against the man's temple. "Your friends outside didn't think we had the guts either."

McKenzie walked up to Paul. "Give me your gun."

She turned around. "That's my mother. Let her go. Now!"

McKenzie joined Josey and pushed her pistol into Johnson's mouth and then pulled the butt upwards into his nose. He gagged and screamed. Blood spurted over McKenzie, Karley and Josey. The knife fell out of his hands and hit the floor. Johnson's hand reached for his nose. Josey grabbed the injured man's weapon. He threw it to Paul and then he grabbed the handcuff keys before he shoved Johnson to the floor.

Tristan ran to his wife and yanked her away. Josey threw Tristan the keys. He unlocked the handcuffs and his wife collapsed into his embrace. Marion and Jade helped bring Karley to a table at the far end of the room. As if possessed, Karley regained her strength. She turned around, looked at Johnson and moved away from her husband. McKenzie continued to point her gun at the sniveling man on the floor. Johnson looked up at the woman he had threatened to murder.

"Give me the gun," said Karley.

"Please don't. I was only doing my duty. Please—"

"Duty to fucking whom? Whose duty threatens to annihilate innocent people? You threatened me, my family and all of these other people. For what?"

"McKenzie, let me have the gun."

"Mom—"

Alex Hall approached McKenzie. "I'll take it.

Shaking, McKenzie handed Alex the gun. "Thank you."

McKenzie turned to her mother. "Mom, I need you."

Karley looked at the sitting figure on the floor. Her upper lip trembled."You're not worth it." She spat into the upturned face. She turned away, put her arm around her daughter and together they walked away.

George and Harry stood up and then the others followed. "I think you're free to... to get up... Move... But, I don't see Smith."

"Dead," said Hank Harbor.

He held the door as Rob ushered in Cindy, Abbi, Cameron, Kayla and Connor. Rob held Jade as the families reunited.

Alex handcuffed Johnson.

"There are two others outside," said Hank. "They're not going anywhere. I'd say let him join his friends."

Alex headed for the door. "Works for me. Bruce, Al—you guys want to call for help?"

Marion helped Ike stand up.

"Christ, I could use a drink," he said.

Chapter 54

"They were trying to bury the bodies over there," said Josey.

"God," said the man in a suit. "I've seen a lot of things but nothing like this."

The man picked up one of the boards. He looked at the bloodied nails. "You killed those two over there using this?"

McKenzie nodded.

"And then you managed to disable the other two. Those guys were trained mercenaries, for God's sake. How did you do it?"

"I don't know," said McKenzie. "We just did."

McKenzie folded her hands against her shoulder. She turned away.

"I don't want to be down here anymore. I am so tired."

Josey put his arm around McKenzie. She started to shake.

"Can we go?" asked Josey. "Please?"

"Yes, of course. I'm sorry. I have what I need for now. Go back to your families. Have breakfast."

The teenage girl and boy started walking toward the Lodge.

"Wait," said the man. "Thank you. I mean, you have stopped something very bad."

McKenzie and Josey continued walking.

"They're all yours," said Peter Schmidt. Three men in suits led Johnson, Harper and Robbins to a Ford Transit Van. He turned to Rob and Ike.

"I'm sorry you had to go through this. When I heard about what happened here, I wanted to come personally. If there's anything—"

"Yeah right," snarled Ike. "You're probably so deep in this the shit's coming up over your Christly hip boots."

"Why do you think that, Ike? I just want to help."

"For starters, Doc told me about the Christly bullshit about mad cow disease. What the hell's your job anyway? What'd you be doin' if these fuckheads had done us all in?"

"Ike, I understand that you are… upset but I don't know—"

"Course you do. You're a big cheese, ain't you? They was goin' to burn us to a crisp. I found the propellant. They was goin' to make it look like an accident. Couldn't have no Christly bullets in our bodies or nothin'. Assholes!"

"Why?" asked Peter.

"Oh for Christ's sake, you know exactly why!" said Ike. "The god-damned catamount, and you damned well know it. You ain't the chowderhead you pretend to be."

"Listen," said Peter. "Cool down, Ike. I'm here to help. Look at those people. They all want to get back to their lives. You want to get back to yours. Some of them may need help. I'm sure the kids will. We have trained counselors available for free for anyone who needs support. We need a little more time to take care of things outside but it's time to move on."

"Cover up, you mean," said Ike. "You gonna make us all shut up?"

"No Ike, you can say whatever you want to whomever you want."

"Is this going to be in the news, Peter?" asked Rob

"Not through us. I don't think exposing a rogue group is in the interest of the country, do you? We have to make hard decisions sometimes."

"Oh, that's what big cheeses do. Still sounds like a Christly cover up to me."

"Ike, it's a free country. You can do or say whatever you want, but there can be consequences. Think about it. Do we want people to think they're going to be attacked by mountain lions when they come to the North Country? What about Stillwater? This place is starting to look like you have to take your life into your hands if you come here. There are already enough paranoia and conspiracy theories out there."

"This one happens to be true," said Rob.

"Happens to be," agreed Peter. "However, there are different truths out there. Choose the one you like. If you don't choose the one we like, life can be damned hard."

"Is that a threat?" asked Ike.

"No, it isn't. Just another truth."

"Besides you knew about the catamount. How come you weren't kidnapped? Just wonderin' that's all." Ike walked away.

"We'll be done soon," said Peter. He offered Rob his hand.

Rob turned away and went over to Jade.

Jade finished setting one of the tables. She moved to the next one. Rob picked up some silverware. "Want help?"

"Marion should have breakfast ready any minute. Everyone is cleaning up. Hank's out with his dogs. The older couple is using their camper. I told them they could hook up to the water. We had enough rooms for everybody else. I'm not sure what they are all going to do. I told them they can stay as long they want to. I've offered to refund the Meuret's and the Nash's money. Was that the right thing to do?"

"Of course."

"We're expecting everyone for breakfast. After that—"

"One step at a time," said Rob. "What about Phil Ramsey? How is he?"

"He said he was okay. He took one of the rooms. What about Ike?"

"Sore and pissed off. Other than that, he seems to be his normal self. He's in helping Marion, whether she wants him to help or not. I'll be right back."

Bruce, Al and Alex entered the room together and sat down at one of the dining room tables near the kitchen. Rob pulled up a chair.

"What now?"

"Seems like we've been dismissed," said Alex.

"Seems that yesterday didn't happen," said Bruce. "We have orders to report back to be reassigned. Or probably retire."

"Kind of young for that. All three of you?" asked Rob.

"Yup, new territories," said Al. "Time for a change."

"Yes sir, it's best for everyone involved," said Alex. "That's what I've been told. The retirement package is awful attractive."

"Don't want us around," said Bruce. It's going to be hard to stay."

Marion, Jade and Ike came into the dining room carrying trays.

"Ready for breakfast?" asked Ike.

Alex opened his hands, palms up. "Sure. Yes. Why not?"

Rob got up. "So, are you going to do it?"

"Do what?"

"Retire?"

"Don't know," said Alex. "For now, guess I'll eat. I'm hungry, I think."

"What about you, Rob? What are you going to do?"

"Looks like carry on. This is all I got."

The Meurets and the Nashes chose two large tables next to each other. Abbi, Cameron, Paul, Kayla, McKenzie and Connor all sat with their parents. Ed, Marty, Josey and Cindy took a table near the two families. George, Doc and Harry grabbed another table. Hollis and Margret Hawkins sat next to Eli Hodge and Phil Ramsey. Hank found a table off to the side.

When she was finished serving, Jade brought her plate of food to Hank's table. Ike and Marion and Rob joined the Rollins' family. Rob surveyed the dining room. The lodge was quiet as everyone contemplated or started to eat their pancakes and scrambled eggs. People were here, as they should be, but Rob's dream felt like the life had been sucked out of it.

Chapter 55

"When are you going to leave?" asked Jade.

"After I eat."

"You don't want to stay another day and get a night's sleep?"

"No, I'll catch up on my sleep. It's time to go."

"Are you okay? I mean, have you ever—"

"Killed a man before?"

"Yes."

"No, I haven't. I hope I never have to do it again."

"Are you okay?"

"No, Jade I'm not exactly okay. I've justified my hunting as being part of the food chain—and it is. That hasn't changed. I despised that man and I have, I believe, eliminated some kind of evil. When the arrow hit him, it was like an orgasm. Now I feel like something essential has drained from me. I'm very tired but it's not the kind of tired that can be satisfied by a good night's sleep. But I will be okay. I'm not the first person to kill another human being and I won't be the last.

"The fact is that I saved lives. I don't understand what they... What happened here is absurd, downright stupid. It shouldn't have happened. The catamounts are gone. The agents—or whatever they were—are all gone. We're still here. No one wants to arrest or even question me or those two kids. I can only imagine how McKenzie and Josey feel. I hope they'll be okay.

"For me, it's time to go home. Elizabeth is going to be waiting. We're both ready for more. In a strange way, I have you to thank for that. Thank you for letting me into your life. It's time to let someone into mine. You showed me what I have been missing. So all of this wasn't for nothing, at least not for me."

Jade took Hank's right hand. "Thank you, Hank. I'll remember you for the rest of my life. Godspeed!

"You will see me again," said Hank.

Jade kissed the top of the guides hand and then walked across the room and sat down with Rob, Ike, Marion, Ed, Marty, Josey and Cindy.

"We saved you some pancakes and eggs," said Cindy.

"Thank you, sweetheart," said Jade. She smiled, then she squeezed Rob's thigh for a moment before starting in on her breakfast.

McKenzie sat on the porch steps. She felt the warmth of the sun on her face. Each year, as spring approached in New Hampshire, that feeling was luxurious. Even now, well into the beginning of summer, this radiance promised a moratorium from the long New England winter. Adults often talked about how short the summers are: "Fourth of July and summer's over!" To McKenzie, the end of vacation time had seemed so far into the future that she could enjoy the here and now. School in the fall, college and career were distant concerns.

Now, none of what had been so important seemed real. She still felt the sun on her exposed face and relished it, but it was not enough. Something deep and dark had revealed itself: she was capable of killing. The man deserved it. He represented... God knows what he represented but he would have willingly and with intention killed her and everyone she loved. If he had, would he have felt like she did—not remorse, but regret? Possibly, but she doubted it.

More than anything, I resent that those men forced me to respond with violence. I never thought... They were bad men who were going to do horrible things to good people. Am I guilty of a crime? Do I feel guilty? I want to go back to the time at the waterfalls. Get high. No moose, no catamount, no Mr. Smith. Go fishing again. Catch my first trout. Share that moment with Josey. Those men robbed me—

McKenzie heard the door close behind her. She turned around. She looked up at Josey. He sat down next to her.

"Are you all right?" he asked.

"Kind of. Not really," she said. "How about you?"

"Pretty fucked up," said Josey. "Did all of this really happen? It must have been a bad dream."

"Yes, it happened," said McKenzie.

"Let's go for a walk," said Holly. "I need to go outside."

Pat, Holly, Karley and Tristan went out on the porch. They stepped by McKenzie and Josey.

"You guys okay?" asked Pat.

"We're good, Mr. Meuret," said McKenzie.

"Are you sure?"

"Yes," said Josey.

"We're going for walk," said Karley. "We'll be back in a bit."

"Okay," said McKenzie.

The four adults followed a path into the forest. McKenzie and Josey watched them disappear into the trees.

"Is anyone staying?" asked Rob.

"I don't know," said Jade. "Hank's getting ready to leave. He wants to say goodbye to you. I already did. We said goodbye to Al, Bruce and Alex earlier. They were going to take Phil Ramsey to a hospital. The couple in the camper left. Doc, George and Harry went to Doc's place. Harry's wife is going to meet him there."

"What about his truck?"

"Oh, I'm sure Peter Schmidt has taken care of that—or will be. I think he even offered the guy a new truck."

"Really? Did he agree to that?"

"Not sure. As far as I know, he never gave Peter an answer"

"Interesting. What about the fisherman?"

"His name's Eli. His wife is coming to pick him up. His truck is still at the Schmidt's house."

"What's it doing there?"

"Peter and his recently deceased friends kept Eli locked in a room at the farm. They had Phil Ramsey, too."

"Yeah," said Rob. "I didn't think Peter was here out of the kindness of his heart. Do we know what the Nashes and the Meurets are going to do?"

"Not yet? And us?"

"For the moment, one step at a time. Do you want to leave?

"Good Lord, no!" said Jade. "Do you?

"No."

"And what about what happened here? Are we going to keep quiet?"

"I haven't decided yet… something."

"Ike wants revenge," said Jade.

"Yeah," said Rob, "for right now. How about you and me? Are we okay?"

"More than that," said Jade. "We're going to make this work—you and I, along with Ike and Marion."

"Good," said Rob.

"Ed, Marty and Cindy are going to the camp. I think Josey wants to stay until McKenzie leaves. I'll go see when Ed and Marty plan to go. It looks to me like they might be getting back together. I'd like to see that."

"Me, too," said Rob. "I'll be right back. I want to say goodbye to Hank."

The sun's warmth radiated on the two couples who were sitting on an old abandoned rowboat. For the moment, the water resembled a sheet of dark polished glass. Pat, Holly, Karley and Tristan looked out on Lake Mackapague.

"It's beautiful here," said Holly.

"Yes, it is," said Tristan. "It's not all that often that the water looks like that, though. Sometimes, it looks more like the ocean. More than once, we had to stay on an island out there until the wind let up."

"It was still beautiful," said Karley. "And we had fun in the tent."

"We'll have to give that a try sometime," said Pat. "So what are guys going to do? Are you going to stay?"

Tristan picked up a small stone and threw it into the water. The ripple grew and then disappeared.

"How about you?"

"Believe it or not, our kids want to stay and camp overnight," said Pat.

Tristan threw another rock into the water. "Really?"

"Josey?" asked Holly.

"Pretty obvious," said Karley. "Your son Paul seems to have bonded with the two of them as well. McKenzie said she would rather deal with her feelings here than sitting around at home. I think I know what she means. We're thinking about staying. We don't live that far from here, so we could always change our minds. It's probably different for you two. Of course, you have to get a rental car at some point. Maybe you could get Bill Holiday's truck."

"We might have to. We could throw the kids in the back, I guess. We're going to have to buy a new car," said Pat , "but we can deal with that in a few days. What do you think, Holly?"

"You know what, I want to stay. What are we going to do at home? I'd rather spend the next five days with Tristan and Karley. Besides, nobody expects us to be back there. That was the whole point of this trip."

"Me too," said Pat. "The hell with it, let's stay. It's not like we have plane tickets or anything. We can always pack up and leave, but I bet we're not going to want to."

Tristan threw yet another rock into the lake. "And this is still a beautiful place and I know a good place to go sunbathing."

"Sounds like a plan," said Pat. "Let's go tell Rob and Jade. I don't know about you but we don't want our money back."

"No," said Karley. "No, we don't."

"So, when are you guys off?" asked Jade.

"I guess we're pretty much there," said Ed. "Josey's going to stay if the Nashes stay."

"He's obviously old enough to make his own decision," said Marty. "I wouldn't have said that before, but—"

"I think Josey and McKenzie need each other right now. I hope Tristan and Karley decide to stay for a little while."

"Mom, Dad," said Cindy. "Let's go home."

Marty took Cindy hand. "Massachusetts?"

"No, I mean the cabin. Can I go say goodbye to Kayla. She doesn't live that far away. I hope we can get together again. Then can we go?"

"I'm sure you can," said Marty.

Cindy went over to her friend. Marty got up. She hugged Jade.

"Thanks for everything, Jade. Take care of Rob and stay in touch. I love both of you. I guess what doesn't kill you makes you stronger. And maybe it wakes you up."

"Maybe," said Jade, "but right now, I'd take some peace and quiet."

Ike and Marion sat on the loading dock to the kitchen. Ike was smoking his pipe.

"You know I used to love it when you smoked your pipe when we first met," said Marion. "It kind of stinks now. Maybe I should get you a new one."

"Nope, I kind of like this one. I'm kind of stuck in my ways. You looking to replace me, too?"

Marion laughed. "Nah, we've been through way too much together. I wouldn't have anything to say to someone new. Besides, for some unknown reason, I'm more in love with you now that we're old. Can't explain it, but there you are. We're kind of an item."

"I guess probably," said Ike. "Couldn't do without you."

"How's your stomach?"

"Kinda sore, but nothing a bit of whiskey won't cure."

"Well then, old man, we've got a lodge to run. Seems that some of our guests are staying. Rob and Jade are busy spooning."

"We could do some spooning ourselves sometime, young lady."

"Looking forward to it, but first we have work to do."

"Yes, ma'am. But, you gotta know, I'm still kinda pissed off."

"We all are," said Marion.

Chapter 56

"Here's to Charley," said George.

Everyone in the room lifted their plastic cups.

"To Charley."

"I don't know how he drank this stuff," said Ed.

"There's a whole closet full of this stuff," said Rob. "It'd be kind of a slap in the face to have brought our own whiskey."

The small gathering consisting of Doc Varney, George Mason, Rob Schurman and Jade Morrison, Ike and Marion Roberts, Ed and Marty Rollins, Phil Ramsey, Harry Huston and his wife sat around a heavily scarred and scratched pine table. They all finished the last of the small measure of cheap whiskey they had used as a toast.

"Seems we underestimated old Froggy," said Doc.

"Helped save my life," said Harry.

"Helped save us all," said George.

"That stuff's not that bad," said Ike. "I'll take a little more."

George held up the bottle.

"Anyone else?"

Everyone else declined. George passed the bottle to Ike.

"I'm glad the state let him be buried on the property," said Harry. "Seems kid of appropriate. It's all he really had. I know I'll be visiting from time."

"He did have that substantial stash of rot gut," said Ike. "Kinda wish I hadn't had that second drink."

"You didn't have to fill the whole cup," said Marion.

"Are you going to claim Charley's stash, Ike?" asked Rob.

"Are you kiddin'? This place is haunted. I saw that old man and woman hanging around here."

"What's he talking about?" asked Phil Ramsey.

"Oh, he thinks he sees the old Abenaki and his wife. No one else sees them. Just him."

"He's probably got one foot in the grave," said Doc. "That's why he sees spirits that no one else sees."

"You got a long way to go to outlive me," grumbled Ike. "They was here."

"Was?" asked George.

"Yup, they're gone"

"Where?"

"How the Christ should I know? Just know they ain't here no more."

"So is the place haunted or not?" asked Phil.

Ike shrugged. "Might be, might not be."

"Are you going to come visit Charley?" asked Harry.

"Nope!"

"Why not?"

"No offence to Charley, but I ain't goin' to push my luck."

"Well," said George, "I hope that Charley and whomever else may or not be here rest in peace."

Everyone at the table echo that sentiment in unison.

"Rest in peace, Charley. You were a good man."

Epilogue

That November, the Vice President of the United States won the election. Ike commented that maybe this guy might shake things up in Washington.

A pickup truck drove up a long hill, turned right and stopped in front of a weather-beaten cemetery. Two men got out. They approached one of the graves toward the back. The inscription on the aged stone read: "The Lone Indian of the Magalloway. Died about 1850." The two men added some coins to those already sitting on top of the stone.

"Do you know why people leave money on his grave?" asked one of the men.

"I don't. When I'm in the area, I like to come here when I have time. Leaving a little change just seems like the right thing to do."

"I hope he is resting in peace," said the other man.

"I think he is."

About the author

Rick Davidson is a retired teacher and professional photographer. For several years Rick and his wife Jane taught English as a Second Language in Germany. They have traveled extensively throughout Europe. They now reside in Freedom, New Hampshire where they raised three daughters and are the proud grandparents of seven wonderful grandchildren. Rick studied philosophy and English at Bowdoin College. Rick regularly wanders around northern New England photographing with Jane and often with his long-time friend and fellow "itin-

photo by Jane Davidson

erant photographer" Bill Thompson. He also enjoys fly fishing and spending time on the mid coast of Maine. Many of the characters from *Catamount, A North Country Thriller, Murder at Stillwater Lodge* and *Catamount Unleashed* are living on in Rick's next North Country thriller.